JAMES PATTERSON

VIOLETS ARE BLUE

headline

First published in Great Britain in 2001
by HEADLINE BOOK PUBLISHING

First published in paperback in Great Britain in 2002
by HEADLINE BOOK PUBLISHING

A HEADLINE paperback

10 9 8 7

ISBN 0 7472 6691 3

Typeset in Palatino Light by
Letterpart Ltd Reigate, Surrey

Printed and bound in Great Britain by
Clays Ltd, St Ives plc

HEADLINE BOOK PUBLISHING
A division of Hodder Headline
338 Euston Road
London NW1 3BH

www.headline.co.uk
www.hodderheadline.com

VIOLETS
ARE BLUE

This is for my friend, Kyle Craig, who doesn't work for the FBI, but who has, I think, a really cool name. I should mention a few other patrons of the arts: Jim Heekin, Mary Jordan, Fern Galperin, Maria Pugatch, Irene Markocki, Barbara Groszewski, Tony Peyser, and my sweet Suzie.

Prologue

Without Any
Warning

Chapter One

Nothing ever starts where we think it does. So of course this doesn't begin with the vicious and cowardly murder of an FBI agent and good friend named Betsey Cavalierre. I only thought that it did. My mistake, and a really big and painful one.

I arrived at Betsey's house in Woodbridge, Virginia, in the middle of the night. I'd never been there before, but I didn't have any trouble finding it. The FBI and EMS were already there. There were flashing red and yellow lights everywhere, seeming to paint the lawn and front porch with bright, dangerous streaks.

I took a deep breath and walked inside. My sense of balance was off. I was reeling. I acknowledged a tall, blonde FBI agent I knew named Sandy Hammonds. I could see that Sandy had been crying. She was a friend of Betsey's.

On a hallway table I saw Betsey's service revolver. Beside it was a printed reminder for her next shooting qualifier at the FBI range. The irony stung.

I forced myself to walk down a long hallway that led from the living room to the back of the house, which looked to be close to a hundred years old. It was filled with the kind of country clutter that she'd loved when she was alive. The master bedroom was situated at the end of the hall.

I knew instantly that the murder had happened in there. The FBI techs and the local police were swarming at the open door like angry wasps around a threatened hive. The house was strangely, eerily quiet. This was as bad as it gets, worse than anything else. Ever.

Another one of my partners was dead.

The second one brutally murdered in two years.

And Betsey had been much more than just a partner.

How could this have happened? What did it mean?

I saw Betsey's small body sprawled on the hardwood floor and I went cold. My hand flew to my face, a reflex over which I had no control.

The killer had stripped off her nightclothes. I didn't see them anywhere in the bedroom. The lower body was coated with blood. He'd used a knife. He'd punished Betsey with it. I desperately wanted to cover her, but I knew I couldn't.

Betsey's brown eyes were staring up at me, but they saw nothing. I remembered kissing those eyes, and that sweet face. I remembered her laugh, high-pitched and musical. I stood there for a long time, mourning Betsey, missing her terribly. I wanted to turn away, but I didn't. I just couldn't leave her like this.

As I stood in the bedroom, trying to figure out something coherent about Betsey's murder, the cell phone in my jacket pocket went off. I jumped. I grabbed it, but then hesitated. I didn't want to answer.

'Alex Cross,' I finally spoke into the receiver.

I heard a machine-filtered voice and it cut right through me. I shuddered against my will.

'I *know* who this is and I even know where you are. At poor, dear, *butchered* Betsey's. Do you feel a little bit like a puppet on a string, Detective? You should,' said the Mastermind, 'because that's what you are. You're my favorite puppet, in fact.'

'Why did you kill her?' I asked the monster on the other end of the phone line. 'You didn't have to do this.'

He laughed a mechanical laugh and the hairs on the back of my neck stood up. 'You ought to be able to figure that out, no? You're the famous Detective Alex Cross. You have all those big, important cases notched on your belt. You caught Gary Soneji, Casanova. You solved Jack and Jill. Christ, you're impressive.'

I spoke in a low voice. 'Why don't you come after me right now? How about tonight? As you say, you know where I am.'

The Mastermind laughed again, quietly, almost under his breath. 'How about I kill your grandmother and your three kids tonight? I know where *they* are, too. You left your partner with them, didn't you? You think he can stop me? John Sampson doesn't have a chance against me.'

I hung up and sprinted out of the house in Woodbridge. I called Sampson in Washington and he picked up on the second ring.

'Everything okay there?' I gasped.

'Everything's fine, Alex. No problems here. You don't sound too good, though. What's up? What happened?'

'He said he's coming for you and Nana and the kids,' I told John. 'The Mastermind.'

'Not going to happen, sugar. Nobody will get past me. I hope to hell he tries.'

'Be careful, John. I'm on my way back to Washington *right now*. Please be careful. He's crazy. He didn't just kill Betsey, he defiled her.'

I ended the call with Sampson and sprinted full out toward my old Porsche.

The cell phone rang again before I got to the car.

'Cross,' I answered, still running as I spoke, trying to steady the receiver against my chin and ear.

It was him again. He was laughing maniacally. 'You can relax, Dr Cross. I can hear your labored breathing. I'm not going to hurt them tonight. I was just fucking with you. Having some fun at your expense.

'You're running, aren't you? Keep running, Dr Cross. But you won't be fast enough. You can't get away from me. It's you I want. You're next, Dr Cross.'

Part One

The California Murders

Chapter Two

United States Army Lieutenant Martha Wiatt and her boyfriend, Sergeant Davis O'Hara, moved at a fast pace as the evening fog began to roll in like a sulfurous cloud across Golden Gate Park in San Francisco. The couple looked sleek, even beautiful, in the waning light of day.

Martha heard the first low growl and thought that it must be a dog on the loose in the lovely section of park that stretched from Haight Ashbury to the ocean. It came from far enough behind them that she wasn't worried.

'The Big Dawg!' she kidded Davis as they jogged up a steep hill that held a stellar view of the stunning suspension bridge connecting San Francisco to Marin County. 'Big Dawg' was a pet expression they used for everything over-sized – from jet-liners, to sexual apparatus, to very large canines.

Soon the thick fog would blanket the bridge and bay completely, but for now it was a gorgeous sight, incomparable, one of their favorite things in San Francisco.

'I love this run, that beautiful bridge, the sunset – the whole ball of wax,' Martha said in a steady, relaxed cadence. 'But enough bad poetry. It's time for me to kick your well-formed, athletic-looking butt, O'Hara.'

'That sounds like cheap-shot female chauvinism to me,' he grunted, but he was grinning, showing off some of the whitest teeth she had ever seen, or run her tongue across.

Martha kicked up her pace a notch. She'd been a cross-country star at Pepperdine University, and she was still in great shape. 'And that sounds like the beginnings of a gracious loser's speech,' she said.

'We'll see about that, won't we. Loser buys at The Abbey.'

'I can already taste a Dos Equis. Mmm, mmm, good.'

Suddenly the two runners' playful exchange was interrupted by a much louder growl. It was closer, too.

It didn't seem possible that a dog had covered so much ground so fast. Maybe there were a couple of 'Big Dawgs' loose in the area.

'There aren't any cats in this park?' Davis asked. 'I mean, like a *mountain* lion variety of cat?'

'No. Of course not. Get real, pal. We're in San Francisco, not the middle of Montana.' Martha shook her head.

Moisture jumped off her close-cropped reddish-brown hair. Then she thought she heard footsteps. *A runner and a large dog?*

'Let's get out of these woods, okay?' Davis said.

'I hear you. I don't necessarily disagree. Last one to the parking lot is dog chow.'

'Not funny, Lieutenant Martha. Bad joke. This is getting a little spooky.'

'I don't know about big cats around these parts, but I think I just spotted a little pussy.'

Another loud growl – and this time it was really close. Right on the heels of the two of them. Gaining ground fast.

'C'mon! Let's go. Let's move it,' said Martha Wiatt. She was a little afraid now, running as fast as she could, and that was very fast.

Another eerie growl pierced the gathering fog.

Chapter Three

Lieutenant Martha Wiatt had definitely picked up her pace. She put some distance between herself and Davis. It wasn't that hard. She did triathlons *for fun*. He worked behind a desk, though, God knows, he certainly looked good for an accountant.

'C'mon, c'mon. Keep up with me, Davis. Don't fall back,' she called over her shoulder.

Her boyfriend for the past year didn't answer. Well, that settled any future debate about who was in better shape, who was the real athlete. Of course, Martha had known that all along.

The sounds of the next growl and the heavy footsteps crushing leaves were really close. They were catching up to her.

But *what* was catching up to her?

'Martha! There's something behind me. Oh God! Run!

Run, Martha!' Davis shouted. 'Get the hell out of here!'

Adrenaline charged through her. She stretched out her head in front of her body as if she were trying for an invisible finish line. Her arms and legs moved in synch like efficient pistons. She leaned her weight forward, the way all good runners do.

She heard screams behind her and looked back – but she couldn't see Davis anymore. The screams were so terrifying that she almost stopped running. But Davis had been attacked by something vicious. Martha rationalized that she had to get help. The police. Somebody.

Her boyfriend's screams were ringing in her ears and she was running in total panic, unaware of where she was going. She stumbled over a pointy rock and cartwheeled down a steep hill, crashing into the base of a small tree, but at least it stopped her fall.

In a daze, she managed to pull herself up. Jesus, she was pretty sure she'd broken her right arm. Cradling it with the left, she ran forward in a clumsy stumble.

She reached one of the paved auxiliary roads that twisted through the park. Davis's screams had stopped. What had happened to him? She had to get help.

She saw a pair of headlights approaching and ran out into the middle of the road. She straddled the double center lines and felt like a total madwoman. *For God's sake, this is San Francisco!*

'Please stop, please stop. Hey! Hey! Hey!' She waved her good arm and shouted at the top of her voice. 'Stop! I need help!'

The white van sped straight for her, but then, thank God, it skidded to a stop. Two men jumped out and ran to her. They would help. The van said 'Red Cross' on its hood.

'Help me. Please,' Martha said. 'My boyfriend is hurt.'

Things went from bad to worse. One of them hit her with a closed fist. Before Martha realized what was happening, she went down hard. Her chin struck the pavement, bouncing like a wet ball. She was knocked almost unconscious by the powerful blow.

She looked up, tried to focus her eyes, and wished she hadn't. Blazing red eyes stared down at her. A mouth was open wide. *Two* mouths. She had never seen such teeth in her life. They were like sharpened knives. The incisors were huge.

She felt the teeth bite into her cheek, then her neck. *How could that be?* They tore into her and Martha screamed until her throat was raw. She rolled and twisted and kicked out at her attackers, but it did no good. They were incredibly strong. Both of them were growling.

'Ecstasy,' one of them whispered against Martha's ear. 'Isn't it exquisite? You're so lucky. You were chosen out of all the beautiful people in San Francisco. You and Davis.'

Chapter Four

It was a perfect, blue-skied morning in Washington – well, almost perfect. The Mastermind was on my cell phone. 'Hello, Alex. Did you miss me? I missed you, partner.'

The bastard had been making obscene, threatening phone calls to me every morning for over a week. Sometimes he just cursed at me for several minutes; this morning, he sounded positively civil.

'What's your day look like? Any big plans?' he asked.

Actually, yes. I was planning to catch him. I was inside an FBI van that was already on the move. We were tracing his call and would have the exact location very soon. A court order had been put through the FBI and the phone company was involved in 'trapping' the call. I was in the rear of the speeding van with three Bureau agents and my partner, John Sampson. We had left my house on Fifth

Street as soon as the call came in; we were heading onto I-395 North. My job was to keep him on the line until the trace was completed.

'Tell me about Betsey Cavalierre. Why did you pick her instead of me?' I asked him.

'Oh, she's much, much prettier,' the Mastermind said. 'More *fuckable*.'

One of the techie agents was talking in the background. I tried to listen to both conversations. The agent said, 'He's living up to his name. We've got a wire tap and *should* be able to trace the call immediately. It *isn't* happening for some reason.'

'Why the hell not?' Sampson asked and moved closer to the agents.

'Don't know exactly. We're picking up different locations, but they keep changing. Maybe he's on a cell phone in a car. Cell phones are harder to trace.'

I could see that we were getting off the D Street Exit. Then we headed into the Third Street tunnel. Where was he?

'Everything all right, Alex? You seem a little distracted,' the Mastermind said.

'No, I'm right here with you. Partner. Enjoying our little breakfast club.'

'I don't know why this is so goddamn hard,' the FBI techie complained.

Because he's the Mastermind, I wanted to yell at him.

I saw the Washington Convention Center on the right. The van was really clipping along, doing sixty or seventy on the city streets.

We passed the Renaissance Hotel. Where the hell was the Mastermind calling from?

'I think we have a fix on him. We're real close,' one of the young agents said in an excited voice.

Suddenly the FBI van stopped; it was chaos inside. Sampson and I pulled out our guns. We had him. I couldn't believe we had him.

Then everyone inside the van groaned and cursed. I looked outside and saw why. I shook my head in disgust.

'Jesus Christ, do you believe this shit!' Sampson yelled and pounded the wall of the van. We were at 935 Pennsylvania Avenue, the J. Edgar Hoover Building. FBI headquarters.

'What's happening now?' I asked the agent in charge. 'Where the hell is he?'

'Shit, the signal is roaming again. It's moving outside Washington. Okay, now it's back in the city. Christ, it just skipped out of the country.'

'Goodbye, Alex. For now anyway. As I told you before, you're next,' the Mastermind said. Then he hung up on me.

Chapter Five

The rest of my day was long, hard, and depressing. More than anything, I needed a break from the Mastermind.

I'm not exactly sure when, where or how I got up the nerve, but I had a date that night. It was with a lawyer for the DA's office here in Washington. Elizabeth Moore was wickedly funny and nicely irreverent. She was a large woman with a really sweet smile that made *me* smile. We were having dinner at Marcel's in Foggy Bottom, a good spot for this kind of thing. The food is French, with a Flemish flair. The night couldn't have been going any better. I thought so, and I was pretty sure that Elizabeth would agree.

After the waiter left with our orders for dessert and coffee, Elizabeth put her hand lightly on top of mine. Our table was lit by a simple crystal votive candle.

'All right, Alex. We've gone through all the preliminaries.

I *enjoyed* the preliminaries,' she said. 'Now what's the catch? There has to be a catch. Has to be. All the good ones are taken. I know that from experience. So why are you still playing the dating game?'

I understood exactly what Elizabeth meant, but I pretended to look slightly puzzled.

'Catch?' I shrugged, then I finally started to smile.

She laughed out loud. 'You're what – thirty-nine, forty?'

'Forty-two, but thanks,' I said.

'You passed every test I could possibly throw at you . . .'

'Such as?'

'Such as picking a great spot for dinner. Romantic, but not too romantic. Such as being right on time when you arrived to pick me up. Such as *listening* to some of the things that actually interest me. Such as being very handsome – not that it matters to me. Yeah, right.'

'I also like children, wouldn't mind having more,' I added. 'I've read all of Toni Morrison's novels. I'm a decent plumber. I can cook if I have to.'

'The *catch*?' she said again. 'Let's leave it.'

Our waiter returned, and right as he was pouring a steaming cup of coffee for Elizabeth, the beeper on my belt went off.

Oh Jesus.

Busted!

I looked across the table at her – and I blinked. I was

definitely the first one to blink.

'You mind if I take this? It's important. I recognize the number – the FBI in Quantico. I won't be long. I'll be right back.'

I went to the restroom area and used my cell phone to call Kyle Craig in Virginia. Kyle has been a solid friend for many years, but ever since I became liaison between the Bureau and the DC police, I've seen way too much of him. He keeps dragging me into the nastiest murder cases on the FBI's docket. I hated taking his calls. *Now* what had happened?

Kyle knew who was calling back. He didn't even bother to say hello. 'Alex, do you remember a case you and I worked about fourteen months ago? A runaway girl was found hung from a lighting fixture in her hotel room. Patricia Cameron? There have been two murders in San Francisco that match up. Happened last night in Golden Gate Park. This is a very bad scene – the worst I've heard about in a while.'

'Kyle, I'm having dinner with an attractive, very nice, interesting woman. I'll talk to you tomorrow. *I'll call you.* I'm off duty tonight.'

Kyle laughed. I amused him sometimes. 'Nana already told me. Your date's a lawyer, right? Listen to this one. The devil meets with this lawyer. Says he can make the lawyer a senior partner, but the lawyer has to give him his soul *and* the soul of everybody in his family. The lawyer stares at the devil and asks, "So what's the catch?" ' After he told his joke, Kyle went on to tell me more than I wanted to hear about the similarities connecting the awful murders in San Francisco to the one I had investigated in DC. I remembered the victim, Patricia Cameron. I could still see her face. I shook off the image.

When he was finished, and Kyle tends to be thorough if a bit long-winded, I went back to join Elizabeth at our table.

She smiled ruefully and shook her head. 'I think I just figured out the catch,' she said.

I did my best to laugh, but my insides were already tied up in knots. 'Honestly, it's not as bad as it looks.'

It's much worse, Elizabeth.

Chapter Six

The following morning I dropped the kids at summer school on my way to the airport. Jannie is eight; Damon just turned ten. They're really good kids, but they're kids. You give them a tiny advantage, they take a lot, and then they take a little more. Someone, I don't remember who, said that 'American children suffer too much mother and too little father.' With my kids, it's been the exact opposite.

'I could get used to this,' Jannie said as we pulled up in front of the Sojourner Truth School. Helen Folasade Adu – *Sade* – was singing softly on the CD. Very nice.

'Don't get used to it. It's a five-block walk from our house to school. When I was a little boy in North Carolina, I used to walk five miles through tobacco fields to school.'

'Yeah, right,' Damon scoffed. 'You forgot that you used to walk *barefoot*. Left that part out.'

'I did. Thanks for reminding me. I used to walk barefoot through those nasty tobacco fields to school.'

The kids laughed and so did I. They're usually good to be around, and I'm always videotaping them. I do it in the hopes that I'll have nice movies to watch when the two of them go bad in their teenage years. Also, I'm afraid I might get CRS someday – the *can't remember shit* disease. It's going around.

'I have a big concert on Saturday,' Damon reminded me. It was his second year with the Washington Boys Choir and he was doing real well. He was going to be the next Luther Vandross, or Al Green, or maybe he was just going to be Damon Cross.

'I'll be home by Saturday, Damon. Trust me, I wouldn't miss your concert.'

'You missed quite a few already,' he said. It was a sharp little dig.

'That was the old me. This is the new and improved Alex. I've also *attended* several of your concerts.'

'You're so funny, Daddy,' Jannie said, and laughed. Both kids are smart, and smart-assed as well.

'I will be home for Damon's concert on Saturday,' I promised. 'Help your grandma around the house. She's almost a hundred years old, you know.'

Jannie rolled her eyes. 'Nana's eighty years young, or so she says. She *loves* to cook, do the dishes, and clean up after us,' she said, imitating Nana's wicked cackle. 'She truly does.'

'Saturday. I can't wait,' I said to Damon. It was the whole truth and nothing but. The Boys Choir was one of Washington's secret treasures. I was ecstatic that Damon was good enough to sing with the group, but most of all that he loved what he was doing.

'Kisses,' I said. 'Hugs too.'

Damon and Jannie groaned, but they leaned in close and I wondered how much longer they would be willing to give me hugs and pecks on the cheek. So I took an extra few while I could get them. When the good times come with your kids, you've got to make them last.

'I love you two,' I said before I let them go off to school. 'What do you say?'

'We love you too,' Damon and Jannie chorused.

'That's why we let you embarrass us to death in front of our school and all our friends,' Jannie said, and she stuck out her tongue.

'This *is* your last ride to school,' I told her. Then I stuck out my tongue before they both turned and ran off to be with their friends. They were growing up way too fast for me.

Chapter Seven

I called Kyle Craig from the airport and he told me his élite crew at Quantico was busy checking for related murders and biting attacks from sea to shining sea. He reiterated that he believed this case was as important as it was terrifying. I wondered what else he knew. Usually more than he tells.

'You're up early, Kyle, and you're busy. This case has caught your full attention. Why is that?'

'Of course it has. It's totally unique. I haven't seen anything remotely like it. Inspector Jamilla Hughes will meet your flight if she can. It's her case and she's supposed to be competent. She's one of two women in Homicide in San Francisco, so she probably is fairly good.'

On the plane trip from DC I read and reread the faxes I'd gotten that morning about the horrific murders in Golden Gate Park. Inspector Hughes' preliminary crime-scene notes were precise and detailed, but most of all gut-wrenching.

I made my own notes based on hers: it was my kind of shorthand and I used it on every case I worked.

Male and female victims found dead at 3:20 A.M. in Golden Gate Park, San Francisco. Why there? Visit park if possible.

Victims hung by feet from oak tree. Why hung? To drain the bodies? Why drain the bodies? Rite of purification? Spiritual cleansing?

Bodies naked and covered in blood. Why naked? Erotic? Sex crimes? Or just brutal? Exposing the victims to the world for some reason?

Male's legs, arms, chest severely gouged – victim appears to have been bitten repeatedly. Male actually died from bites!!!

Female bitten – but not as severely. Also cut with sharp object. Died from massive blood loss, Class IV. Female lost over 40% of her blood.

Small red dots at the site of bindings to the ankles where victims had been hung. Called petechiae by the ME.

Teeth marks on male appear to be those of large animal. Is that even remotely possible? What animal would attack a jogger in a big city park? Seems far-fetched to say the least.

White substance on male victim's legs and stomach. Could be semen. What game were the killers playing? Auto-erotic?

I remembered the related case in Washington. How could I forget it?

A sixteen-year-old runaway girl from Orlando, Florida, had been found dead and severely mutilated in a hotel room downtown. Her name was Patricia Dawn Cameron. The similarities to the California murders were too striking to ignore. The girl in DC had suffered savage bites all over her body. She had been hung by her feet from a hotel room lighting fixture.

Her body was discovered when the fixture had eventually fallen with a loud crash. Patricia Cameron had died of blood loss, another Class IV. She had lost nearly seventy percent of her blood supply.

The first question was an obvious one.

So why did somebody need all that blood?

Chapter Eight

I was still thinking about the strange, terrible bites, and all that blood, as I walked off the plane and into crowded San Francisco International Airport. I looked around for Inspector Jamilla Hughes. Rumor had it that she was an attractive black woman.

I noted that a businessman near the gate was reading *The Examiner*. I could see the bold headline on the front page – HORROR IN GOLDEN GATE PARK, TWO MURDERED.

I didn't see anyone waiting, so I began to look for signs directing me to public transportation. I only had a carry-on bag; I had promised to be home by Saturday for Damon's concert. I had my marching orders and I planned to keep my promises from now on. *Cross my heart.*

A woman walked up to me as I started away from the gate. 'Excuse me, are you Detective Cross?'

I had noticed her just before she spoke to me. She was wearing jeans, a black leather car coat over a powder blue T-shirt. Then I spotted the tell-tale holster under her jacket. She was probably in her mid-thirties, nice looking, down-to-earth, pleasant for a homicide detective, who often come on a little gruff.

'Inspector Hughes?' I asked.

'Jamilla.' She extended her hand and smiled as I took it. Nice smile, too. 'It's good to meet you, Detective. Ordinarily, I'd resist the sell out of any idea that originated with the FBI, but your reputation precedes you. Also, the murder in DC was awfully similar, wasn't it? So – welcome to San Francisco.'

'Good to be here.' I returned the smile as I shook hands with her. Her grip was strong, but not overly so. 'I was just thinking about the murder in DC,' I told her. 'Your crime-scene notes brought it all back to me. We never got anywhere with the murder of Patricia Cameron. You can add that to the file on my so-called reputation, the one that preceded me.'

Jamilla Hughes smiled again. Sincere. Nothing overdone about it; nothing overdone about her either. She didn't particularly look like a homicide detective, and that was probably good. She seemed a little too normal to be a cop.

'Well, we'd better hurry. I've contacted a veterinary dental specialist and he's meeting us at the city morgue.

He's a good friend of the medical examiner. How's that for showing you the sights of San Francisco?'

I shook my head and grinned. 'Actually, it's exactly what I came out here to see. I think I read about it in one of the tour books. When you're in San Francisco don't pass up a chance to see the morgue.'

'It's not in the tour books,' Jamilla said, 'but it should be. It's a whole lot more interesting than any trolley-car ride.'

Chapter Nine

Less than fifty minutes later, Jamilla Hughes and I were inside the morgue at San Francisco's famed Hall of Justice. We had joined the chief medical examiner, Walter Lee, and the dental expert, Dr Pang.

Dr Allen Pang took his time examining both bodies. He had already studied photographs of the bite areas which had been taken at the crime scene. He was a small man, completely bald, with very thick black-rimmed glasses. At one point during his examination, I noticed Inspector Hughes give a wink to the ME. I think they found Dr Pang just a little strange. So did I, but he was very thorough, and obviously serious about the job he had taken on.

'Okay, okay. I'm ready to talk about the nature of the bites now.' He finally turned to us and made his pronouncement. 'I understand you're making casts of the bite marks, Walter?'

'Yes, we lifted the marks with fingerprint powder. The casts should be ready in a day or two. We swabbed to gather saliva, of course.'

'Well, good. That's the right approach, I think. I'm ready to state my piece, my educated guess.'

'That's excellent, Allen,' Lee said in a soft, very dignified voice. He wore a white coat with the nickname Dragon stitched on one pocket. He was a tall man, probably six-two, and weighed at least two-fifty. He carried himself with confidence. 'Dr Pang is a friend I have used before,' Lee continued. 'He's a veterinary dental expert from the Animal Medical Center in Berkeley. Allen is one of the best in the world, and we're lucky to have him on this case.'

'Thank you for your time, Dr Pang,' Inspector Hughes said. 'This is terrific of you to help.'

'Thank you.' I joined in with the hallelujah chorus of praise.

'It's perfectly all right,' he said. 'I'm not exactly sure where to start, other than to say that these two homicides are most interesting to me. The male was severely bitten, and I'm relatively sure the attacker was, well, it was a tiger. The bites on the female were inflicted by two humans. It's as if the humans and the large cat were running together. Like they were a pack. Extraordinary. And bizarre, to say the least.'

'A *tiger*?' Jamilla was the one to express the disbelief we were all feeling. 'Are you sure? That doesn't seem possible, Dr Pang.'

'Allen,' Walter Lee said. 'Explain, please.'

'Well, as you know, humans are heterodonts; that is, they have teeth of different sizes and shapes, which serve different functions. Most important would be our canines, which are situated between the lateral and the first premolar on each side of each jaw. The canines are used to tear food.'

Walter Lee nodded, and Dr Pang continued. He was speaking solely to the ME at this point. I caught Jamilla's eye, and she gave me a wink. I liked that she had a sense of humor.

Dr Pang now seemed in his own world. 'In contrast to humans, some animals are homodents. Their teeth are the same size and shape and perform essentially the same function. This is not true of large cats, however, especially tigers. The teeth of tigers have been adapted for their feeding habits. Each jaw contains six pointed cutting teeth; two very sharp, recurved canines; and molars that have evolved into cutting blades.'

'Is that important in terms of these murders?' Jamilla Hughes asked Dr Pang. I had a version of the same question.

The small man nodded enthusiastically. 'Oh, of course. Certainly. The jaw of a tiger is extremely strong, able to clamp down hard enough to crush bone. The jaw can only move up and down, not side to side. This means the tiger can only tear and crush food, not chew or gnaw.' He demonstrated with his own teeth and jaw.

I swallowed hard, and found my head shaking back and forth. *A tiger was involved in these murders? How could that possibly be?*

Dr Pang stopped talking. He reached up and scratched his bald pate rather vigorously. Then he said, 'What completely baffles me is that someone commanded the tiger away from its prey after it struck – *and the tiger obeyed*. If that didn't happen, the prey would have been eaten.'

'Absolutely amazing,' the medical examiner said, and gave Dr Pang a pat on the back. Then he looked at Jamilla and me. 'What's the saying – "catch a tiger, if you can"? A tiger shouldn't be all that hard to find in San Francisco.'

Chapter Ten

The large, white, male tiger was making a chuffing sound, a muted, backward whistle. The sucking noise came from deep inside its wide throat. The sound was almost unearthly. Birds took flight from a nearby cypress oak. Small animals scampered away as fast as they could.

The tiger was eight feet long, muscular, and weighed just over five hundred and eighty pounds. Under ordinary circumstances its prey would have been pigs and piglets, deer, antelope, water buffalo. There were no ordinary circumstances in California. There were lots of humans, though.

The cat pounced quickly, its lithe, powerful body moving effortlessly. The young blond male didn't even try to resist.

The tiger's massive jaw opened wide, then clamped down onto the man's head. The cat's jaws were strong enough to pulverize bone.

The man screamed, 'Stop! Stop! *Stop!*'

Amazingly the tiger stopped.

Just like that. On verbal command.

'You win,' the blond man laughed and patted the animal, which released his head.

The man twisted sharply to the left. His movements were almost as quick and effortless as the cat's. Then he pounced. He attacked the tiger's vulnerable creamy-white underside, grabbing onto flesh with his teeth. 'Got you, you big baby! You lose. You're still my love slave.'

William Alexander stood off in the distance, watching his younger brother with a mixture of curiosity and awe. Michael was a beautiful man-child, incredibly graceful and athletic, strong beyond belief. He wore a black pocket T-shirt and powder blue shorts. He was already six feet three and a hundred-eighty-five pounds. He was flawless. Both of them were, actually.

William walked away, staring into the distance at the rich, green hills. He loved it out here. The beauty and the solitude, the freedom to do anything he wanted to do.

He was very quiet inside – an art that he was still mastering.

When he and Michael were small boys, this whole area had been a commune. Their mother and father had been hippies, experimenters, freedom lovers, massive drug-takers. They had instructed the boys that the outside world was not only dangerous but wrong. Their mother had taught William and Michael that having sex with anyone, even with her, was a good thing, as long as it was consensual. The brothers had slept with their mother, and their father, and many others in the commune. Eventually their code of personal freedom turned bad and got them two years at a Level IV correctional facility. They had been arrested for possession, but it was aggravated assault that put the brothers behind bars. They were suspected of much more serious crimes, but none could be proved.

As William stared off at the foothills, he marveled at the concept of the *unbridled mind*. Day by day he left behind the shabby baggage of his past life. Soon he would have no false morals, or ethics, or any of the other bullshit inhibitions taught in the civilized world.

He was getting closer to the truth. So was Michael.

William was twenty.

Michael was only seventeen.

They had been killing together for five years, and they kept getting better and better at it.

They were invincible.

Immortal.

Chapter Eleven

That night, the two brothers hunted in the town of Mill Valley in Marin County. The area was beautiful, small mountains teeming with strapping, healthy evergreen and eucalyptus trees. The redwood house was maybe a hundred yards ahead, up a steep, rocky slope that they climbed with ease. A brick walkway led to an entryway with double wooden doors.

'We have to go away for a while.'William spoke without turning around to Michael. 'We have a mission from the Sire. San Francisco was just the start.'

'That's excellent,' Michael said, and he began to smile. 'I enjoyed what went down there very much. Who are these people, the ones in the big, fancy house?'

William shrugged. 'Just prey. They're nobody.'

Michael began to pout. 'Why won't you tell me who they are?'

'The Sire said not to talk, and not to bring the cat.'

Michael asked no further questions. His obedience to the Sire was complete.

The Sire told you how to think, feel, and act.

The Sire was accountable to no one, to no other authority.

The Sire despised the straight world, as did they.

This definitely looked like the 'straight world'. The large house had all the trappings: gardens tended and watered daily; a small pond filled with koi; several layers of terraces leading up to a large house with over a dozen rooms – for just two people. How obnoxious could anyone be?

William walked right in the front door and Michael followed. The foyer had a twenty-foot ceiling, a ridiculous crystal chandelier, a spiral staircase to heaven.

They found the couple in the kitchen, preparing a late meal, both of them sharing the preparations like the goodie-goodies that they were.

'Yuppies at play,' William said, and smiled.

'Whoa!' the male said, and threw up both of his hands. He was close to six-four and well-built. He was working like kitchen help at the vegetable sink. 'What the hell do you guys think you're doing? Let's take it outside.'

'*You're* the trouble-making lawyer,' William said, and pointed at the female. She was early thirties, short blond hair, high cheekbones, slender, with small breasts. 'We came for supper.'

'I'm a lawyer, too,' the domineering male said. 'I don't think you two were invited. I'm sure of it. Get out! You hear me? Hey, you assholes, hit the road.'

'You threatened the Sire.' William continued to talk to the female. 'So he sent us here.'

'I'm going to call the police.' The woman finally spoke. She was upset now, the nubs of her breasts rising and falling against her shirt. She had a small cell phone in her hand and William wondered if she had pulled it out of her ass. The thought made him smile.

He was on her in an instant and Michael took down the husband almost as easily. The brothers were incredibly fast and strong – and they knew it.

They growled loudly, but that was only an element of surprise, a scare tactic.

'We have money in the house. My God, don't hurt us,' the male shrieked loudly, almost like a woman.

'We're not after your obscene money – we have no use for it. And we're not serial killers, or anything common like that,' William told them.

He bit down into the struggling woman's luscious pink neck – and she stopped fighting. Just like that, she was his. She gazed into his eyes, and she swooned. A tear ran down her cheek.

William didn't look up again until he had fed. 'We're vampires,' he finally whispered to the murdered couple.

Chapter Twelve

On my second day in San Francisco, I worked out of a small cubicle near Jamilla Hughes' desk at the Hall of Justice. I attended a couple of her briefings on the Golden Gate Park murders, which were thorough and highly professional. She was impressive.

Everything about the murder case was weird and wrongheaded, though. No one had a fix on it yet; no one had a good idea, at least none that I'd heard so far. The only thing we knew for sure was that people were being murdered in particularly horrible ways. It happens more and more frequently these days.

Around noon, I got a call on my cell phone. 'Just checking in,' the Mastermind said. 'How is San Francisco, Alex? Lovely city. Will you leave your heart there? Do you think it's a good place to die?

'Or how about Inspector Hughes? Do you like her?

She's very pretty, isn't she? Just your type. Are you going to fuck Jamilla? Better hurry then. Tempus fugit.' He hung up.

I went back to work. Lost myself for a couple of hours. Began to make some minor progress.

Around four o'clock, I was staring out at the start of rush hour San Francisco-style – pretty mild, actually – while I talked to Kyle Craig. He was still at Quantico, but he was definitely heavily involved in the case.

Kyle was in a position to choose the cases he became personally connected with, and he told me this was going to be one of them. We'd be working together again. I looked forward to it.

I caught a movement out of the corner of my eye and saw Jamilla approaching. She had her leather jacket half on and was struggling into the second sleeve. Going somewhere? 'Hold on, Kyle,' I said into the receiver.

'We have to go,' she said, 'to San Luis Obispo. They're going to exhume a body. I think it's related.'

I told Kyle that I had to leave right away. He wished me happy hunting. Jamilla and I took the elevator down to the parking garage beneath the Hall of Justice. The more I saw of her work, the more I was impressed; not just by her savvy, but by her enthusiasm for the job. A lot of detectives lose that after a couple of years. She obviously hadn't. *Are you going to fuck Jamilla? Better hurry then.*

'Are you always this pumped up?' I asked her once we

were inside her blue Saab and heading out toward Highway 101.

'Yeah. Pretty much,' she said. 'I like the work. It's tough, but interesting, honest most of the time. I could do without the violence.'

'This case in particular. The hangings give me the creeps.'

She looked over at me. 'Speaking of life-threatening situations, you'd better buckle up. We've got a hike ahead of us, and I used to drive funny cars as a hobby. Don't be fooled by the Saab.'

She wasn't kidding. According to the road signs, it was about 235 miles to San Luis Obispo. Heavy rain peppered the car most of the way. She still got us there by eight-thirty.

'In one piece, too.' She nodded and winked as we whisked off the highway at the San Luis Obispo exit.

It looked like an idyllic spot, but we were there to exhume the corpse of a young girl. She had been hung and her blood had been drained.

Chapter Thirteen

San Luis Obispo is a very pretty college town, at least from the outside looking in. We found Higuera Street and drove down it to Osos, past small local shops, but also Starbucks, Barnes & Noble, the Firestone Grill. Jamilla told me that you could always tell the time of day in San Luis Obispo by the scents and aromas: like barbecue smoke in the afternoon on Marsh Street, or the aroma of wheat and barley at night outside the Slo Brewing Co.

We met Detective Nancy Goodes at the police station in town. She was a petite, attractive woman, with a nice California tan, very much in charge of her homicide investigation. In addition to contacting us about this exhumation, she was also the lead on the murders of two students from Cal Poly that didn't seem related to our case, but who could tell for sure. Like most homicide detectives these days, she was busy.

★ ★ ★

'We've got the permissions we need to exhume the body,'
Goodes told us on the way out to the cemetery. At least the
rain had stopped for now. The air was warm, thanks to
Santa Ana winds.

'What can you tell us about the murder, Nancy? You
worked the case yourself, right?' Jamilla asked.

The detective nodded. 'I did. So did just about every
other detective in town. It was very sad, and an important
case here. Mary Alice Richardson went to the Catholic
high school in town. Her father's a well-liked doctor. She
was a nice kid, but a bit of a wild child. What can I tell you,
she was a *kid*. Fifteen years old.'

'What do you mean she was a wild child?' I asked
Detective Goodes.

She sighed and worked her jaw a little. I could tell this
case had left a wound. 'She missed a lot of school, two or
three days a week sometimes. She was bright enough, but
her grades were just terrible. She hung with other kids
who liked to experiment – drugs like Ecstasy, raves, black
magic, heavy drinking, all-night parties. Maybe even a
little free-basing. Mary Alice was only arrested once, but
she was giving her parents a lot of premature gray hairs.'

Jamilla asked, 'Were you at the crime scene, Nancy?' I
noticed that she was respectful of the other detective at all
times. Very non-threatening toward Nancy.

'Unfortunately, I was. That's one of the reasons I worked so hard getting the permissions we needed to dig up her body. Mary Alice died a year and three months ago, but I will never, ever forget how we found her.'

Jamilla and I looked at each other. We hadn't heard the particulars of the murder yet. We were still playing catch-up.

Goodes continued. 'It was pretty clear to me that she was meant to be found. Two kids from Cal Poly were the ones who actually discovered the body. They were parking out near the hills. It's a popular spot for submarine races. They went for a little moonlit stroll. I'm sure they had nightmares after what they saw. Mary Alice was hanging from a cypress tree by her bare feet. Naked. Except the killers left her earrings, and a small sapphire in her belly button. This wasn't a robbery.'

'How about her clothes?' I asked.

'We found the clothes: UFO parachute pants, Nikes, Chili Peppers T-shirt. No trophies were taken to our knowledge.'

I glanced at Jamilla. 'The killer trusts his or her memory. Doesn't need trophies for some reason. Or so it seems. None of this follows any of the usual paths for serials.'

'No, it doesn't. I agree with that one hundred percent. Do you know what scarification is?' Detective Goodes asked.

'I've come across it,' I said. 'Scars, wounds. Most often on the legs and arms. Occasionally the chest or back. They avoid the face, because then people might make them stop. Usually the scars are self-inflicted.'

Detective Goodes nodded. 'Mary Alice had either cut herself over the past couple of months, or someone else did it for her. She had over seventy separate cuts on her body. Everywhere but the face.'

The detective's white Suburban pulled onto a gravel road, then we passed between rusted wrought-iron gates.

'We're here,' Nancy Goodes announced. 'Let's get this over with. Cemeteries make me twitchy. I hate what we're going to do. This makes me so sad.'

It made me sad, too.

Chapter Fourteen

I have yet to meet a relatively sane person who is anything but twitchy in a cemetery late at night. I consider myself to be mildly sane, therefore I was twitchy. Detective Goodes was right, this was a very sad affair, a tragic conclusion to a young girl's life.

The backdrop for the cemetery was the rolling foothills of the Santa Lucia Mountains. Three patrol cars from the police department in San Luis Obispo were already parked around the gravesite of Mary Alice Richardson. The medical examiner's van was parked nearby. Plus two beat-up trucks without any clear identification on them.

Four cemetery workers were digging in the bright light cast from the patrol-car headlamps. The soil looked rich and loamy and was thick with worms. When the hole was of sufficient depth, a backhoe was brought in to finish the job.

. The police observers, including myself, had nothing to do but stand impatiently around the grave. We drank coffee, exchanged small talk, cracked a few dark jokes, but nobody really laughed.

I turned my cell phone off. I didn't need to hear from the Mastermind, or anybody else, here in the cemetery.

Around one in the morning, the container of the casket was finally uncovered by the cemetery workers. A lump rose in my throat, but I looked on. Beside me stood Jamilla Hughes. She was shivering some, but sticking it out. Nancy Goodes had retreated to her Suburban. Smart lady.

A crowbar was used to pry off the top of the liner. It made an unpleasant groaning noise, like someone in deep pain.

The hole in the ground was approximately six feet deep, eight feet long, less than four feet wide.

Neither of us spoke. Every detail of the exhumation held our attention now. My eyes blinked too rapidly in the eerie light. My breathing was uneven and my throat felt a little raw.

I was recalling crime-scene pictures of Mary Alice that I'd seen. Fifteen years old. Hung two feet off the ground by her ankles, left that way for several hours. Drained of nearly all her blood. Another Class IV death. Viciously bitten and stabbed.

The victim in Washington hadn't been stabbed. So what

did that mean? Why the variations on the murder theme? What did they do with all the blood? I almost didn't want to know the answers to the questions throbbing inside my head.

Tattered gray canvas straps were carefully secured to the casket and it was finally, slowly raised out of the ground.

My breathing was ragged. Suddenly I felt guilty about being here. I had the thought that we shouldn't be disturbing this poor girl in her grave. It was an unholy thing to do. She had been violated enough.

'I know, I know. This sucks. I feel the same thing,' Jamilla said out of the side of her mouth. She lightly touched a hand to my elbow. 'We have to do it. No other choice. We have to find out if it's the same killers.'

'I know. Why doesn't that make me feel any better about this?' I muttered. 'I feel all hollowed out.'

'That poor girl. Poor Mary Alice. Forgive us,' Jamilla said.

A local funeral director, who had consented to be on hand, carefully opened the casket. Then he stepped back, as if he had seen a ghost.

I moved forward to get my first look at the girl. I nearly gasped, and Jamilla's hand went to her mouth. A couple of the cemetery workers crossed themselves and bowed their heads low.

Mary Alice Richardson was right there staring up at us. She was wearing a flowing white dress and her blond hair was carefully braided. The girl looked as if she had been buried alive. There had been virtually no decay of the body.

'There's an explanation for this,' the funeral director said to us. 'The Richardsons are friends of mine. They asked me if anything could be done to preserve their daughter for as long as possible. Somehow they knew their little girl would be seen again.

'The condition of the body, once interred, can be in any state of decay. It depends on the ingredients. I used an arsenic solution in the embalming process, the way we used to in the old days. You're looking at the result.'

He paused as we continued to stare.

'This is the way Mary Alice looked the day she was buried. This is the poor girl they murdered and hung.'

Chapter Fifteen

We got back to San Francisco at seven in the morning. I didn't know how Jamilla could drive, but she did just fine. We forced ourselves to talk most of the way back, just to keep awake. We even had a few laughs. I was bone-tired and could barely keep my eyes open. When I finally closed them inside my hotel room, I saw Mary Alice Richardson in her coffin.

Inspector Hughes was drinking coffee at her desk when I arrived at the Hall of Justice at two o'clock that afternoon. She looked fresh and alert. None the worse for wear. She seemed to work as hard as I did on a case, maybe harder. I hoped it was a good thing for her.

'Don't you ever sleep?' I asked as I stopped to talk for a moment. My eyes went to the clutter at her work-space. I noticed a photograph of a smiling, very good-looking man propped on her desk. I was glad that she had time for a love life at least. It made me think of Christine Johnson, who was now living out here on the West Coast. I felt a stab of rejection. The love of my life? Not anymore. Unfortunately, not anymore. Christine had left Washington and moved to Seattle. She liked it there a lot, and was teaching school again.

Jamilla shrugged. 'I woke up around noon, couldn't get back to sleep. Maybe I'm too tired. The ME in Luis Obispo says he'll send us a report late today. But listen to this. I just got an e-mail from Quantico. There have been eight murders in California and Nevada that bear some resemblance to the Golden Gate Park ones. Not all of the victims were hung. But they were bitten. The cases go back six years. So far. They're looking back even further than that.'

'What cities?' I asked her.

She glanced down at her notes. 'Sacramento – our esteemed capital. San Diego. Santa Cruz. Las Vegas. Lake Tahoe. San Jose. San Francisco. San Luis Obispo. This is so goddamn creepy, Alex. One murder like this would be enough to keep me sleepless for a month.'

'Plus the murder in Washington,' I said. 'I'm going to ask the Bureau to look at the East Coast.'

She grinned sheepishly. 'I already did. They're on it.'

I teased, 'So what do we do now?'

'What do cops always do when they wait? We eat doughnuts and drink coffee,' she said and rolled her dark brown eyes. She had a natural, very attractive beauty, even on just a few hours' sleep.

The two of us had a late breakfast at Roma's around the corner. We talked about the case, then I asked her about other cases she'd solved. Jamilla had a lot of confidence, but she was also modest about her contributions. I liked that about her. She definitely wasn't full of herself. When she had finished her omelet and toast, she sat there nervously tapping her finger against the table. She had several tics, seemed wired most of the time. I knew she was on the job again.

'What's the matter?' I finally asked. 'You're holding something back, aren't you?'

She nodded. 'I got a call from KRON-TV. They're close to doing a story revealing that there have been several murders in California.'

I frowned. 'How the hell did they find out?'

She shook her head. 'Who knows? I'm going to give a reporter I know at *The Examiner* the okay to break the story first.'

'Hold on a second,' I said. 'You sure about that?'

'I'm sure. I trust my friend as much as I trust anybody. He'll ground the story in reality at least. Now help me figure out if there's anything we want the killers to read in the newspapers. It's the least my friend can do for us.'

When we got back to the Hall of Justice there was bad news. The killers had struck again.

Chapter Sixteen

I t was another bad one, another hanging. Two hangings, actually.

Jamilla and I split up as soon as we arrived at the murder scene in Mill Valley. We had different ways of doing things, different crime-scene techniques. Some-how, though, I thought we would arrive at the same conclusions about this one. I could see the signs already – all of them bad.

The two bodies were hung upside down from a rack used to hold copper pots. The scene of the murders was a contemporary kitchen inside a large, very expensive house. Dawn and Gavin Brody looked to be in their mid-thirties. Like the other victims, they'd been drained of most of their blood.

The first curiosity: although the Brodys were naked, the killers had left behind their jewelry. A pair of Rolex watches, wedding bands, a large diamond engagement ring, hoop earrings studded with countless small diamonds. The killers weren't interested in jewels or money, and possibly they wanted us to know it.

So where were the victims' clothes? Had they been used to clean up the mess, to mop up blood? Was that why the killers had taken the clothing with them?

They seemed to have interrupted the Brodys, who were both successful lawyers, while they were preparing a meal. Was there some symbolism involved here? Or dark humor? Was it a coincidence, or had they purposely attacked the couple at dinner time? Eat the rich?

Several small town police officers and FBI techies were crowded into the kitchen with us. I figured that the damage had already been done by the Mill Valley police. They were well-intentioned, but had probably never worked a major homicide before. I saw a few dusty footprints on the natural stone kitchen floor. I doubted they belonged to the killers, or the Brodys.

Jamilla had made her way around the large kitchen and now she came up to me. She'd seen enough already. She shook her head, and really didn't have to say what she was thinking. The local police had messed up this crime scene pretty badly.

'This is beyond strange,' she finally said in a low whisper.

'These killers have so much hatred in them. I've never seen anything like it. The rage. Have you, Alex?'

I looked into Jamilla's eyes, but said nothing. Unfortunately, I had.

Chapter Seventeen

The story detailing a 'rampage' of West Coast murders dominated the front page of the San Francisco *Examiner*. All hell had broken loose. Literally.

William and Michael watched it unfold on TV that night. They were impressed with themselves, though they had expected the news story to break soon. They were counting on it in fact. That was the plan.

They were *the special ones*. The chosen team to get the job done. Now they were on their mission. On the road again.

They were chowing down at a diner in Woodland Hills, north of LA, off Highway 5. People in the restaurant noticed the two of them. How could they not? Both were over six feet two, blond ponytails, strapping, well-muscled bodies, dressed completely in black. William and Michael were the archetypes of modern boyhood: *wild animal* meets *entitled prince*.

The news was playing out on TV. The murders were the lead story of course, and the sensationalized coverage lasted for several minutes. Frightened people in Los Angeles, Las Vegas, San Francisco and San Diego were interviewed on camera and had the most incredibly insipid things to say.

Michael frowned and looked over at his brother. 'They got it all wrong. Mostly wrong anyway. What idiots, what fucking drones.'

William took a bite of his dreary sandwich, then he stared up at the TV again. 'Newspapers and TV always get it wrong, little brother. They're part of the larger problem, of what has to be fixed. Like those two lawyers in Mill Valley. You finished here?'

Michael wolfed down the remainder of his extra-rare cheeseburger in a voracious bite. 'I am, and I'm also hungry. I need to feed.' His beautiful blue eyes were glazed.

William smiled and kissed his brother on the cheek. 'C'mon then. I have a good plan for tonight.'

Michael held back. 'Shouldn't we be a little careful? The police are out looking for us, right? We're a big deal now.'

William continued to smile. He loved his brother's naïveté. It amused him. 'We are an incredibly big deal. We're the next big thing. C'mon, little brother. We both need to feed. We deserve it. And besides, the police don't know who we are, always remember this, the police are incompetent fools.'

William drove their white van back down the road they had traveled on through Woodland Hills, before they stopped at the diner. He was sorry they hadn't brought the cat, but this trip was too long. He pulled into an obnoxiously lit shopping mall and studied the signs: Wal-Mart, Denny's, Staples, Circuit City, Wells Fargo Bank. He despised every one of them as well as the people who shopped there.

'We're *not* looking for prey here?' Michael asked. His bright blue eyes darted around the mall and he looked concerned.

William shook his head. The blond ponytail wagged. 'No, of course not. These people aren't worthy of us, Michael. Well, maybe that blonde girl in the tight blue jeans over there is marginally worthy.'

Michael cocked his head sideways, then licked his lips. 'She'll do. For an appetizer.'

William hopped out of the van and walked to the far end of the parking lot. He was strutting a little, smiling, his head held high. Michael followed. The brothers crossed through the back yard of the Wells Fargo Bank. Then the full parking lot of the Denny's restaurant that William thought smelled of bacon grease and fat people.

Michael began to smile when he saw what his brother was up to. They had done this kind of thing before.

A somber black-and-white sign loomed straight ahead of them. It was backlit. *Sorel Funeral Home.*

Chapter Eighteen

It took William less than a minute to crack open the back door into the funeral home. It wasn't a problem since security was minimal.

'Now, we feed,' he said to Michael. He was starting to get excited and his sense of smell led him to the embalming room. He discovered three bodies stored in the refrigerators. 'Two males and a female,' he whispered.

He quickly examined the bodies. Two had been embalmed, one hadn't. They were fresh. William knew about necrology, including what went on in funeral homes. The embalming process involved draining blood from the veins, then injecting a formaldehyde-based fluid. Tubes connected to pumps were inserted into the carotid artery and the jugular vein. The next step involved emptying the internal organs of their fluids. After that, much of the work was cosmetic. The jaws of the dead were wired shut. The lips were arranged and sealed with some kind of glue. Eye caps were placed under each eyelid to prevent the eyeballs from sinking into the head.

William pointed to a centrifuge, which was used to drain bodies of blood and other fluids. He began to laugh. 'We won't be needing *that* tonight.'

All his senses were heightened. He felt larger than life. His night vision was excellent. Nothing more than the illumination from a table lamp would be needed.

He walked to the last of three stainless steel tables and took the unembalmed body in his arms. He carried the dead, a woman in her early forties, to a nearby porcelain table.

William looked at his brother and gently rubbed his hands together. He took a deep breath. They had raided funeral homes before, and though it didn't compare to a fresh kill, prey was prey.

Besides, the dead woman was a fairly good physical specimen for her age. She was attractive and compared favorably to the female they had attacked and fed upon in San Francisco. There was a nametag on the body: *Diana Ginn.*

'I hope some funeral director didn't have Diana first,' William said to his brother. Pathetic geeks sometimes took jobs at funeral homes so that they could ravage the dead at their leisure. They'd do unnecessary searches into vaginal and anal cavities. Another kinky pastime was to have sex with the dead in a coffin. It happened more than people could imagine.

William found that he was excited. There was nothing to compare to this. He climbed up on the embalming table and positioned himself above the woman.

Diana Ginn's naked body was ashen, but pretty enough in the dim light. Her lips were full and blue. He wondered how she had died, since she didn't look sick. There were no obvious wounds. She hadn't been in an accident.

William carefully pried open the eyelids, looked into her eyes. 'Hello, my sweet girl. You're beautiful, Diana,' he whispered dreamily. 'That isn't just a cheap pickup line. I mean it. You're extraordinary. You're worthy of tonight, of Michael and me. And we will be worthy of you.'

He let his fingers lightly graze her cheeks, then the long neck, her breasts, which weren't pert now but more like sacs of pudding. He studied the intricate lines of her veins. So beautiful. He was almost dizzy with lust for Diana Ginn.

While William crouched low over the body, his brother lightly stroked the woman's bony feet, her thin ankles, then slowly, lovingly moved his hands up the long legs. He was moaning softly, as if he were trying to waken her from the deepest sleep.

'We love you,' Michael whispered. 'We know you can hear us. You're still here in your body, aren't you? We know, Diana. We know exactly how you feel. We're the undead.'

Chapter Nineteen

I continued to be impressed with the tremendous discipline and hard work of Jamilla Hughes. What drove her? Something buried in her past? Something more obvious in the present? The fact that she was one of two women homicide inspectors in the San Francisco Police Department? Maybe all of the above? Jamilla had already told me that she hadn't taken a day of comp time in almost two years. That sounded kind of familiar.

A couple of times during the next day at the Hall of Justice I mentioned her incredible work ethic, but she shrugged it off. She was well respected by the other homicide inspectors. She was a regular person. No false airs. No bullshit about her. I found out that she had a nickname. It suited her – *Jam*.

I spent a couple of hours in the afternoon finding out what I could about tigers. Area zoos and shelters were being canvassed in an attempt to locate every single tiger in California. The murderous cat was our best lead so far.

I was keeping my own list of facts, different things that struck me.

Someone had been able to command and control the tiger before and after it had attacked and bitten Davis O'Hara in Golden Gate Park. An animal trainer? A vet?

The jaw of a tiger was so strong that it could crush bone, and then pulverize it. And yet, someone had been able to call the tiger off its prey.

All tiger species were considered endangered. Their existence was being challenged by both loss of habitat and poaching. Could the killers also be environmentalists?

Tigers were being poached for their suspected healing powers. Almost every part of the cat was considered valuable, and in some cases, sacred.

Tigers had magical significance in some cultures, especially in parts of Asia. Could that be important to the case?

I had lost track of the time, and when I looked up from my note-taking it was already getting dark outside. Jamilla was striding down the corridor in my direction.

She had on a long black leather jacket, and looked ready to leave. She'd put on lipstick. Maybe she had a date. She looked terrific. 'Tyger, Tyger, burning bright,' she recited a line from Blake's poem.

I answered with the only other line I could remember.

'Did He who made the Lamb make thee?'

She looked pensive, then she smiled. 'What a team. The poet detectives. Let's get a beer.'

'I'm pretty beat and I have a few more files to check. I think I'm still jet-lagged.' Even as I was saying the words, I wasn't sure why the hell I was saying them.

She put up her hand. 'All right already. You could have just said *no, you're not my type*. Jeez, man. I'll see you in the morning. But thanks for all your help. I mean that.' I saw her smile as she turned, then walked away, down the long hall to the elevators. But then I saw her shake her head.

After she was gone, I sat at the desk overlooking the streets of San Francisco. I sighed, and then I shook *my* head. I could feel a familiar weariness settling in. I was alone again and I had no one to blame. Why had I turned Jamilla down for a couple of beers? I liked her company. I didn't have any other plans; and I wasn't *that* jet-lagged.

But I thought I knew the reason. It wasn't too complicated. I had gotten close to my last two partners on homicide cases. Both Patsy and Betsey were women I liked. Both had died.

The Mastermind was still out there.

Could he be in San Francisco right now?

Was Jamilla Hughes safe in her own city?

Chapter Twenty

The ringing of the telephone in my hotel room woke me early the next morning. I was groggy, still half-asleep when I picked up.

It was Jamilla, and she sounded a little breathless. 'I got a call late last night from my friend Tim at *The Examiner*,' she told me. 'He's got a lead for us. This could be good stuff.' She quickly filled me in on the sketchy details of an attempted murder, an old case. We had a witness this time. She and I were going on the road again. She didn't ask if I wanted to go – it was apparently a done deal.

'I'll pick you up in half an hour, forty minutes at the latest. We're going to LA. Wear black. Maybe you'll get discovered.'

United flies an hourly shuttle between San Francisco and Los Angeles. We just made the nine o'clock and were in

LA an hour or so later. We didn't stop talking for the entire trip. We rented a car at Budget and headed to Brentwood. I was as pumped up about the new lead as she was. The FBI was also in on the game in LA.

On the way to Brentwood, she checked in with her pal Tim at *The Examiner*. I wondered if Tim was a boyfriend. 'You find out any more for us?' she asked. She listened, then repeated what she heard for me. Part of it we already knew.

'Two men attacked the woman we're going to see. She managed to get away from them. Lucky girl, incredibly lucky. They bit her severely. Chest, neck, stomach, face. She thought the perps were in their mid-forties to mid-fifties. The attack occurred over a year ago, Alex. It was a big story in the supermarket tabloids.'

I didn't say anything, just listened to her, took it all in. This case was so strange. I hadn't seen anything quite like it.

'They were going to hang her from a tree. There was no mention of a tiger in any of the articles my friend was able to dig up. A detective from the LAPD is meeting us at the station house. I'm sure we'll hear more details from him. He was the lead detective on the case.'

She looked over at me. She had something here, something good. 'Here's the kicker, Alex. According to my source, the woman believes her attackers were vampires.'

Chapter Twenty-One

We met with Gloria Dos Santos at the police station in the Brentwood section of LA. It was a one-story concrete building, about as non-descript as a post office. Detective Peter Kim joined us in a small interview room, which was about six by five feet, soundproof, with padded walls. Kim was slender, around six feet, in his late twenties. He dressed well, and seemed more like an up-and-coming Los Angeles business executive than a policeman to me.

Gloria Dos Santos obviously knew Kim, and they didn't seem too fond of each other. She called him 'Detective Fuhrman', and she used the name over and over, until Kim told her to 'can it' or he would lock her the hell up.

Dos Santos wore a short black dress, high black boots, leather wristbands. There were about a dozen earrings in strategic locations on her body. Her frizzy black hair was piled high, but some also cascaded down to her shoulders. She was only an inch or two over five feet and had a hard face. Her lashes were thick with mascara and she used purple eye shadow. She looked to be in good physical shape – like all the other victims so far.

She stared at Kim, then at me, and finally at Jamilla Hughes. She shook her head and smirked. She didn't like us, which was fine – I didn't much like her either.

She sneered. 'Can I smoke in this rat-trap? I'm going to smoke, like it or not. If you don't like it, then I'm going the hell home.'

'So smoke,' Kim said. 'But you're not going home under any fucking circumstances.' He took out some David's ranch-style seeds and started to eat them. Kim was a strange boy himself.

Dos Santos lit up a Camel and blew out a thick stream of smoke in Kim's face.

'Detective *Fuhrman* knows everything that I know. Why don't you just get it all from him? He's brilliant, y'know. Just ask him about it. Graduated with some cumma honors from UCLA.'

'There are a few things we aren't clear about,' I said to her. 'That's why we came all the way from San Francisco to see you. Actually, I came from Washington, DC.'

'Long trip for nothing, Shaft,' she said. Gloria Dos Santos had a zinger for every occasion. She wiped her hand over her face a few times as if she were trying to wake herself up.

'You're obviously high as a kite,' Jamilla cut in. 'That doesn't matter to us. Relax, girl. These men who attacked you hurt you pretty bad.'

Dos Santos snorted. 'Pretty bad? They broke two ribs, broke my arm. They knocked me down 'bout six times. Fortunately, they knocked me right down a goddamn hill, side of a mountain, actually. I started rolling. Got up. Ran my ass off.'

'The initial report said that you didn't see either of them very well. Then you claimed that they were in their forties or fifties.'

She shrugged. 'I don't know. It was foggy. That's an impression I had. Earlier that night, I went to the Fang Club on West Pico. It's the only place where you can meet real vampires and live to tell about it. So they say. I was going to a lot of Goth clubs back then – Stigmata, Coven 13, Vampiricus over in Long Beach. I worked at Necromane. *What's Necromane?*' she asked, as if it were a question we would want answered. She was right. 'Necromane is a boutique for people who are really into the dead. You can buy real human skulls there. Fingers, toes. A full human skeleton if that's your thing.'

'It's not,' Jamilla said. 'But I've been to a shop like that in San Francisco. It's called the Coroner.'

The girl looked at her contemptuously. 'So I'm fucking impressed? You must be very cool. You must live right on the edge.'

I spoke again. 'We're trying to help you. We—'

She cut me off. 'Bullshit, you're trying to help yourselves. You've got another big case. Those kinky murders in San Francisco, right? I can *read*, man. You couldn't care less about Gloria Dos Santos and her problems. I got lots of them. More than you know. Who gives a shit, right?'

'Two people were killed in Golden Gate Park. It was a massacre. Did you read that? We think it might be the same men who attacked you,' I told her.

'Yeah, well let me tell you something you better get straight. The two men who attacked me were *vampires*! Got that? I know this is impossible for you to wrap your little minds around, but there are vampires. They set themselves apart from the human world. That means – they aren't like you!

'Two of them almost killed me. They were hunting in Beverly Hills. They kill people *every fucking day in LA*! They drink their blood. They call it feeding. They chew on their bones like it's KFP, that's Kentucky Fried People, chumps. I can see you don't believe me. Well, *believe me*.'

The door to the interview room opened quietly. A uniformed patrolman popped in and whispered something to Detective Kim.

Kim frowned and looked at us, then at Dos Santos. 'There was a killing on Sunset Boulevard a short time ago. Someone was bitten and then hanged at one of the better hotels.'

Gloria Dos Santos's face twisted horribly. Her eyes grew small and very angry. She flew into a rage, started to scream at the top of her voice. 'They followed you here, you assholes! Don't you get it? They followed you! Oh my God, they know I talked to you. Oh Jesus Christ, they'll get me. You just got me killed!'

Part Two

Blood Lust

Chapter Twenty-Two

I always liked working tough murder cases with Kyle Craig, so I was glad that he would be joining Jamilla Hughes and me in Los Angeles later that day. I was surprised, however, when I saw him already at the murder scene in Beverly Hills when we arrived. The body had been found at the Chateau Marmont, the hotel where John Belushi had overdosed and died.

The hotel looked like a French castle and rose seven stories over the Sunset Strip. As I entered the lobby, I noticed that everything looked to be authentic 1920s, but dated rather than antique. Supposedly, a studio boss had once told the actor William Holden, 'If you have to get into trouble, do it at the Chateau Marmont.'

Kyle met us at the door of the hotel room. His dark hair was slicked back and it looked like he'd gotten a little sun. Unusual for Kyle. I almost didn't recognize him.

'This is Kyle Craig, FBI,' I told Jamilla. 'Before I met you, he was the best homicide investigator I ever worked with.'

Kyle and Jamilla shook hands. Then we followed him into the hotel room. Actually, it was a hillside bungalow: two bedrooms, a living room with a working fireplace. It had its own private street entrance.

The crime scene was as depressingly bad as the others. I recalled something typically pessimistic that a philosopher had written. I'd once had this same thought at a grisly crime scene in North Carolina: 'Human existence must be a kind of error. It is bad today and every day it will get worse, until the worst of all happens.' My own philosophy was a little cheerier than Schopenhauer's, but there were times when he seemed on the mark.

The worst of all had happened to a twenty-nine-year-old record company executive named Jonathan Mueller, and in the worst possible way. There were bites on his neck. I didn't see any knife cuts. Mueller had been hung from a lighting fixture in the hotel room. His skin was waxy and translucent and I didn't think he had been dead very long.

The three of us moved closer to the hanging body. It was swaying slightly, and still dripping blood.

'The major bites are all in his neck,' I said. 'It looks like role-playing vampires again. The hanging has to be their ritual, maybe their signature.'

'This is so goddamn creepy,' Jamilla whispered. 'This poor guy had the blood sucked out of him. It almost looks like a sex crime.'

'I think it is,' Kyle said. 'I think they seduced him first.'

Just then the cell phone in my jacket pocket went off. The timing couldn't have been worse.

I looked at Kyle before I answered the call. 'It could be him,' I said. 'The Mastermind.'

I put the receiver to my ear.

'How do you like LA, Alex?' the Mastermind asked in his usual mechanical drone. 'The dead pretty much look the same everywhere, don't they?'

I nodded at Kyle. He understood who was on the line. The Mastermind.

He motioned for me to give him the phone and I handed it over. I watched his face as he listened, then frowned deeply. Kyle finally took the phone away from his ear.

'He broke off the connection,' he said. 'It was like he knew you weren't on the line anymore. How did he know, Alex? How does the bastard know so much? What the hell does he want from you?'

I stared at the slowly revolving corpse, and I didn't have any answers. None at all. I felt drained myself.

Chapter Twenty-Three

I t was Friday already and we were in the middle of a nasty, sordid mess that wasn't going to be over soon. In the afternoon I had to make a tough phone call home to Washington. Nana Mama answered after a couple of rings, and I immediately wished that one of the kids had picked up instead.

'It's Alex. How are you?'

She said, 'You're not coming home for Damon's concert tomorrow, are you, Alex? Or did you forget all about the concert already. Oh, Alex, Alex. Why have you forsaken us? This isn't right.'

I love Nana tremendously, but sometimes she goes too far to make her point. 'Why don't you put Damon on the phone?' I said. 'I'll talk to him about it.'

'He's not going to be a boy for very much longer. Pretty soon he'll be just like you, won't listen to a word anybody says. Then you'll see what it's like. I guarantee you won't like it,' she said.

'I feel bad enough already, guilty enough. You don't have to make it worse, old woman.'

'Of course I do. That's my job, and I take it as seriously as you obviously take yours,' she said.

'Nana, people are dying out here. Someone died a horrible death in Washington to get me involved in this mess. It keeps happening. There's a connection I have to find, or at least try to.'

'Yes, people are dying, Alex. I understand that. And other people are growing up without their father around as much as they need him to be – especially since they don't have a mother. Are you aware of that? I can't be mother and father to these children.'

I shut my eyes. 'I hear what you're saying. I don't even disagree with you, believe it or not. Now, would you please put Damon on?' I asked again. 'As soon as I get off the phone, I'll go out and see if I can find a mother for my children. Actually, I'm working with a very nice female detective. You'd like her.'

'Damon's not here. He said if you called, and weren't coming home, to tell you *thanks a lot.*'

I shook my head, and finally smiled in spite of myself. 'You got his inflection down perfectly. Where is he?'

'He's playing basketball with his friends. He's very good

at that, too. I think he'll be an outstanding two guard. Have you even noticed?'

'He has soft hands and a quick first step. Of course I've noticed. You know which friends he's out with?'

'Of course I do. Do *you*?' Nana shot back. She was relentless when she was on the attack. 'He's with Louis and Jamal. He picks good friends.'

'I have to go now, Nana. Please give Damon and Jannie my love. Give little Alex a big hug.'

'Alex, you give them love and hugs yourself,' she said. Then she hung up the phone on me. She had never done that before. Well, she hadn't done it very often.

I sat there, pinned to my chair, thinking over what had just been said, wondering whether or not I was guilty as charged. I knew that I spent more time with the kids than a lot of fathers, but as Nana had so skillfully argued, they were growing up fast, and without a mother. I had to do an even better job and there were no goddamn excuses.

I called home a few more times. There was no answer, and I figured I was being punished. I finally caught up with Damon around six that night. He had just gotten home from a rehearsal for his concert with the Boys Choir. I heard his voice come on the line, and I sang a little Tupac rap ditty he likes.

He thought that was funny so I knew everything was okay. He had forgiven me. He's a good boy, the best I could have hoped for. I suddenly remembered my wife, Maria, and was sad that she wasn't here to see how well Damon was turning out. *You would really like Damon, Maria. I'm sorry you're missing it.*

'I got your message. I'm sorry, Damon. I wish I were going to hear you tomorrow. You know I do. Can't be helped, buddy.'

Damon sighed dramatically. 'If wishes had wings,' he said. It was one of his grandmother's pet sayings. I had been hearing it for years, ever since I was around his age.

'Beat me, whip me, beat me,' I told him.

'Naw. It's all right, Daddy,' Damon said, and sighed again. 'I know you have to work, and that it's probably important stuff. It's just hard for us sometimes. You know how it is.'

'I love you, and I should be there, and I won't miss the next concert,' I said to him.

'I'll hold you to that,' Damon said.

'I'll hold myself to it,' I told him.

Chapter Twenty-Four

I was still at the precinct house in Brentwood at around seven-thirty that night. I was tired and finally looked up from a thick sheaf of police reports on the sadistic murders that had taken place in nine West Coast cities, plus the one in DC, that we knew about. The case was scaring the hell out of me, and certainly not because I believed in vampires.

I *did* believe in the weird and horrible things people could sometimes do to one another: savage bites, sadistic hangings, draining blood out of bodies, tiger attacks. For once, I couldn't begin to imagine what the killers might be like. I couldn't profile them. Neither could the FBI's Behavioral Science Unit. Kyle Craig had admitted as much to me. That was one reason why he was out here himself. Kyle was stumped, too. There was no precedent for this string of murders.

Jamilla appeared at my desk around quarter to eight. She had been working down the hall. She has a very pretty face, but tonight she just looked tired. There is a simple fact of life about police work. Adrenaline starts flowing during bad cases. It makes everybody's feelings more intense. Attractions grow and can cause unanticipated problems. I had been there before, and maybe so had Jamilla. She acted like it. Perhaps that was why we were a little tentative around one another.

She leaned over my desk and I could smell a light cologne. 'I have to go back to San Francisco, Alex. I'm heading out to the airport now. I left *beaucoup* notes for you and Kyle on some of the files I was able to get through. I'll tell you what, though, it doesn't seem, *to me*, that all the murders were committed by the same killers. That's my contribution for today.'

'Why do you say that?' I asked. Actually, I'd had the same feeling. Nothing to substantiate it, though. Just a gut reaction to the evidence we had gathered so far.

Jamilla rubbed the bridge of her nose, then she wrinkled it some. Her mannerisms were funny, and made me smile. 'The patterns keep changing. Especially if you look at the most recent murders versus the ones from a year or two ago. In the earlier murders the killers were methodical, very careful. The last couple of murders are slapdash, Alex. More violent, too.'

'I don't disagree. I'll look at all the files carefully. So will Kyle and his folks at Quantico. Anything else bothering you?' I asked.

She thought about it. 'A strange crime was reported this morning. Might be something. Funeral home in Woodland Hills. Somebody broke in, ravaged one of the bodies. Could be a copycat. I left the file for you. Anyway, I have to run if I want to catch the next shuttle . . . You'll keep in touch?'

'Of course I will. Absolutely. You're not getting off the hook this easily.'

She waved once, and then she was gone down the hallway.

I hated to see her leave.

Jam.

Chapter Twenty-Five

Ten minutes after Jamilla left to catch her plane back to San Francisco, Kyle appeared at my desk. He looked like a rumpled, tweedy, forty-something professor who had just emerged from his library carrel after days of researching a scholarly piece for the criminal justice journals.

'You crack the code?' I asked him. 'If you did, can I get a flight out of here tonight? I'm catching hell at home for being here.'

'I didn't crack a goddamn thing,' he complained. Then he yawned. 'My head feels a little cracked. Like there's a slow leak or something.' He rubbed his knuckles back and forth against his skull.

'You believe in New Age vampires yet?' I asked. 'Role-players?'

He gave me one of his crooked little half-smiles. 'Oh, I

always believed in vampires. Ever since I was a boy in Virginia and then North Carolina. Vampires, ghosts, zombies, other diabolical creatures of the night. Southerners believe in such things. It's our Gothic heritage, I suppose. Actually, ghosts are more our specialty. I definitely believe in ghosts. I wish this was only a ghost story.'

'Maybe it is. I saw a ghost the other night. Her name was Mary Alice Richardson. These bastards hung and murdered her during one of their pleasure fests.'

Around nine, Kyle and I finally left the station house in Brentwood to get some grub and maybe a few beers. I was pleased to have some time with him. Bad thoughts were buzzing in my head: disconnected feelings, suspicions, and general paranoia about the case. And, of course, there was always the Mastermind to worry about. He might call, or send a fax, or e-mail.

We stopped at a small bar called The Knoll on the way back to the hotel. It looked like a quiet place to have a drink and talk. Kyle and I often did this when we were on the road together.

'So how are you doing, Alex?' Kyle asked after he'd taken a sip of Anchor Steam. 'You all right? Holding up so far? I know you don't like being away from Nana and the kids. I'm sorry about that. Can't be helped. This is a big case.'

I was too tired to argue with him. 'In the words of Tiger Woods, "I didn't have my A game today." I'm a little stumped, Kyle. This is all new and all bad.'

He nodded and said, 'I don't mean today. Overall. In general. On balance. How the hell are you doing? You seem tense to me. We've all been noticing it, Alex. You don't volunteer much at St Anthony's anymore. Little things like that.'

I looked at him, studied his intense, brown eyes. He was a friend, but Kyle was also a calculating man. He wanted something. What was he after? What thoughts were going through his mind?

'On balance, I'm totally fucked. No, I'm okay. I'm happy with the way the kids are doing. Little Alex is the best antidote for anything. Damon and Jannie are doing fine. I still miss Christine, I miss her a lot. I'm troubled about how much time I spend investigating the sickest, most fucked-up crimes that anyone can conjure up. Other than that, I'm just fine.'

Kyle said, 'You're in demand because you're good at this. That's just the way it is. Your instincts, your emotional IQ, *something* sets you apart from the other cops.'

'Maybe I'd rather not be so good anymore. Maybe I'm not. The murder cases have affected every aspect of my life. I'm afraid they're changing who I am. Tell me about Betsey Cavalierre. Anything on the case? There must be something.'

Kyle shook his head. His eyes showed concern. 'There's

absolutely nothing on her murder, Alex. Nothing on the Mastermind either. That prick still calling you any time of day or night?'

'Yeah. He never mentions Betsey or her murder anymore.'

'We could set up another trace on your phones. I'll do that for you.'

'It won't do any good.'

Kyle continued to look deep into my eyes. I sensed he was concerned, but it was hard to tell with him. 'You think he might be watching you? Following you?'

I shook my head. 'Sometimes I get that feeling, yeah. Let me ask you something, since I have you here. Why do you keep pulling me into these messed-up cases, Kyle? We worked Casanova down in Durham, the Dunne and Goldberg kidnapping, the bank robberies. Now this piece of shit.'

Kyle didn't hesitate to spell it out. 'You're the best I know, Alex. Your instincts are almost always on target. You give these investigations the best shot they could get. Sometimes you solve them, sometimes not, but you're always close. Why don't you come join us at the Bureau? I'm serious, and yes, this *is* an offer.'

There it was, Kyle's agenda for the meeting. He wanted me at Quantico with him.

I roared with laughter, and then he did too. 'To tell you the truth, I don't feel close on this one, Kyle. I feel lost,' I finally admitted.

'It's still early in the game,' he said. 'The offer stands, win or lose out here. I want you to come to Quantico. I want you working close to me. There's nothing that would make me happier.'

Chapter Twenty-Six

This was a good break. Better than they could have expected or hoped for. William and Michael followed the two hotshot police dicks from the station house in Brentwood. They stayed a reasonable distance back in their van. The brothers didn't particularly care if they lost them. They knew which hotel they were staying at. They knew how to find them.

They even knew their names.

Kyle Craig, FBI. A DIC from Quantico. A 'big case' man. One of the Bureau's best.

Alex Cross, Washington PD. Forensic psychologist to the stars.

There was a saying that William wanted to whisper in their ears: *If you hunt for the vampire, the vampire will hunt for you.*

That was the truth, but it also sounded too much like a

rule. William fucking hated rules. Rules made you predictable, less of an individual. Rules made you less free, less
authentic, less yourself. And in the end, *rules could get you
caught*.

William touched down lightly, tentatively, on the van's
brake pedal. Maybe they shouldn't hunt the two cops
down, then kill them like dogs, he was thinking. Maybe
they had better things to do while they were in LA.

There was a special place here where he and Michael
often went. It was called the Church of the Vampire, and it
was for those who were 'searching for the Dragon within'.
It actually was a church: vast, high-ceilinged rooms filled
with funky old Victorian furniture, elaborate golden candelabras, human skulls and other bones, tapestries that
portrayed stories of famous old blood seekers. The usual
dreaded role-players came to the Church, but so did real
vampires. Like William and Michael.

Exciting, very exotic, sado-erotic things happened inside
the Church of the Vampire. Excruciating pain was trans-
formed into ecstasy. William remembered his last visit, and
it sent electricity shooting through his body. He had found
a blond boy of seventeen. An angel, a prince. The boy was
dressed all in black that night; he even had black eye
contacts, absolutely gorgeous from every angle. To show
William that he was a real vampire, the darling boy had
punctured his own carotid artery and then drunk his own

blood. Then he had asked William to drink, to be one with him. When he and Michael had hung the boy to drain him completely, it was out of love and adoration of the angel's perfect body. They were merely fulfilling their nature – to be sado-erotic.

William came out of his delicious reverie as the two cops entered a bar called The Knoll. It was just off Sunset Boulevard. Very mundane, a nothing spot. Perfect for the two of them.

'They're going drinking together,' William said to Michael. 'Cop camaraderie.'

Michael snickered and rolled his eyes. 'They're just two old men. They're harmless. Toothless,' he said, and laughed at his joke.

William watched Alex Cross and Kyle Craig disappear inside. 'No,' he finally spoke again. 'Let's be careful with them. One of them is extremely dangerous. I can feel his energy.'

Chapter Twenty-Seven

I finally had a lead, courtesy of Jamilla's contact at the San Francisco *Examiner*. The chase was on, or so I hoped. The next morning I drove up Route 1 to Santa Barbara, which is located approximately sixty miles north of LA.

It was sobering and a little depressing to watch the sky actually grow bluer as I traveled away from Los Angeles and the copper-gray cover of smog thickly spread over the city.

I was to meet a man named Peter Westin at the Davidson Library in the University of California, Santa Barbara. The library was supposed to contain the most extensive collection of books on vampires and vampire mythology in the United States. Westin was the expert who had been recommended by Jamilla's contact. She warned me that Westin was thoroughly eccentric, but a definitive source on vampires, past and present.

He met me in a small private sitting room just off the library's main reading room. Peter Westin looked to be in his early forties and was dressed completely in deep purple and black. Even his fingernails were painted a shade of mauve. According to Jamilla, he owned a clothing and jewelry shop in a small mall on State Street in Santa Barbara, El Paseo. He had long black hair streaked with silver, and he was dark and dangerous looking.

'I'm Detective Alex Cross,' I said as I shook hands with Westin. His grip was strong, lacquered fingernails or no.

'I am Westin, descended from Vlad Tepes. I bid you welcome. The night air is chill and you must need to eat and rest,' he said in overly dramatic tones.

I found myself smiling at the prepared speech. 'Sounds like something the count might have said in one of the old Dracula movies.'

Westin nodded, and when he smiled I saw that his teeth were perfectly formed. No fangs.

'In several of them, actually. It's the official invitation of the Transylvania Society of Dracula in Bucharest.'

I immediately asked, 'Are there American chapters?'

'American and Canadian. There's even a chapter in South Africa, and in Tokyo. There are several hundred thousand men and women with an avid interest in vampires. Surprise you, Detective? You thought we were a more modest cult?'

'It might have a week ago, but not now,' I said. 'Nothing surprises me much anymore. Thanks for talking to me.'

Westin and I took seats at a large oak library table. He had selected a dozen or more volumes on vampires for me to read, or at least leaf through.

'I especially recommend Carol Page's *Bloodlust: Conversations with Real Vampires*. Ms Page is the real deal. She gets it,' he told me, and handed over *Bloodlust*. 'She has met vampires, and records their activities accurately and fairly. She started her investigation as a skeptic, much like yourself I expect.'

'You're right, I'm very skeptical,' I admitted. I told Peter Westin about the most recent murder in Los Angeles, and then he let me ask whatever questions I wished about the vampire world. He answered patiently, and I soon learned that a vampire subculture exists in virtually every major city as well as some smaller ones, such as Santa Cruz, California; Austin, Texas; Savannah, Georgia; Batavia, New York; Des Moines, Iowa.

'A real vampire,' he told me, 'is a person born with an extraordinary gift. He, or she, has the capacity to absorb, channel, transform, and manipulate pranic energy – the life force. Serious vampires are usually very spiritual.'

'How does drinking human blood fit in?' I asked Peter Westin. Then I quickly added, 'If it does.'

Westin answered quietly. 'It is said that blood is the

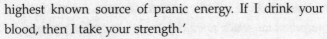
highest known source of pranic energy. If I drink your blood, then I take your strength.'

'My blood?' I asked.

'Yes, I would think you'd do nicely.'

I recalled the nocturnal raid on the funeral parlor north of LA. 'What about the blood of corpses? Those dead for a day or two?'

'If a vampire, or a poseur, was desperate, I suppose blood from a corpse would suffice. Let me tell you about real vampires, Detective. Most of them are needy, attention seeking and manipulative. They are frequently attractive – primarily *because* of their immorality, their forbidden desires, rebelliousness, power, eroticism, their sense of their own immortality.'

'You keep emphasizing the word *real*. What distinction are you trying to make?'

'Most young people involved with the underground vampire lifestyle are merely role-players. They are experimenting, looking for a group that meets their needs of the moment. There's even a popular mass-market game – Vampire: The Masquerade. Teenagers especially are attracted to the vampire lifestyle. Vampires have an incredible alternative way of looking at the world. Besides, vampires party late into the night. Until the first light.' His lips curled into a smile.

Westin was definitely willing to talk to me, and I

wondered why. I also wondered how seriously he took the vampire lifestyle. His clothing shop in town sold to young people looking for alternative trappings. Was he a poseur himself? Or was Peter Westin a real vampire?

'The mythology of the vampire goes back thousands of years. Actually, it's present in China, Africa, South and Central America. And central Europe, of course. For a lot of people here in America it's an aesthetic fetish. It's sexual, theatrical, and very romantic. It also transcends gender, which is an attractive idea these days.'

I felt it was time to stop his spiel and focus on the murders. 'What about the murders – the actual violence taking place in California and Nevada?'

A mask of pain came over his face. 'I've heard Jeffrey Dahmer called a vampire/cannibal. Also, Nicolas Claux, whom you may not be familiar with. Claux was a Parisian mortician who confessed to murders in the mid-nineties. Once he was captured he took great pleasure in describing eating the flesh of corpses on his mortician's slab. He became known all over Europe as the Vampire of Paris.'

'You've heard of Rod Ferrell in Florida?' I asked.

'Of course. He's a dark hero for some. Very big on the Internet. He and his small cult bludgeoned to death the parents of another member. They then carved numerous occult symbols into the dead bodies. I know all about Rod Ferrell. He was supposedly obsessed with opening the

Gates of Hell. Thought he had to kill large numbers of people, and consume their souls, to be powerful enough to open up Hell. Who knows, maybe he succeeded,' Westin said.

He stared at me for a long moment. 'Let me tell you something, Detective Cross. This is the absolute truth. I believe it's important for you to understand. It is no more common for a vampire to be a psychopath or a killer than it is for any random person on the street.'

I shrugged. 'I guess I'd have to check your research statistics on that one. In the meantime, one or more vampires, real ones, or maybe just role-players, have murdered at least a dozen people,' I said.

Westin looked a little sad. 'Yes, Detective, I know. That's why I consented to talk with you.'

'Are you a vampire?' I asked him one final question.

Peter Westin paused before he finally answered. 'Yes. I am.'

The words cut through me. The man was completely serious.

Chapter Twenty-Eight

That night in Santa Barbara, I was just a little more afraid of the dark than I had ever been. I sat in my hotel room and read a touching novel called *Waiting* by Ha Jin. I was waiting as well. I called home twice that night. I wasn't sure if I was lonely, or still feeling guilty about missing Damon's concert.

Or maybe Peter Westin had frightened me with his vampire stories and books, and the haunted look in his dark eyes. At any rate, I was taking vampires more seriously now that I had met him. Westin was a strange, eerie, unforgettable man. I had the feeling that I would meet, or at least talk to him again.

My inner fears didn't go away that night, and not even with the first light of morning shining brightly over the Santa Ynez Mountains. Something strange and quite awful was happening. It involved twisted individuals, or maybe an underground cult. It probably had something to do with the vampire subculture. But maybe it didn't, and that was even more disturbing to think about. It would mean we were in a totally gray area with the investigation.

By seven-thirty in the morning, my rented sedan was easing into soupy gray fog, and then the morning traffic clog. I was singing a little Muddy Waters blues, which nicely matched my mood.

I left Santa Barbara and headed toward Fresno. I had another 'expert' to meet.

I drove for a couple of hours. I got on 166 at Santa Maria and continued east through the Sierra Madres until I reached Route 99. I took it north. I was seeing California for the first time and liking most of what I saw. The topography was different to back East, and so were the colors.

I fell into a comfortable driving rhythm. I listened to a Jill Scott CD. For long stretches of the road trip I thought about the way my life had been going over the past couple of years. I knew that some of my friends were starting to worry about me, even my best friend, John Sampson, and I wouldn't exactly classify him as a worrier. Sampson had told me more than once that I was putting myself in harm's way. He even suggested that maybe it was time for a career change. I knew I could go with the FBI, but that didn't seem like much of a sea change. I could also go back into psychiatry full time – either see patients, or possibly teach, maybe at Johns Hopkins, where I'd gotten my degree and still had pretty good connections.

Then there was Nana Mama's favorite tune: I needed to find someone and settle down again; I needed somebody to love.

It wasn't as if I hadn't tried. My wife, Maria, had been killed in a drive-by shooting in DC that had never been solved. That had happened when Damon and Jannie were little, and I guess I'd never really gotten over it. Maybe I never would. Even now, if I let myself, I could get torn up thinking about Maria and what had happened to her, to us, and how goddamn senseless it had been. What a terrible waste of a human life. It had left Damon and Jannie without their mother.

I had tried hard to find someone, but maybe I just wasn't meant to be lucky twice in my lifetime. There had been Jezzie Flanagan, but that couldn't have turned out worse. And then Christine Johnson, little Alex's mother. She was a teacher and now lived out here on the West Coast. She was doing well, loved Seattle, and had 'found someone'. I still had terribly mixed feelings about Christine. She'd been hurt because of me. My fault, not hers. She had made it clear she couldn't live with a homicide detective. And then, not too long ago, I had started to become involved with an FBI agent named Betsey Cavalierre. Now Betsey was dead.

Her murder case remained unsolved. I was afraid to even have drinks with Jamilla Hughes. The past was starting to haunt me.

'Some detective,' I muttered as I spotted the overhead sign: *Fresno*. I had come here to see a man about some teeth.

Fangs, actually.

Chapter Twenty-Nine

The *tattoo/fang and claws* parlor was located on the fringe of a lower middle-class commercial district in downtown Fresno. It was a ramshackle storefront, with an old dentist's chair prominently displayed in the window. In the chair was a girl who couldn't have been more than fourteen or fifteen. She sat with her skinny, pimpled neck bowed toward her lap, wincing with each needle puncture.

On a tall stool beside her sat a young guy with a bright blue and yellow bandanna wrapped tightly around his head. He was applying the tattoo. He reached for a bottle of ink. The array of tattoo inks beside him reminded me of the spin art booth at a school fair.

I watched from the street for the next few minutes. I couldn't help thinking about the role of physical pain in making tattoos, but also in the murders so far.

I knew the basic tattoo process and watched as the

resident artist adjusted a gooseneck lamp toward the nape of the girl's neck. He used two foot-operated tattoo machines: one for outlining, the other for shading and coloring. The round shader between the machines held fourteen different needles. The more needles, the more colorful the flash.

A middle-aged man with a crew cut was passing by on the street, and paused just long enough to mutter, 'That's nuts, and so are you for watching.'

Everybody's a critic these days. I finally went inside and saw the result of the tattoo master's art: a small Celtic symbol, green and gold. I asked him where I could get fangs and claws. He moved his head, his chin actually, to indicate a hallway to his left. Never said a word.

I walked past display cases: tongue and navel studs, including glow-in-the-dark studs; massive knuckle rings; sunglasses, pipes, beaded thingees; a poster for two popular claws – Ogre and Faust.

You're getting warmer, I thought as I entered the hallway, and then met the fang master face to face.

He was expecting me, and he started talking as soon as I entered his small shop.

'You've finally arrived, pilgrim. You know, when you go to the most interesting, and most dangerous, vampire clubs, the ones in LA, New York, New Orleans, Houston, you see fangs everywhere. It's the scene, and what a scene, my man. Goth, Edwardian, Victorian, bondage apparel, anything goes. I was one of the first to custom-make fangs out here. Started in Laguna Beach, worked my way north. And now, here I am, the Fresno Kid.'

As he spoke, I became aware of his teeth, elongated molars. Those teeth looked as if they could inflict severe damage.

His name was John Barreiro, and he was short, painfully thin, and dressed mostly in black, much like Peter Westin. He was probably the most sinister-looking person I had ever met.

'You know why I'm here – the Golden Gate Park murders,' I said to the fangmaker.

He nodded and grinned wickedly. 'I know why you're here, pilgrim. Peter Westin sent you. Peter's very persuasive, isn't he? Follow me.' He took me into a small over-crowded room in the rear of the store. The walls were dark blue, the lighting crimson.

Barreiro had a lot of nervous energy, he moved around constantly as he spoke. 'There is a fabulous Fang Club in Los Angeles. They like to say it's the only place where you can meet vampires and live to tell about it. On weekend nights you might see four, five hundred people there. Maybe fifty of the fuckers are real vampires. Almost everyone wears fangs, even the vampire wannabes.'

'Are your teeth real?' I asked him.

'Let me give you a little nip and we'll see,' the fang-maker said and laughed. 'The answer to your question is yes. I had my incisors capped, then filed to a sharp edge. I bite. I drink blood. I am the real deal bad dude, Detective.'

I nodded, didn't doubt it for a second. He looked and acted the part.

'If I might take a simple cast of your canines, I could make a pair of fangs just for you. That will really separate you from your detective peers. Make you peerless.'

I smiled at his wit, but I let him talk.

'I make several hundred sets of fangs every year. Uppers and lowers. Sometimes double fangs. Occasionally, I make a pair in gold and silver. I think you'd look great with silver canines.'

'You've read about the other killings around California?' I asked.

'I've heard about them, yes. Of course. From friends and acquaintances like Peter Westin. Some vampires are excited by what's happened. They think it signals a new time; perhaps a new Sire is coming.'

I stopped him. A sudden chill ran through me. Something he'd just said. 'Is there a leader of the vampires?'

Barreiro's dark eyes narrowed to slits. 'No. Of course there isn't. But if there was, I wouldn't talk to you about it.'

'Then there *is* a Sire,' I said.

He glared at me and began to move about again.

I asked, 'Could you make tigers' teeth – for a man to wear?'

'I could,' he said. '*I have*.'

Suddenly he lunged up at me with surprising speed. He grabbed my hair with one hand, my ear with the other. I'm six three and a lot heavier than him. I wasn't ready for this. The small man was swift, and he was very strong. His open mouth moved toward my throat, but then he stopped.

'Don't ever underestimate us, Detective Cross,' John Barreiro hissed, then let me go. 'Now, are you sure that you don't want those fangs? No charge. Maybe for your own protection.'

Chapter Thirty

William drove the dusty white van through the Mojave Desert at close to a hundred miles an hour. The Marshall Mathers LP was playing at maximum volume. William was really pushing it along Route 15, heading toward Vegas, the next stop on their tour.

The van was an ingenious idea. It was a damn bloodmobile with all the requisite Red Cross stickers. He and Michael were actually certified to take blood from anyone who volunteered to give it.

'It's up ahead a couple of miles, 'William told his brother, who was sitting with one bare leg out the open window.

'What's up ahead? Prey, I hope. I'm bored out of my skull. I need to feed. I'm thirsty. I don't see anything up there.' Michael whined like the spoiled rotten teenager that he was. 'Don't pull any Slim Shady shit on me. I don't see a thing up ahead.'

'You will soon,' William said mysteriously. 'This should snap you out of your funk. I promise it will.'

Minutes later, the van pulled into a commercial parachute center known as a drop zone. Michael sat up, whooped loudly and beat on the dashboard with the palms of his hands. He was such a *boy*.

'I feel the need for speed,' Michael yelled, doing his best imitation of the young Tom Cruise.

The two brothers had been parachuting since they got out of prison. It was one of the best legal highs around, and it took their mind off killing. They hopped out of the van and headed inside a flat-roofed concrete building that had definitely seen better decades.

William paid twenty dollars directly to the pilot for a ride in a Twin Otter plane. There were two of them sitting near the tiny runway at the airstrip, but there was only one pilot and no one else at the parachute center.

The pilot was a dark-haired girl not much older than William. Early twenties at most. She had a tight sexy body but a mean little weasel's face with badly pocked cheeks. He could tell that she liked his and Michael's looks, but hey, who wouldn't?

'No boards, so you're not sky surfing. What are you boys into?' the pilot asked in a strong southwestern accent. 'Name's Callie, by the way.'

'We're into just about everything!' Michael volunteered

and laughed. 'I mean that too, Callie. I'm serious. We're into just about everything that's worth getting into.'

'I don't doubt it,' Callie said, and held Michael's eye for a few seconds. 'Well, let's do it then,' she said, and they climbed up into the Otter.

Less than ninety seconds later, the small plane was pounding down the hardscrabble runway. The brothers were laughing and hollering at the top of their voices.

'You guys really seem pumped up, I'll give you that. You're free-fallers, right? You're both certifiable,' Callie shouted over the airplane noise. She had a throaty rasp that William found, frankly, a little irritating. He wanted to rip a gaping hole in her neck, but he resisted the urge.

'Among other things, yes. Take her up to sixteen thousand,' William shouted back to her.

'Whoa! Thirteen thousand's plenty. You know, temperature at thirteen thousand feet's under forty degrees. You lose 'bout three degrees every thousand feet. Hypoxia sets in at sixteen. Too much for you thin-skinned boys.'

'We'll tell you when it's too much for us. We've done this kind of thing before,' said Michael, a little angry now, his teeth bared, but maybe she took it for a seductive little smile. It wouldn't be the first time that had happened.

William slid the pilot another twenty dollars. '*Sixteen* thousand,' he said. 'Trust me. We've been there before.'

'Okay, you'll be the ones with frostbitten fingers and

ears,' Callie told them. 'I warned you.'

'We're hot-bodied boys. Don't worry about us. You an experienced pilot?'

Callie grinned. 'Well, we'll just have to see, won't we. Let's just say that I'm probably not losing my cherry up here.'

William watched the gauges to make sure she took them high enough. At sixteen thousand feet, the Otter leveled off smoothly. Not too much wind up there today and a view to die for. The plane was practically flying itself.

'This is not a real good idea, guys,' the pilot warned again. 'It's cold as a motherfucker out there.'

'It's a great idea! And so is *this*!' William shouted.

He took her on the spot, biting deeply into Callie's exposed throat. He held her neck firmly with his teeth and strong jaw and began to drink, to feed at sixteen thousand feet.

It was the height of sado-eroticism. Callie screamed and kicked, struggled fiercely, but she couldn't get him off. Bright red blood splattered around the cockpit. He was so powerful. She tried desperately to get out of her cramped pilot's seat and dislocated her hip.

Her knees cracked against the instrument panel several times, and then they stopped suddenly. Her brown eyes glazed over and became still as stones. She gave in. Both of them drank her blood greedily. They fed quickly and efficiently, but couldn't come close to draining the prey inside the cockpit.

William then opened the plane's door. He was struck with a blast of freezing cold air. 'C'mon!' he yelled. The two brothers jumped out of the plane – free falling.

It wasn't an appropriate name for what they were experiencing. The sensation wasn't like falling, it was more like flying your body.

When the two of them went horizontal, they were soaring at about sixty miles an hour. But when they went vertical, they zoomed up to over a hundred, closer to a hundred and twenty, William figured.

The thrill was incredible, absolutely amazing to experience. Their bodies trilled like tuning forks. Callie's fresh blood was still pumping through their systems. The rush was otherworldly.

At those speeds, the slightest leg movement to the left jolted the body to the right.

They got vertical quickly, and stayed that way. Almost all the way down.

They hadn't pulled the cords on their chutes yet. That was the best thrill of all: the possibility of sudden, unexpected death.

The wind pushed and pulled incredibly against their bodies.

The only sound they heard was the wind.

This was ecstasy.

They still hadn't opened their chutes. How long could they wait? How long?

The only thing missing, the only thing that kept this from being close to perfect, William was thinking, was the absence of pain. Pain made any experience better. Pain was the secret to pleasure which so few understood. He and Michael did though.

Finally, they pulled the cords, and they couldn't have waited a second more. The chutes opened, yanked hard at their bodies. The ground was flying up at them.

They landed and rolled, just in time to see the Twin Otter crash and burn, maybe a mile away in the desert.

'No evidence,' William said smugly, his eyes glazed with pleasure and excitement. 'That was such fun.'

Chapter Thirty-One

The Crimson Tide. That's what William called their murderous tour. He and Michael were on a roll now and nothing could stop them until the mission was over. Nothing – not rain, nor sleet, nor the FBI.

The Red Cross van drifted slowly along Fremont Street, the original Strip in Las Vegas. It blended into the garish neoned scene. Made them feel invisible. And like so many young males, William and Michael felt invulnerable. They would never be caught, never be stopped.

The killers took everything in – the ridiculous spouting fountains in front of nearly every casino and hotel, a wedding chapel with 'Love Me Tender' crooning tinnily from a loudspeaker, brightly painted tour buses, like the one ahead of the van, from the United Union of Roofers and Waterproofers.

'This is a true vampire's city,' William proclaimed. 'I can

feel the energy. Even these pathetic worms on the street must feel alive when they're here. It's fabulous – so theatrical, glittery, overly dramatic. Don't you just love it?'

Michael clapped his large hands. 'I'm in heaven. We can be choosy here.'

'That's our plan,' said William, 'to be very choosy.'

At midnight they drove out to the new Strip, Las Vegas Boulevard. They stopped at the Mirage, where the *Daniel and Charles Magic Show* was advertised on a large, neon billboard that rose high over the busy street.

'Is this such a good idea?' Michael asked as they approached the box office inside the hotel. William ignored him and picked up two reserved tickets for the magic show. They were both dressed in black leather with black engineering boots. Nobody really cared what you wore in Vegas anyway. The show was about to begin as they took two seats near the front.

Everything about the theater was spectacular and over the top. An enormous stage had been covered in spray-on black velvet. The backdrop was a thirty-foot-high metallic structure covered in rear-projection pictures that kept changing. Half a dozen techies worked the spotlights. The lighting conveyed spatial grandness if nothing else.

William used the candle on their table to light a cigar. 'It's showtime, my dear brother. Remember what you said – we can be choosy. Don't forget that.'

The magicians' grand entrance onto the stage was a glittery nugget of eye candy. Daniel and Charles literally flew down from the rafters, at least a fifty- or sixty-foot drop.

Then the magicians *disappeared*, and the spellbound audience erupted in applause.

William and Michael cheered as well. The sheer speed with which the hydraulic mechanisms worked was impressive.

Daniel and Charles appeared again. The magicians led two small elephants, a white stallion, and a glorious Bengal tiger onto the stage.

'That's me,' William whispered against Michael's ear. 'I *am* that beautiful cat. I am right at Daniel's side. He should be careful.'

The sound system played Led Zeppelin's 'Stairway to Heaven' in computerized surround-sound. The noise was as gaudy as the visual. A powerful exhaust system vented out the odor of urine and horse and elephant dung. A semi-pleasant vanilla-almond fragrance was pumped in.

On the stage, meanwhile, the two magicians were arguing about something.

William leaned toward a handsome young couple who had just been seated at the cocktail table to his left. The male and female were in their mid-twenties. He immediately recognized them from a hit TV show. He couldn't decide which of the two actors was better looking. They were both so fly, so full of themselves. He knew that their names were Andrew Cotton and Dara Grey. Hell, he read *EW* and the tabloids in his spare moments.

'Isn't this amazing?' he said. 'I love magic. It's so kinky, and *funny*. This is hilarious!'

The female glanced his way. Dara Grey was about to put him in his place when she looked into William's eyes. Just like that – he had her. Only then did he bother to check out the rest of her: an electric blue slip dress, vintage belt and jeweled shoes, embroidered Fendi bag. Nice, very nice. He wanted to feed on her.

This was going to be so good, so delicious.

Now he would seduce the boyfriend. Andrew, dear sweet Andrew.

Then – then they would party until dawn.

Chapter Thirty-Two

The two magicians continued to taunt each other mercilessly on stage. William's eyes drifted back toward the bright lights and the loud bickering. He smiled, couldn't help it. The magicians were part of tonight too, a big part, actually. Important as hell.

Daniel and Charles were in their early forties. They were handsome in a crude sort of way, confident, especially in the eyes of the tawdry Vegas crowd.

Daniel spoke to the audience as if he were a trial lawyer cleverly engaging a jury. He waved a long, highly polished sword, using it for emphasis.

'We are performance artists, possibly the best now working in the world. We've played at Madison Square, and the Winter Garden in New York, the Magic Castle, the Palladium in London, the Crazy Horse Saloon in Paris. We've headlined in Frankfurt, Sydney, Melbourne, Moscow, Tokyo of course.'

Charles seemed bored by his partner's self-serving speech. He sat down on the edge of the stage and yawned until his tonsils showed.

'They don't care about your pedigree, Daniel,' Charles finally spoke. 'Most of these bumpkins wouldn't know Houdini from Siegfried and Roy. Do a cheap trick, that's what they're here for. Tricks are for kids, and they're all kids! Do a trick! Do a cheap, slick trick!'

Daniel suddenly pointed the tip of his sword at his partner. He waggled it threateningly. 'I'm warning you, chump.'

William looked over at the couple sitting beside him. 'This part is pretty good,' he whispered, 'believe it or not.'

He caught the man's eye, but the actor quickly pulled his gaze away. *Too late. He had him too. The male wanted to get into his pants. Who could blame him? God, he wanted to feed. Right here, right now.*

Onstage, Daniel had begun to yell at Charles. 'I've had enough of your high-handed, condescending bullshit, partner. I've had enough of you! More than enough!'

'*That's too bad,*' William mimicked the next few words spoken onstage, '*because I've only just begun to torment you, and them! The bumpkins!*'

The two actors sitting next to them laughed at William's accurate play by play. He had them utterly charmed. Now the male almost couldn't take his eyes off William. Poor, poor Andrew.

Suddenly, up on the stage, Daniel rushed at Charles. He thrust the sword right into Charles's chest. Charles's scream was piercing and real. Blood erupted from his chest, spilled and splashed everywhere. The frightened audience gasped, and the room went quiet. They were in shock.

William and Michael giggled, couldn't stop. So did the couple beside them. Others *shushed* them.

Daniel began to drag Charles's body across the stage, careful to emphasize how heavy the man was. Very dramatic stuff. He stopped at a small prop that was actually a butcher-block table. He draped the body across the table.

He took an ax, hoisted it high, and chopped Charles's head off!

The room exploded with screams. Some people covered their eyes. 'This is not funny,' someone shouted.

William roared with laughter and clapped and stamped his feet. The loud *shushing* continued all around him. People were horrified, but they wanted more. The two actors beside him were laughing as hard as he was. The woman playfully swatted William's arm.

Daniel now placed Charles's head inside a wicker basket. He did it very theatrically. Then he bowed. The audience finally got it. They had caught up.

William frowned and lowered his head. 'The good part is over. The rest is anti-climax.'

Daniel carried the wicker basket back across the entire length of the stage. He walked very slowly. With great care, he spilled out Charles's head onto a silver platter.

'Just happened to have a platter handy!' William whispered to the couple.

Daniel turned to the audience. 'Any of you figure this out yet? No? . . . Really? . . . He's *dead*.'

'Liar! No he's not!' William shouted from his seat. 'Your act is dead, but Charles is alive! Unfortunately.'

Suddenly, the head on the silver platter moved. Charles's eyes opened. The audience went wild. The illusion was quite stunning, and certainly novel enough.

Charles said, 'My God, look what you've done, Daniel. All these witnesses saw you. You'll never get away with this, you murderer.'

Daniel shrugged. 'Oh, but I will. Nobody out there really cares about you, or anyone else for that matter. They don't like you. They don't even like themselves. You deserved this, Charles.'

The head on the platter spoke again. 'A public beheading? Help me, Daniel.'

'What's the magic word, Charles?' asked Daniel.

'Please help me,' Charles answered. 'Please, Daniel. Help me?'

Daniel carefully placed the basket over Charles's head, and then he carried it back across the stage where, with broad flourishes and theatrical gestures, he reattached Charles's head to his body. Charles then rose up and grasped his partner's hand.

The two magicians stood together and bowed. 'Ladies and gentlemen, we are Daniel and Charles, the best magicians in the world!' they shouted to the rafters.

The applause inside the room was loud and sustained. People stood and clapped and cheered. The magicians took several more bows.

'Boo! Boo! They're fakes!' William and Michael hooted from their seats. They saw a couple of hotel security geeks approaching their table.

William leaned toward Andrew Cotton and Dara Grey. 'You like magic, theater, adventure?' he asked. 'I'm William Alexander and this is my brother, Michael. Let's go somewhere. Let's get the hell out of here. We'll have some real fun.'

The actors rose, and as they were leaving with William and Michael, the security people arrived.

'We want our money back,' William said to them. 'Daniel and Charles are *fakes*.'

Chapter Thirty-Three

'Your place or ours?' William asked the actors, keeping the question as non-threatening as he possibly could. He didn't want to lose Dara and Andrew now. He had plans for them.

'Where are you staying?' Dara asked. She was incredibly sure of herself, a goddess in her own mind, a diva. Yet another one.

William answered, 'Michael and I are at Circus Circus.'

'We're at the Bellagio. We're camped out in a suite. Let's go there. It's fabulous, the best in Vegas. We have drugs,' Andrew said. 'MDMA. You like?'

'We have lots of fun toys,' Dara said and gently brushed William's blond hair with her fingers. He could have killed her for the affront. Instead, he took her hand and kissed it. She was so full of life, and rich, warm blood.

The suite at the Bellagio was on a high floor and it

looked out across a man-made lake with fountains that shot water hundreds of feet into the air. The fountains were choreographed to a song from *A Chorus Line*. William thought it was an incredible amount of water to be wasting in the desert. He glanced around the room and was surprised that he didn't totally hate it – there were no nylon rugs or ultra acrylic-coated walls anyway. Bowls of fruit and fresh flowers had been left out in several places. God, he was hungry, famished, but not for grapes and apples.

Dara slid out of her Bob Mackie party dress as soon as she pranced in the door. The young actress's body was tanned and toned. She shrugged off an expensive bra.

Her small breasts were pert, the nipples erect. She kept on her creamy white thong underwear. And her high heels – Jimmy Choo's.

William smiled at the actors – their primping, their practiced, shallow attempts at seduction and eroticism. He wouldn't be surprised if a make-up person popped out of a closet, and suddenly wondered what Brad Pitt and Jennifer Aniston were like together in bed? Probably a beautiful, blond bore.

'Your turn,' Dara said teasingly to the brothers. 'Let's see what you have. Strut your stuff. Let's all get in the mood.'

'You won't be disappointed,' William said. He smiled and began to peel off his clothes. He took his time with the boots, then slowly unzipped his tight black leather jump-suit. 'You sure you don't want to take this monkeysuit off for me?' he asked Dara.

Her eyes were wide. So were Andrew's.

William unbound Michael's ponytail, letting his brother's wavy blond hair flow down onto his shoulders. He kissed Michael's cheek, then his shoulder blade. He began to undress him.

'Oh my, my, my,' Dara whispered, 'you two *are* beautiful.'

They were both hard. Michael and William were large and their penises pulsed and throbbed as they stood there naked. They weren't shy. The brothers were used to nudity since their boyhoods. They were also accustomed to having sex with strangers.

Dara looked around and said, 'I feel outnumbered, but not over-matched.' She took some coke from her purse.

William gently stayed her hand. 'You won't need that. Lie down on the bed. Trust me a little. Trust yourself, Dara.'

Like a magician, William produced four silk scarves – red, blue, and silver. He tied Dara to the bedposts. She struggled some, pretended to be afraid. They all enjoyed watching her act, and Michael put his arm around Andrew, who was getting lost in the shuffle. He was high, too. His blue eyes were glazed.

'Why don't you get comfortable,' Michael whispered. 'You're among friends.'

Andrew slid a pair of handcuffs from a black leather bag on the floor. 'These are for you. Just for fun. Okay?'

Michael obediently thrust his hands out, ready to be cuffed. 'Just for fun,' he said, and laughed.

'This is going to be so great,' Andrew said, his tongue more than a little thick. 'I can feel a rush already. I think I'm starting to peak.'

'No, you aren't even close,' Michael told him.

It happened so fast that it almost didn't seem possible. Suddenly, Michael had locked the handcuffs onto Andrew's wrists. Then he took the actor down on the carpet. He was all over Andrew. He and William gagged him with silk scarves. They moved so fast. They took off his clothes. They tied his ankles with more scarves.

'Trust us, Andrew. This will be great. You can't imagine,' William whispered. Then he watched Michael bite into Andrew's throat. Just a sip. A few delicious drops. An aperitif.

Andrew Cotton's beautiful eyes became wild with fear and confusion. The look was priceless. He knew that he was going to die. Soon, very soon. Maybe in just a couple of minutes.

Dara couldn't see what was happening on the floor. 'Hey. What are you men doing down there? Is it dirty? Are you buggering one another? I'm feeling neglected up here. Somebody come to bed with me. Bugger me.'

William rose up to her and his penis was large and beautiful, his stomach impossibly flat, his smile enchanting, irresistible, and he knew it.

'Up popped the devil,' he said.

'Kiss me, devil,' she whispered, and fluttered her eyelashes. 'Make love to me. Forget about old Andrew. And Michael. You're not in love with your own brother, are you?'

'Who wouldn't be?' William asked.

He knelt over her and then he lowered his body very slowly. He closed his arms around her. Suddenly, Dara was shaking. She knew, without really knowing. Like so many men and women William had feasted on, she wanted to die, without knowing what it was that she wanted. He knew she could see herself reflected in his deep brown eyes. He knew Dara felt she had never looked more desirable.

And he did desire her. Right now, he wanted Dara more than anything else on the earth. He inhaled her scents – flesh, soap, a citrus fragrance, the rich blood coursing through her veins. Then his tongue gently lapped at her earlobe. He knew that Dara felt as if she had been touched *inside*. It wasn't physically possible – but she had felt William's tongue deep inside her.

Suddenly, Michael was lifting Andrew up onto the immense bed. There was room for everyone. Andrew was bound in colorful scarves and shiny silver handcuffs. There was a harsh, red mark on his neck. And blood running down his chest. The actor was already dead.

Dara was beginning to understand everything. William was right – this was so much better without the cocaine. He was touching her everywhere and he was so warm, so hot, this was exquisite. She was writhing, ready to come already, bursting with yearning and desire.

'This is just the beginning,' William whispered against her throat. 'Your pleasure is only just starting. I promise, Dara.'

He licked away her bittersweet perfume. He kissed her again and again. Then he bit down into her throat.

It got better and better.

The ecstasy of pain.

Dying like this.

No one understood that until the end.

Chapter Thirty-Four

It had happened again. Jesus. Two more ungodly murders.

An FBI helicopter was waiting for me at the airport in Fresno. I was flown to Las Vegas where an FBI sedan was waiting. The driver, an agent named Carl Lenards, informed me that Director In Charge Craig was already at the crime scene. Then Lenards filled me in on the rest.

The latest murders had taken place at a five-diamond luxury hotel, the Bellagio. When it had opened in 1998, the Bellagio was the most expensive hotel ever built. It was upscale, and family friendly, until now anyway. There was hardly a trace of the old Las Vegas – no naked ladies, no mobsters in shiny, sharkskin suits.

Las Vegas police cars and EMS vehicles were parked all over the approach driveway from Boulevard South, Route 604. There were also at least a half dozen TV vans on the property. I estimated that five to six hundred onlookers were gathered outside the hotel. Why was the crowd so large? Exactly what had happened inside? All I had so far were sketchy details of the murders. I knew that the bodies had been drained. *But not hung.*

As I made my way through the onlookers, I saw something that bothered me, shook me up even more than the news of the murders.

There were at least a dozen men and women dressed in Goth attire: black frock coats, top hats, leather pants, long boots. One of them smiled right at me. He showed off a set of sharpened, very nasty-looking fangs. He had on blood-red contacts that glowed. He seemed to know who I was. 'Dude,' he smirked. 'Welcome to hell.'

There was nothing I could do about the ghouls. I kept on walking toward the Bellagio. These strange role-players seemed to have no qualms about being at the crime scene. Were the killers here? Were they watching? What did they expect to see next? What did the murders mean?

I hoped that the Vegas police or the FBI was filming the crowd gathering outside the hotel. I figured that Kyle would have taken care of that. I was here for one reason: I can put together details at a murder scene that other cops usually can't. It was why Kyle Craig had asked for me. He understood my strengths, and probably also my weaknesses.

The suite where the couple had been murdered was

large and relatively tasteful by resort standards. The first thing anyone entering the room would notice was a marble bathtub in a tinted glass window overlooking a man-made lake and several fountains.

Two bodies were in the tub. I could see the tops of their heads and a couple of bare feet. As I got closer, I saw that the man and woman had been bitten, and also cut several times. The nude corpses were eerily white.

There hadn't been anywhere to hang them inside the suite.

There wasn't much blood in the tub itself, but it had been stoppered. The room was buzzing with police activity. Too much to suit me. There were LVPD detectives, paramedics, crime-scene scientists, a pathologist, the Coroner's investigative team, and the FBI, of course.

I needed quiet.

I studied the pale, pathetic bodies for several minutes. As was the case with all of the victims so far, the man and woman had been attractive.

Perfect specimens. Chosen for that reason? If not, then why?

The girl looked to be in her early twenties. She was petite, blonde, slender, probably under a hundred pounds. The span of her shoulders was only about a ruler's length. Her breasts were small, and had been bitten, almost shredded. There were bite gouges up and down her legs. The male also appeared to be in his early twenties. He was blond, blue-eyed, with a corn-fed look; his body was toned and sculpted. He too had been bitten. His throat had been slashed and so had his wrists.

I could see no defensive bruises on either of their hands. *They hadn't fought back.* They knew the attackers.

'You saw the ghouls lurking outside?' Kyle asked. 'The semi-human freak show?'

I nodded. 'It's daylight, though. The ones out there must be harmless. The ghouls in their crypts are the ones we need to find.'

Kyle nodded, then he walked away.

After most of the police technicians left I wandered around the hotel suite for hours. It's a ritual for me, part of my own obsession. Maybe I feel I owe it to the dead. I stopped and stared out at the view of the lake that the victims had enjoyed. I noticed everything – the creamy whites, blushing pinks, and Sixties Parrish yellows that engulfed the room. Framed mirrors spotlighted with recessed lights. Fresh fruit and flowers.

The victims had unpacked and put away their clothes. I went through the labels: Bob Mackie dresses, high-heel shoes by Jimmy Choo and Manolo Blahnik, a couple of skirts. Expensive, chic, the best of everything.

The last thing either of them had expected was to die.

A stack of fifty- and hundred-dollar markers from the Venetian and New York-New York were in plain view on the dresser. The killers had left the chips. Also, two full vials of cocaine in the woman's purse. A carton of Marlboro Lights.

Was it to tell us they weren't interested in money and drugs? In gambling? In cigarettes? What are they interested in – murder? Blood?

There were ticket stubs inside the woman's purse. Souvenirs? Passes to MGM Grand Adventures. Tickets for shows at Circus Circus, the Folies Bergère in the Tropicana, the magicians Siegfried & Roy. A half-full bottle of Lolita Lempicka perfume.

The male kept a few restaurant receipts: Le Cirque in the Bellagio, Napa, the Palm, Spago at Caesars.

'There are no tickets or receipts for last night,' I said to Kyle. 'We need to find out where they went. Could be where they met the killers. They must have gotten friendly with them. They let the killers in here.'

Chapter Thirty-Five

The cell phone in my pocket went off. *Shit! Damn it!* Why do I carry these infernal gadgets? Why does anybody in their right mind need to constantly be on call?

I glanced at my watch as I took the phone in hand. It was already seven in the morning. What a life. So far, we knew that Andrew Cotton and Dara Grey had gone to the Rum Jungle for drinks and then a magic show at the Mirage. They were seen talking to two people, but it had been dark in the theater. That was what we had so far, but it was still early.

I had been at the Bellagio murder scene since a little past four in the morning. The case was really getting under my skin. The murders were brutal, primal.

'Alex Cross,' I spoke into the phone. I turned toward the picture window revealing the lake and the desert in the distance. The view was soothing, an incredible contrast with what had happened in the hotel room.

'It's Jamilla, Alex. Did I wake you?'

'No, not hardly. I wish you had. I'm at a murder scene. I'm in Las Vegas, staring out at the desert. You're up pretty early yourself,' I said.

It was good to hear her voice. She sounded sane and normal. She *was* sane and normal. I was the one in trouble.

'Oh, I sometimes get in to the office before six. That way I can get a day's work done before everybody else arrives here. Alex, I have some information to share on the biting attacks.'

From the sound of her voice, I suspected this wasn't going to make things any easier for me.

'Go ahead, Jamilla. I'm listening.'

'Okay,' she said. 'I've been working with a couple of medical examiners from the other places where the blood-suckers struck. I think we may have hit on something important in San Luis Obispo and then again in San Diego.'

I was listening; Jam had my full attention.

'In both of the cities, the medical examiners really got into the case, really tried to help. As you know, we exhumed in San Luis Obispo. Then Guy Millner, the ME in San Diego, did the same. I won't bore you with all the details right now, though I can overnight it to your hotel.'

'That would be great. Obviously, no faxes on any of this material.'

'Here's what we've found out. In both these murders, the teeth marks are different to those in San Francisco or LA. The marks were made by human teeth. But the killers were not the same ones. The evidence is pretty conclusive.

'Alex, there are at least *four* killers out there working. *At least* four. We've identified four different sets of human teeth so far.'

I was trying to make some sense of what I'd just heard. 'These are bodies that were exhumed? Human teeth could leave bite marks on bone?'

'Yes. The MEs all agreed on that. The enamel on teeth is the hardest substance in the human body. Also, as you know, the killers might have been wearing enhancers.'

'Fangs?'

'Right. There was *gnawing* on the bones found in San Luis Obispo and San Diego. That's another reason why there were clear marks.'

'Gnawing?' I winced.

'You're the psychologist, not me. Gnawing entails strong, repetitive, intentional action. It could definitely account for teeth marks. One of the victims was an adolescent, the other was in his fifties. That helped us some, too. According to my sources, the adolescent's bones had less density; so did the older person's due to osteoporosis. Thus the clear marks. But why gnaw on the bones? You tell me.'

I was thinking about it. 'How about this. Inside the bone is the marrow. And the marrow is rich in blood vessels.'

'Oh, Alex, *yuk*,' Jamilla said. 'That could be it. How perfectly awful.'

Chapter Thirty-Six

The murders of the two actors exploded media awareness of the case.

Suddenly, we had hundreds of tips to check and way too many bogus leads to follow. According to the tips, Dara Grey and Andrew Cotton had been spotted in nearly every club and hotel in Vegas. It was just what we didn't need to deal with. We had decided not to release the information that there might be more than one set of killers. California and Nevada weren't ready for it.

Kyle Craig had decided to stay out west for the next couple of days. So did I, of course. I didn't have much of a choice. The case was too hot, and seemed to be revving up even more. Over a thousand local police and FBI agents were involved on some level.

Then the killings simply stopped.

The pattern that had seemed to be escalating and

building ended; the killers, who had seemed to be getting bolder, just vanished. Or maybe we weren't finding the bodies anymore.

I was talking daily to profilers in Quantico, but none of them could discern a pattern that made sense to any of us. Jamilla Hughes couldn't come up with interesting leads and theories either.

Everyone was completely stumped.

The killers just stopped killing.

Why? What was going on? Had the publicity scared them off? Or was it something else? What? Where had the killers disappeared to? How many were there?

It was time for me to go home. That was the good news, and I took it for what it was. Kyle agreed, and I headed back to Washington with the uncomfortable feeling that I had failed, and that maybe the murderers would get away with what they had done.

I got to the house on Fifth Street at four on a Friday afternoon. The home front looked a little worn, but also comfortable. I made a mental note to paint the outside this coming spring. The gutters needed work. Actually, I looked forward to it.

Nobody was home. Nobody was there. I'd been away for twelve days.

I had wanted to surprise the kids, but I guess that was

another bad idea. They seemed to be coming in clusters lately.

I wandered around the house, taking it all in, noting little things that were different. The kids' all-the-rage Razor scooter had a broken back wheel. Damon's white choral robe, sheathed in a plastic dry-cleaning bag, hung over the banister.

I was feeling guilty as it was, and the quiet, empty house didn't help. I looked at a few framed photos on the walls. My wedding photo with Maria. School portraits of Damon and Jannie. Snapshots of little Alex. A formal picture of the Boys Choir taken by me at the National Cathedral.

'Daddy's home, Daddy's home.' I sang an old fifties tune as I peeked into the upstairs bedrooms. 'Shep and the Limelights,' I muttered.

Nobody was around to care that I was singing old rock-and-roll tunes and trying to lighten the mood. The Capitol and the Library of Congress were within walking distance, and I knew Nana liked to take the kids there sometimes. Maybe that's where they were.

I sighed and wondered once again whether it was time for me to get the hell out of police work. There was always one catch: I was still passionate about it. Even though I'd failed on the West Coast, I usually got some kind of result. I had saved some lives in the past few years. The FBI brought me in on some of their toughest cases. I figured this was my bruised ego talking, so I stopped the internal bullshit, cut it right off.

I took a hot shower then changed into a Men's March T-shirt, jeans and flip-flops. I felt a lot more comfortable, like I was back in my own skin. I could almost make myself believe that the lurid vampire killers were gone from my life for good. I think that's what I wanted to happen. Just let them crawl back into their hole.

I went down to the kitchen and grabbed a Coke from the fridge. Nana had taped a couple of the kids' master-pieces to the door. 'Inner Galactic Encounter' by Damon, and 'Marina Scurry Saves the Day – Again' by Janelle.

A book was laid out on the kitchen table: *10 Bad Choices That Ruin Black Women's Lives*. Nana was doing a little light reading again. I peeked inside to see if I was one of the ten bad choices.

I wandered out to the sun porch. Rosie the cat was asleep on Nana's rocker. She yawned when she saw me, but didn't get up to rub against my leg. I had been away too long.

'Traitor,' I said to Rosie. I went over and scratched her neck and she was okay with it.

I heard footsteps. I walked to the foyer and opened the front door. Lights of my life.

Jannie and Damon looked at me and screeched, '*Who are you?* What are you doing in our house?'

'Very funny,' I said. 'Come give your daddy a big hug. Hurry, hurry.'

They ran into my arms and it felt so good. I was home, and there was no place like it. And then I had a thought I didn't want to have: did the Mastermind know that I was here? Was our house safe anymore?

Chapter Thirty-Seven

At its best, life can be so simple and good. As it should be. On Saturday morning, Nana and I packed up the kids and we headed over to their favorite place in all of Washington, the huge and wonderful and occasionally elevating Smithsonian complex. We were all in agreement that the Smithsonian, or 'Smitty', as Jannie has called it since she was a very little girl, was where we wanted to be today.

The only issues were where to go first, and, ultimately, where to go during the day.

Since Nana would be there for only a few hours with little Alex, we let her pick out the day's first stop.

'Let me guess,' Jannie said, and rolled her eyes. 'The Museum of African Art?'

Nana Mama shook a finger at Jannie. 'No, Ms Weisenheimer. Actually, I'd like to go to the Arts and Industries

Building. That's my choice for today, young lady. Surprised? Shocked that Nana isn't the creature of habit you thought she was?'

Damon piped up. 'Nana wants to see the History of Black Photographers. I heard about it at our school. They got cool black cowboy pictures. Isn't that right, Nana?'

'And much, much more,' said Nana. 'You'll see, Damon. You'll be proud and amazed, and maybe stimulated to take a few more photographs than you do. You too, Jannie. And Alex as well. Nobody takes pictures in this family except me.'

So we went to the Arts and Industries Building first and it was very good, as it always is. Inside, the dull roar of air-conditioning and the cries of a gospel album mixed nicely. We saw the black cowboys, and also a lot of exceptional photos from the Harlem Renaissance.

We stood in front of a twelve-foot photo of ambitious-looking black men in suits, ties and top hats taken from a bird's eye view. A stunning shot that would be hard to forget.

'If I saw that scene on the street,' Jannie said, 'I would definitely take the picture.'

After Arts and Industries we appeased Jannie and returned to the Einstein Planetarium, where we watched 'And a Star to Steer Her' for the fourth or fifth time, or maybe the sixth or seventh time, but who's counting. Nana took little Alex home for his nap then, and we trekked on over to the Air and Space Museum. Now began the portion of our journey that Jannie called 'Damon's macho planes-and-trains trip'.

But even Jannie enjoyed Air and Space. The Wright Brothers' plane floated high above us, suspended by long wires, and it was magnificent – light spruce beams and stretched white sheets of canvas. To its right, the Breitling Orbiter 3, another important page from aeronautic history – the first nonstop balloon flight around the world. And then – 'one small step for man' – the thirteen-thousand-pound Apollo 11. You can be cynical about all this or go with it. I choose to go with it. Makes life a lot easier and more rewarding.

After we had studied several of the aeronautic miracles, Damon insisted we catch *Mission to Mir* on the IMAX screen at the Langley Theater.

'I'm going to outer space one day,' he announced.

'I have news,' Jannie said, 'you're already there.'

In honor of Nana, we stopped at the Museum of African Art and the kids got a kick out of the masks and ceremonial clothes, but especially the old currency exhibit – cowrie shells, bracelets, and rings. It was incredibly quiet inside, spacious, colorful, cool as could be. The last stop of the day was to see the Dinosaur House at the Museum of Natural History. But then both Jannie and Damon said we *had* to see the tarantula feeding at the Orkin Insect Zoo. There was a sign on walls painted to resemble a rain forest: *'Insects won't inherit the earth – they own it now.'*

'You're in luck,' Jannie teased her brother. 'Your kind rules.'

Finally, around six, we crossed Maryland Avenue to the Mall. The kids were quiet, tired and hungry by then – and so was I. We ate a picnic supper under spreading shade trees at the foot of the Capitol.

It was the best day I'd had in weeks.

No calls from anybody.

Chapter Thirty-Eight

As he had done so many times before, probably a dozen times by now, the Mastermind watched Alex Cross and his family.

Love equals hate, he thought. What an incredible equation, but so true, absolutely true. It made the world go round and it was a lesson Alex Cross needed to learn. Christ, he was such a fucking optimist. It was infuriating.

If anyone had cared enough to carefully study *his* past they would have discovered the keys to everything that had happened so far. His personal crime and murder spree was one of the most daring in history. It had lasted for over twenty-eight years. He could count the mistakes he'd made on one hand. The keys were right there for anybody to see:

Narcissistic personality disorder.

That's where it all began. That's where it would end.

A grandiose sense of self-importance.

That was him, all right.

Expects to be recognized as superior without commensurate achievements.

Preoccupied with fantasies of unlimited success, power, brilliance, or ideal love.

Interpersonally exploitive.

Yes, indeed. He lived for it.

Lacks empathy.

To put it mildly.

But please note, Dr Cross and others who might wish to study the long and winding trail – this is a personality disorder. There is no psychosis involved. I am an organized, even obsessive, thinker. I can work out elaborate plots that serve my need to compete, criticize, and control. The three Cs. I am rarely impulsive.

Questions you should be asking about me:

Are my parents alive? Answer: *Yes and no.*

Was I ever married? Answer: *Yes.*

Any siblings? Answer: *Oh, absolutely.* Note bene.

If I'm married, do I have any children? Answer: *Two genuine American beauties. I saw that movie by the way. Loved Kevin Spacey. Adored him.*

And am I attractive, or physically flawed in some minor way? Answer: *Yes and yes!*

Now do the homework! Draw the love and the hate

triangles in my life, Doctor. You're *in* the triangles, of course. But so is your family – Nana, Damon, Jannie, and Alex Jr. Everything you care about and think that you stand for is right there in those beautiful triangles, wrapped up in my obsessions.

So unravel it, before it's too late for both of us. Not to mention everybody you care about in the world.

I'm right outside your house on Fifth Street, and it would be so easy to barge inside right now. It would have been easy to kill you and the family at the Smithsonian, the 'Smitty', as your daughter calls it.

But that would be too easy, too small, and *as I've been trying to tell you—*

The phone in the Mastermind's hand was ringing, calling, reaching out to touch somebody. Patiently, he let it continue.

Finally, Cross picked up.

'*I have a grandiose sense of self-importance,*' the Mastermind said.

Chapter Thirty-Nine

I settled back into my duties in Washington, where I took some abuse from my detective pals about how much I seemed to enjoy working with the Federal Bureau lately. They didn't know that I had been approached about becoming an FBI agent, and was actually thinking it over. But I was still drawn to the mean streets of DC.

I had a decent week on the job, and when another Friday rolled around, I also had a date. It had struck me a long time ago that the best thing that had ever happened to me was being married to Maria and having two great kids with her. It's not an easy thing to play the dating game at any age, especially when you have kids, but I was committed to it. I definitely wanted to be in love again if I could, to settle down, to change my life. I suppose that most people do.

Occasionally I would hear my aunts say, 'Poor Alex, he

doesn't have anyone to love, does he? He's all alone, poor baby.'

That wasn't exactly true. Poor Alex, my butt. I have Damon, Jannie, and little Alex. I also have Nana. And I have lots of good friends in Washington. I make friends easily – like Jamilla Hughes. So far, I haven't had trouble getting a date either. So far.

Macy Francis and I had known each other since we were little kids growing up in the neighborhood. Macy went on to get a couple of degrees in English and Education at Howard and Georgetown. I went to Georgetown, then Johns Hopkins for my doctorate in psychology.

About a year ago, Macy returned to the Washington area to teach English Lit. at Georgetown. We met again at one of Sampson's parties. We talked for an hour or so that night and I found that I still liked her. We agreed to get together again soon.

I'd called Macy when I got home from my bust of a trip to California. We met at the 1789 restaurant for drinks and maybe dinner. Macy's choice. It was near her place in Georgetown.

The restaurant is set in a Federal-style town house at Thirty-sixth and Prospect. I got there first, but Macy arrived a few minutes later. She came up, gave me a sweet kiss on the cheek before we sat down in the cozy pub. I liked the fleeting touch of her lips, the smell of a citrus fragrance on her neck. She had on a lilac turtleneck sweater – sleeveless, a black skirt that lightly hugged her, suede slingback heels. She had small diamond studs in her ears.

As far back as I can remember, Macy had always dressed well. She'd always looked nice, and I guess I had always noticed.

'You know, I'll tell you a secret, Alex,' Macy said once we had ordered glasses of wine. 'I saw you at John Sampson's party, and I thought to myself, Alex Cross looks better than he ever did. I'm sorry, but that's what went buzzing through my head.'

We both laughed. Her teeth were even and shiny white. Her brown eyes were bright and intelligent. She had always been the smartest in her classes.

'I thought the same thing about you,' I told her. 'You like teaching okay, the new job at Georgetown working out? The Jesuits leaving you alone?'

She nodded. 'My father once told me you're lucky if you *ever* find something you like to do. Then it's a miracle if you can find somebody who'll *pay* you to do it. I found it, I guess. How about you?'

'Well,' I said seriously, 'I'm not sure if I love my job, or if I'm just addicted to it. No, actually I do like it most of the time.'

'You a workaholic?' Macy asked. 'Tell the truth now.'

'Oh no . . . well, *maybe* . . . some weeks I am.'

'But not this week? At least not tonight.'

'No, last week was the bad one. This week has been mostly relaxed. Tonight is very relaxed. I need a whole lot more of this,' I said, and laughed.

'You look relaxed, Alex. It's so nice seeing you again.'

Macy and I continued to talk easily. A few people were eating at banquettes in the pub room, but it was mostly quiet. Parents of Georgetown students often take their kids to 1789 for a special meal. It *is* special. I was glad I was meeting Macy here. She'd made a good choice.

'I asked some girlfriends about you,' she confessed, then giggled. 'Alex Cross is "not available" a few of them said. "He's kind of a coconut," one sister said. The other girls said she was crazy as a loon. But – *are you*?'

I shook my head. 'People are funny, how they need to make judgments on everybody else. I still live in the old neighborhood, don't I? No coconuts live in Southeast. I don't think so.'

Macy agreed with that. 'You're right, you're right. Not too many people understood how we grew up here, Alex. I was named after a damn department store. You believe that?'

'I do. I grew up here, Macy.' We clinked our glasses and laughed.

'I guess I'm lucky my name isn't Bloomingdale.'

A couple of times, I brought up dinner, but she was

more comfortable sitting and talking. I know Chef Ris Lacoste, and I love her cooking. I had my heart set on crab cakes garnished with her special slaw. But we drank another couple of glasses of wine, and then Macy started to get a little ahead of me with the wine orders.

'You sure you don't want to eat something?' I asked a little later.

'I think I already told you that I didn't,' she said. Then she forced a smile. 'I like what we're doing here, just talking, chilling. Don't you?'

I did like talking to Macy but I hadn't eaten since breakfast, and I needed to get some solid food in me pretty soon. I was hungering for some of the thick, luscious black bean soup. I glanced at my watch and saw it was already ten-thirty. I wondered what time 1789 stopped serving.

Macy began telling me about her marriages. Her first husband had been a bum and a loser; the second, a younger man from Grenada, was even worse, she said. She was getting a little loud and people at the bar were starting to notice us.

'So here I am, thirty-seven years old. I had to go back to work even though I didn't want to. I'm teaching freshmen, Alex. English composition, World Lit. God knows, seniors are bad enough.'

I was sure she said that she liked teaching, but maybe I heard her wrong, or she was being sarcastic. I wasn't doing much talking anymore, just listening to her stories, and eventually Macy noticed. She put her hand over mine. She had the smoothest brown skin. 'I'm sorry, I got carried away, Alex. I talk too much, don't I? So I've been told. I'm really sorry.'

'We haven't seen each other in a long time. Lots to talk about.'

She looked at me and she had such beautiful brown eyes. I was sorry that she'd been hurt in her marriages, hurt by love. It happens to the best of people sometimes. Macy was obviously still hurting.

'You do look great,' she said. 'And you listen pretty good for a man. That's important.'

'You too, Macy. I like your stories.'

Her hand was back on top of mine, her nails lightly grazing my skin. It felt nice, actually. There was nothing too subtle going on here. She let her tongue wet her upper lip, then she lightly bit down. I was finally starting to forget that I was hungry for the crab cakes and black bean soup at 1789. Macy was quietly staring into my eyes. We were both adults, unattached, and I was definitely attracted to a lot of things about her.

'My place isn't far, Alex,' she said. 'I don't usually do this. Come home with me. Jus' walk me home.'

Her place was only ten blocks away, so I walked Macy there. Actually, she had a little trouble walking and her speech was slurred. I put my arm around her, held her steady.

Macy's apartment was on the ground floor of a town house near the university. It was minimally furnished. The walls were painted a pale green. Against one wall was a black lacquered upright piano. A framed magazine article about Rudy Crew caught my eye. The educator's words were set in large type: 'Education is about the distribution of knowledge . . . and to whom we actually distribute this particular commodity is a major question in this country.'

Macy and I held each other and cuddled for a moment on the living-room couch. I liked her touch, the way she kissed. This wasn't right, though. I knew that I didn't want to be there. Not tonight anyway. Macy wasn't at her best right now.

'Good man's hard to find,' Macy said, drawing me close. She was still slurring her words a bit. 'You have no idea, no idea. So hard out there. It's hell.'

I did have some idea about how hard it was to find someone to be with, but I didn't pursue the point. Maybe some other time.

'Macy, I'm going to head home,' I finally said. 'I liked seeing you again. I liked it a lot.'

'I knew it!' she exploded on me. 'I expected as much! Just *go*, Alex. Go. I don't want to fucking see you again!'

Before the anger had welled in her eyes, I had seen

something beautiful and nearly irresistible. Now it was gone again. Maybe she could get back in touch with it, maybe not. Then Macy started to cry and I knew enough not to try and comfort her. I didn't want to be condescending.

I left the apartment, with its beautiful piano and the wonderful quote from Rudy Crew. This woman wasn't right for me to be with. Not now anyway.

Sad night.

A good woman is hard to find too, I wanted to tell Macy.

God, I hated dating.

Chapter Forty

The night with Macy Francis kept bothering me for the next couple of days. It was like a sad song that played in my head. I hadn't expected it to turn out that way. I hadn't liked what I'd seen, or felt. The look in Macy's eyes stayed with me: a terrible mixture of hurt, vulnerability, and anger that would be hard to soothe.

I grabbed Sampson on Thursday night after work. We agreed to meet at the Mark for drinks. The bar was a couple of streets down from Fifth. Local hangout. Tin ceiling, wideboard pine floors, long, worn mahogany bar, ceiling fan turning lazily.

'Sugar, damn,' Sampson said when he arrived and found me sitting by myself, nursing a Foggy Bottom lager while studying the old Pabst clock on the wall. 'You don't mind me saying, you look like shit, man. You sleeping all right? You still sleeping *alone*, aren't you.'

'Good to see you too,' I said to him. 'Sit down and have a beer.'

Then Sampson wrapped one of his mammoth arms around me. He hugged me as if I were his little kid. 'What the hell is going on with you?' he asked.

I shook my head. 'Don't know exactly. The manhunt on the West Coast went real bad. I mean, it dried the hell up. There's no word on Betsey Cavalierre's murder either. Had a date the other night. Just about has me swearing off dating for the rest of my life.'

Sampson nodded. 'I know the words to that sad song.' He ordered a Bud from the bartender, an ex-cop we both knew – Tommy DeFeo.

'The case I was working on in California ended real badly, John. The killers just disappeared. Thin air. So. How are you doing? You look good. For you.'

He raised an index finger. Then he pointed it right between my eyes. 'I always look good. It's a given. Don't try to change the subject on me. We're into something here.'

'Oh hell, you know I don't like to talk about my troubles, John. So tell me about yours.' I started to laugh. He didn't.

Sampson just looked at me, said nothing, waited me out.

'You'd probably make a decent shrink,' I told him.

'Speaking of which, have you been to see the good Doctor Finaly lately?' Adele Finaly is my psychiatrist.

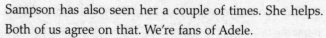

Sampson has also seen her a couple of times. She helps. Both of us agree on that. We're fans of Adele.

'No, she's really pissed off at me. Says I'm not trying hard enough, says I won't embrace my own pain. Words to that effect.'

Sampson nodded and smiled thinly. 'So why is that?'

I made a face. 'I didn't say that I agree with Adele.'

I sipped my Foggy Bottom. It wasn't too bad, and I liked being loyal to a local brewer.

'When I *try* to embrace the goddamn pain, I keep coming back to the conflict between the job and the life I think I want to lead. I missed another one of Damon's concerts while I was out in California. Stuff like that keeps happening.'

Sampson punched my shoulder. 'That's not the end of the world, you know. Damon knows you love his little ass. The young dude and I talk about it sometimes. He's over it. Now you get over it.'

'Maybe it's just that I've worked on too many bad murder cases in the past few years. It's changing me.'

Sampson nodded approval. He liked that answer. 'Sounds like you're feeling a little burnt-out.'

'No. I'm feeling like I'm caught in a scary nightmare that won't go away. Too many coincidences whirling around me. The Mastermind howling my name, threatening me. I don't know how to make it all stop.'

Sampson stared into my eyes. He locked into them. 'Back there a little bit you said coincidences, sugar. *You don't believe in coincidences.*'

'That's what makes it so scary. If you want to know the truth, I think that someone really is after me, and they've been after me for *a long time.* Whoever it is, he's scarier than the vampires. I keep getting calls from the Mastermind, John. He calls me every day. Hardly misses a day. We still can't trace the calls.'

Sampson ran a hand across his forehead. 'I just can't work out who would be stalking you. Who would dare to take on the Dragonslayer? Must be some kind of fool.'

'Believe me,' I said, 'this is no fool.'

Chapter Forty-One

Sampson and I stayed at the Mark later than we should have. We drank a lot of beer, and finally closed the place down at around two. We were smart and sane and sober enough to leave our cars in the parking lot instead of driving home. John and I walked home under a bright moonlit sky. It reminded me of the two of us growing up in Southeast. We had to walk just about everywhere we went. Maybe we'd take a city bus if we were feeling flush. He dropped me off at my house and continued toward the Navy Yard and his place.

Early the next morning, I had to retrieve my car before I went to work. Nana was up with little Alex and I drank a half pot of her coffee, then put the boy in his stroller. He and I walked to my car.

The morning was clear and bright and the neighborhood seemed peaceful and quiet at around seven o'clock.

Nice. I've lived on Fifth Street for thirty years, ever since Nana moved there from her old place on New Jersey Avenue. I still love the neighborhood, and it is home for the Cross family. I don't know if I could ever leave.

'Daddy was with Uncle John last night.' I bent down and talked to the boy as I pushed his blue- and white-striped stroller along. A nice-looking woman passed us on her way to work. She smiled like I was the best man in the history of the world, because I was walking my child this early in the morning. I didn't believe it for a second, but I enjoyed the romanticized fantasy.

Little Alex likes to watch passing people, cars, the clouds streaming above his little head. He loves rides in the stroller and I like pushing him, talking or singing kiddie ditties as we go about our business.

'See the wind blowing the tree leaves?' I said, and he looked up as if he understood every word.

It's impossible to tell how much he understands, but he seems responsive to what I say. Damon and Jannie were the same way, though Jannie was constantly babbling as an infant. She still loves to talk, and to get in the last word, and the next to the last, just like her grandmother, and also, now that I remember, her mother, Maria.

'I need your help, buddy.' I stooped down and talked to little Alex again.

He looked up at me, smiled beautifully. *Sure, Daddy, you can count on me.*

'It's your job to hold me together for a little while. You give me something precious to focus on. Can you do that?'

Alex continued to smile. *Of course I can, Daddy. It's no problem. Consider it done. I am your precious. Lean on me.*

'Good boy, I knew I could count on you. Just keep doing what you're doing. You're the best thing that's happened to me in a while. I love you, little buddy.'

As I was talking to my son, though, a little of the feelings of the night before rolled over me like some cold, wet fog coming up from the Anacostia River. *Coincidences*, I remembered. *The bad things that had happened around me for the past two years. A real bad run. The murder of Betsey Cavalierre. The Mastermind. The vampire killers.*

I needed for it to let up some, needed to come up for air.

When I got to headquarters that morning, a message was waiting for me. There had been another vampire murder. But the game had just changed, taken another turn.

This one had taken place in Charleston, South Carolina.

The killers were on the East Coast again.

Part Three

Murder In The South

Chapter Forty-Two

I flew to Charleston and arrived a little before nine in the morning. The local murder story was splashed boldly across the front pages of the *Post* and *Courier* and also *USA Today*.

I could feel uncertainty and fear in the bright, sterile, overly commercialized confines of the airport. Travelers I passed seemed nervous and wary. Several looked as if they hadn't slept well the night before.

I'm sure that some of them felt that if the mysterious killers could strike in the heart of Charleston, they could do it in an airport waiting room or food court just as easily. No one was feeling safe anywhere.

I rented a car at Charleston airport, and then I set off for a spot called Colonial Lake in town. A male and female jogger had been murdered there at around six the previous morning. The couple had been married for just four months. The similarities to the murders in Golden Gate Park were unmistakable.

I had never been to Charleston, though I'd read books set in the city. I soon discovered for myself that Charleston is physically gorgeous. Once upon a time, it had been a city of incredible wealth, most of which came from cotton, rice, and slaves, of course. Rice had been the biggest export, but slaves, who were brought into Charleston Port and sold throughout the South, were the import that proved the most profitable. Wealthy planters had traveled frequently between the plantations in the lowlands and their homes in Charleston, where the important balls, concerts, and masquerades were held. Relatives of Nana Mama's had been brought into Charleston Port and sold there.

I found a parking spot on Beaufain Street, which was lined with Victorian-style houses. I even spied a few English gardens. This wasn't the kind of place where ghoulish murders ought to happen. It was too pretty, too idyllic. Was that what drew the killers here? Did they appreciate beauty – or hate it? What were they revealing to us with each new murder? What was their dark fantasy? Their horror story?

If Charleston as a whole was suspicious and fearful about the murders, then the streets around Colonial Lake seemed close to terror. People eyed each other warily and coldly. There was nothing even close to a welcoming smile, no southern hospitality on display anywhere.

I had left a message for Kyle to meet me at the lake. It was surrounded by wide sidewalks and wrought-iron benches. Yesterday, it had probably appeared picture perfect and completely safe. Today, bright yellow crime-scene tape was set up near the intersection of Beaufain and Rutledge. The Charleston police had surrounded the area and were watching everybody as if the killers might return today.

I finally saw Kyle waiting under a spreading shade tree and I walked toward him. The morning was warm, but there was a breeze off the ocean that smelled of salt and fish. Kyle had on his usual attire: gray suit, white shirt and nondescript blue tie. He looked like the playwright and actor Sam Shepard, even more so than usual. He also looked gaunt, tired, almost as haunted as I felt. The murders were getting to him, too. Something was.

'It must have been like this yesterday morning, though it was earlier when they struck the couple,' I said as I came up to Kyle. 'No one saw anything? No witnesses in an area like this? That's what I read in the police briefs.'

Kyle sighed. 'We actually have a witness who saw two men hurrying out of the park. Older man in his mid-eighties. He said he thought he saw blood on the shirts of the men, and he felt he was mistaken. Then he found the bodies.'

I quickly surveyed the scene at Colonial Lake again. The sun was shining brightly and I was forced to shade my eyes. Birds were twittering in several of the trees. The park was wide open to scrutiny. 'They were out in broad daylight. Some vampires,' I muttered.

Kyle eyed me. 'You're not starting to believe in vampires.'

'I believe that there are people who practice a vampire lifestyle,' I told him. 'I know some of them believe they're vampires. Some of the role-players even sport very sharp teeth. Fangs. They can be very violent. I haven't seen any shape changers yet. Otherwise our witness might have seen a couple of furry bats winging it out of here instead of two men. That's supposed to be funny, Kyle. What else did our witness say about the men he saw?'

'Not a lot. He thought they were young, Alex. Twenties or thirties, which covers a hell of a lot of territory. They were walking quickly, but didn't seem alarmed that he saw them. He's eighty-six, Alex. He seems, shall we say, distracted by all the attention he's getting.'

'Whoever the killers are, they're certainly bold. Or stupid. I wonder if these are the same bastards we chased through California and Nevada.'

Kyle lit up a little. He had something to tell me. 'My people in Quantico were up half the night. Again. Alex, they've come up with a dozen East Coast cities with unsolved murders that could be connected to the others.'

'What's the time frame of the murders?' I asked.

'That's the really interesting part. This may have been going on for a long time. Nobody seems to have put these cases together before we came along. The time frame is at least eleven years.'

Chapter Forty-Three

That night, Kyle and I had dinner with a good friend in Charleston. Actually, Kyle made the arrangements, including reservations at the Capital Grille on North Tyron.

Kate McTiernan hadn't changed much since we had been thrown together during the Casanova murder spree in Durham and Chapel Hill, North Carolina. When the murderer Casanova had kidnapped Kate in her house outside Chapel Hill he'd believed she was the most beautiful woman in the South.

Not only that, Kate was extremely smart. She was a doctor now, a pediatrician, but she was thinking about becoming a surgeon.

When she arrived at our table, Kyle and I were deep in conversation. Actually, we were arguing about possible next steps in the investigation.

'Hi, guys.' Lustrous brown hair framed Kate's face. She

was wearing it longer these days. Her eyes were dark blue with a nice sparkle. She was still in terrific shape, but I knew she was a softie deep inside.

'Give it up,' Kate said. 'You boys are working way too hard. We're going to have some fun tonight.'

Seeing her there got us both up out of our chairs and grinning like idiots. We'd gone through a lot together, and survived to be together again for this unlikely dinner in Charleston.

'This is a great coincidence. I was at a medical conference just outside town,' Kate said as she sat down with us.

'Alex doesn't believe there are coincidences,' Kyle said.

'Well, fine. So here we are again, brought together by divine intervention or whatever, praise the Lord,' Kate said, and grinned.

'You seem in excellent spirits, Kate,' Kyle said. He was actually pretty buoyant himself.

'Well, Kyle, this is just such a nice, unexpected treat. I get to see the two of you. Plus, I *am* in excellent spirits. I'm getting married next year in the spring. My Thomas proposed two nights ago.'

Kyle fumbled out a congratulation, and I called over our waiter and ordered a bottle of champagne to celebrate. For the next few minutes, Kate told us all about her Thomas, who owned and ran a small, nicely snooty bookstore in North Carolina. He was also a landscape painter, and Kate said he was exceptional at both his jobs.

'Of course I'm hugely biased, but I'm also a picky little bitch, and he really is good. He's a fine person too. How are Nana and the kids? How's Louise, Kyle?' she asked. 'C'mon, tell me everything. I've missed you two.'

By the end of dinner, we were all in good spirits. The champagne and the company did the trick. I had noticed before how Kate could raise up everyone around her – even Kyle, who usually isn't the most social person. All through dinner he rarely took his eyes off her.

The three of us hugged outside of the restaurant at around eleven.

'You two are coming to my wedding,' Kate said, and stamped her foot. 'Kyle will bring Louise, and Alex, you'll bring the new love of your life. Promise?'

We promised Kate. She left us no choice. We then watched her walk away toward her car, an old blue Volvo that she made house calls in.

'I like her a lot.' I couldn't help stating the obvious.

'Yes, I like her too,' said Kyle, who didn't stop watching until Kate's car was gone from sight. 'She's a very special girl.'

Chapter Forty-Four

We were connecting some of the dots now. *Finally*. I hoped we would be able to put together the whole vampire puzzle soon. By the following afternoon, the FBI had identified twelve cities on the East Coast where murders involving vampire-like bites had occurred as early as 1989. I put the names on one of my index cards. Then I stared at the list long and hard. What could possibly link these cities?

Atlanta
Birmingham
Charleston
Charlotte
Charlottesville
Gainesville
Jacksonville
New Orleans

Orlando
Richmond
Savannah
Washington, DC

The breadth of the list was a problem. Scarier and more mystifying was the fact that the murders might have been going on for over a decade.

Next I made an even longer list of cities where non-lethal attacks by supposed 'vampires' had been reported and investigated. I stared at the list and got a little depressed. This was starting to look like an impossible conspiracy.

New York City
Boston
Philadelphia
Pittsburgh
Virginia Beach
White Plains
Newburgh
Trenton
Atlanta
Newark
Atlantic City
Tom's River
Baltimore
Santa Cruz

Princeton
Miami
Gainesville
Memphis
College Park
Charlottesville
Rochester
Buffalo
Albany

The Violent Crime unit in Quantico was working round the clock on the murders. Kyle and I were pretty sure that other cities would turn up, and that the pattern might even go back further than eleven years.

In Atlanta, Gainesville, New Orleans, and Savannah there appeared to have been murders in at least two different years. So far, Charlotte, North Carolina, was the worst hit: there were three suspicious murders going back to 1989. It was even possible that the killing spree had started in Charlotte.

The FBI had moved agents into the twelve cities where the murders had taken place, and special task forces had been set up in Charlotte, Atlanta and New Orleans.

I finished up with my investigation in Charleston. It didn't accomplish too much. At this point, the media didn't have the story about the wide net of murder locations, and we wanted to keep it that way for as long as we could.

That night, I visited Spooky Tooth, the only club in the Charleston area that was a hangout for Goths and vampire wannabes. What I found there was a nest of young people, mostly under twenty. They were still in high school or college. I interviewed the owner of the nightclub, and questioned some of the clientele. They were definitely angry and restless, but no one seemed a likely murder suspect.

I made sure I was back in Washington the next afternoon. At seven-thirty, Nana, Jannie, little Alex and I went to one of the Boys Choir concerts.

The choir sounded better than ever. Damon was one of the featured singers. He had a beautiful solo, 'The Ash Grove'.

'See what you've been missing,' Nana leaned in close and said.

Chapter Forty-Five

William and Michael liked being in the South. It was wild and free-spirited just like they were. Most important, they were right on schedule.

They had arrived in Savannah, Georgia. William drove the van along Oglethorpe Street, and stopped at the famous Colonial Park Cemetery. Then he went on to Abercorn. Then along Percy Street, passing Chippewa and Orleans Squares. He told Michael, lectured to him, 'Savannah is built on its dead. A whole lot of this port city is built on the graveyards.' Also that Savannah had been spared in the Civil War and was now one of the best-preserved southern cities.

William liked this beautiful city very much, and was pleased that they had to take a victim in Savannah. It would be a pleasure to feed here, and to fulfill their mission. He lost track of the street names as he took in the sights of the historic district. Magnificent Federal-period town houses, nineteenth-century churches, fancy scrolled ironwork and Greek motifs, flowers everywhere. He admired the famous old houses: Green-Meldrim, Hamilton-Turner, Joe Odom's first house.

'It's beautiful and elegant,' he told his brother. 'I could live here. You think we should settle down one day? Would you like that?'

'I'm famished. Let's settle down soon,' Michael replied with a laugh. 'Let's settle down and feast on the finest that Savannah has to offer.'

William finally parked the van on a street called West Bay, and he and his brother got out and stretched their arms and legs.

Two young girls in Savannah College of Art and Design T-shirts and blue jean cutoffs came strolling up to the van. They had long, shapely legs, butterscotch tans, and seemed not to have a care in the world.

'Can we give blood here?' the smaller of the girls asked with a conquering smile. She looked to be around sixteen or seventeen. She had lip studs and wild cherry Jello-dyed hair.

'Aren't you the dainty morsel,' said Michael as he locked eyes with the girl.

'I'm a lot of things,' she said, and looked over at her friend, 'but dainty sure isn't one of 'em. Don't you agree,

Carla?' The other girl nodded and rolled her green eyes.

William looked the girls over and thought they could do better in Savannah. These two tramps weren't worthy of him and Michael.

'We're closed for business right now. Sorry.' He was polite and smiled graciously, even seductively. 'Maybe a little later, ladies. Why don't you two come back tonight? How about that?'

The short girl snapped, 'You don't have to get an attitude. We were just making conversation.'

William ran his hand lazily back through his long blond hair. He continued to smile. 'Oh, I know that. So was I. Who could blame me for chatting up two beautiful girls like yourselves. Like I said, maybe we'll see you later tonight. Of course we'll take your blood for the cause.'

William and Michael decided to take a stroll toward the Savannah River and an area called Riverfront Plaza. They barely noticed the freighters and tugs on the water, or the gaily festooned paddleboat, the Savannah River Queen, or even the 'Waving Girl' statue, towering and bronze, a young woman waving a sad farewell to departing sailors. They preferred to check out the men and women walking through the Plaza. They were looking for prey, even though they knew it would be dangerous to strike here in broad daylight. A flea market was in progress and the various local artists had drawn a respectable crowd – a few soldiers, but mostly women, some of them very attractive.

'I do want to take someone. Maybe right here in this oh-so-fucking-pretty river park,' William finally said.

'He'd do nicely,' Michael said, pointing out a slender male in a black T-shirt and blue jean cutoffs. 'Or maybe just a snack. How about that delectable two-year-old in the sandbox there? Yum. Much better than that sickly sugar sweetness I smell everywhere.'

William enjoyed his brother's humor. 'That's pralines you smell. The barbecue is supposed to be especially good here, too. Very spicy,' he said.

'I don't want any stringy pork or beef.' Michael wrinkled his nose.

'Well,' William finally began to relent, 'maybe we could have a quick bite. What do you see that you like? You can have anything that you want.'

Michael pointed out his choice.

'Perfect,' whispered William.

Chapter Forty-Six

This was bad. There had been another grisly vampire-style murder – in Savannah. Kyle and I rushed down to Georgia in a shiny black Bell Jet helicopter that would have done Darth Vader proud. Kyle wouldn't let the case go. He wouldn't let me go either.

Even from the air, the seaport city was stunningly beautiful, with its clusters of mansions, quaint shopping districts, and the Savannah River winding through golden yellow marshes out to the Atlantic. Why were the attacks taking place in crowded, attractive locales? Why these particular cities?

There had to be a reason why this was eluding all of us so far. The killers had to be playing out a complex story/fantasy. What the hell was it?

An FBI sedan was waiting and it rushed us to the Cathedral of St John the Baptist. The church was on East

Harris in the historic district of town. Police cruisers were parked everywhere among the antebellum homes. So were EMS vans.

'The highways around Savannah are completely blockaded,' Kyle told me as we made our way through the heavy traffic near the church. 'This is the most bizarre and lurid thing to happen around here since John Berendt's book. Or, I suppose, the murder that inspired it. Should bring in lots more tourists, though, don't you think? Maybe the vampire tour will come to rival the one for *Midnight in the Garden of Good and Evil*.'

'Not the kind of visitors the chamber of commerce, or especially residents, probably want to see here,' I said. 'Kyle, what the hell is going on? The killers are working right in our face. They're telling us something. They strike in beautiful cities. They murder in public parks, in crowded luxury hotels, even in a cathedral. Do they want to get caught? Or do they believe they *can't* be caught?'

Kyle looked at the church spires up ahead. 'Maybe it's a little of both. I agree, though, they are reckless for some reason I don't quite fathom. That's why you're here. You're the profiler. You're the one who understands how their sick minds work.'

I couldn't get the thought out of my head that these killers wanted to get caught. *Why?*

Chapter Forty-Seven

K yle and I got out of the sedan and hurried toward the Cathedral of St John the Baptist. A gold-and-white banner over the main door proclaimed, 'One Faith, One Family.'

The twin spires of the church rose high over the city of Savannah. The style was French Gothic: grand arches and traceries, impressive stained-glass windows, an Italian marble altar. It occurred to me that the neo-vampire culture admired Gothic clothing, trappings, so why not architecture? I was taking everything in – *everything*. But nothing had clicked yet.

The murder had been discovered less than two hours ago. Kyle and I were in the air minutes after we heard the news from the Savannah police. The story was already all over the TV.

The sweet smell of incense was in my nose. I could see

the victim as soon as we entered the cathedral. I groaned and felt a little sick to my stomach. It was a twenty-one-year-old male, which I had known from the early reports; an art history major at the University of Georgia named Stephen Fenton. The killers had left Fenton's wallet and money. Nothing had been stolen – except his shirt.

The cathedral was large and could probably hold as many as a thousand worshipers. A flow of light from stained-glass windows created a pattern of colored light and dark patches on the floor. Even from a distance, I could see that the victim's neck had been torn open. The shirtless body was toned and sculpted, just like the others. It lay at the foot of a Station of the Cross, the thirteenth. The floor was stained with blood, but not much liquid remained.

Did they drink the blood here in the cathedral? Was this about sacrilege? Religion? The Stations of the Cross?

Kyle and I approached Stephen Fenton. A body bag was already laid out in the nave. Technicians from the Savannah Police Department stood by. They were restless and angry, anxious to do their work and get out of there. We were holding them up. The local medical examiner was doing his examination of the body and told us he was certain two people had attacked Fenton – he had found two different sets of teeth marks.

Kyle and I knelt over the body together. I pulled on a

pair of plastic gloves. Kyle almost never used them. He rarely seemed to touch evidence at a crime scene. I had always wondered why. His instincts were good, though.

But if we were both so good, why didn't we have any clue as to where the killers had gone, or where they might strike next? That was the question that nagged me more and more at each murder site. What was this gruesome rampage about?

'They're so goddamn impulsive,' I muttered to Kyle. 'I suspect they're both under thirty. Maybe early twenties, or even younger. I wouldn't be surprised if they were in their late teens.'

'Makes sense to me. They don't seem to have any fear at all.' Kyle spoke softly as he looked at the student's wounds. 'It's as if a wild animal has been turned loose. Like the tiger. First in California. Now here on the East Coast. The problem is that we don't really know how far back the killings go, or how many killers are involved, or even if they're working out of this country.'

'That's three problems. Three sub-sets that require answers we don't have. Your agents still talking to people at the Goth and vampire clubs? The Internet? Somebody has to know something.'

'If anybody knows, they're keeping it to themselves. I have over three hundred agents *full time* on this case, Alex. We can't keep this heat up.'

I looked up at the wooden Station of the Cross. It depicted Jesus being taken down from the cross and laid in his mother's arms. Crown of Thorns. The crucifixion. Piercings. Blood. Was blood the connection here? Eternal life? I wondered. In Santa Barbara, Peter Westin had mentioned that some vampires were spiritual. Was this a ritual killing or a random one? Should I talk to Peter Westin again? He seemed to know more about vampires than anyone else I'd met.

The victim was still wearing khaki trousers and new Reebok sneakers. I examined the wounds to his neck. There were also gouges on his left shoulder, and parts of the upper chest. One or more of the killers was very angry, close to a rage state.

'Why take the shirt?' Kyle asked. 'Same thing in Vegas.'

'Maybe because it was blood-soaked,' I answered as I continued to look at the student's wounds. 'These are definitely human bites. But they're attacking like animals. Perhaps the tiger that attacked the victims in Golden Gate Park is a model, a symbol, something important? What, though?'

Kyle's cell phone sounded and he flipped it open. I couldn't help thinking of the Mastermind – his constant calls to me. Kyle listened to whoever it was for about twenty seconds.

Then he turned to me. 'We're going to Charlotte right

now. There's been another murder, Alex. They struck again. They're already in North Carolina.'

'God damn them! What the hell are they doing?'

Kyle and I raced toward the doors of the cathedral. We ran as if we were being chased.

Chapter Forty-Eight

Every once in a while, a single murder, or a series of murders, horrifies us, catches the public's imagination in an almost obscene way. Jeffrey Dahmer's bizarre spree in Milwaukee, the murder of Gianni Versace and subsequent killings by Andrew Phillip Cunanan, the Russian, Andrei Chikatilo, reputed to be the worst. Now this bloody rampage on opposite coasts of the United States.

It was fortunate that we had the FBI helicopter to get us out of Savannah and over to Charlotte. While we were still in the air, Kyle was in contact with his operators on the ground, who had surrounded a ramshackle farmhouse about fourteen miles outside Charlotte. I had never seen Kyle so animated and excited about a case before, not even Casanova or the Gentleman Caller.

'Looks like we caught a break,' Kyle said to me. 'No one

will get out of that house until we get there. I like our chances.'

'We'll see,' I said. 'I'm still not convinced these are the people we're after.' I had stopped making assumptions about the killers. Why Charlotte, North Carolina? This would be the fourth attack in the same city. Had everything been leading us to Charlotte? Why?

Kyle listened to another situation report from agents on the scene, then he gave me the relevant details. 'A married couple – the parents of a seventeen-year-old Charlotte boy – were attacked in bed late last night. Both bludgeoned to death. A claw hammer was found at the scene. There were bites on the bodies. There's evidence that either a large animal attacked the two adults, or the assailant was wearing sharpened metal fangs.' Kyle rolled his eyes. He still didn't have much truck with vampires.

'Their son was seen leaving the house, with blood dripping from his mouth. The assailant then fled to an abandoned farmhouse near the Loblolly River outside Charlotte. As far as we know, the people loitering in the house are mostly teenagers. Apparently, some are as young as twelve or thirteen. It's a mess, Alex. Everything is on hold until we get there. The age of some of these kids is a real problem.'

A little more than ten minutes later we landed in a wide meadow brimming with wild flowers. We were less than three miles from the farmhouse. This was Bonnie & Clyde stuff. By the time we got to the thick woods surrounding the house it was past five o'clock. It would be dark soon enough.

The house was a two-story, wood-framed structure obscured by an overgrowth of wisteria and myrtle. Pine cones, hickory nuts, and what are known locally as sweet gum monkey balls covered the ground where we hid and watched. Everything about the place brought back memories of where I had grown up in the South. Not too many happy moments unfortunately. My mother and father had both died in their thirties, well before their time. My therapist has a theory that I see myself dying young because both my parents did. The Mastermind seems to hold a similar theory, and perhaps wants to put it into action soon.

The roof of the old house was sharply pitched; a narrow attic window was broken in two places. The peeling, white-painted clapboards were mostly intact, but the asbestos-shingled roof was bare in spots, revealing tar paper. Creepy, creepy, creepy. What in hell was going on here?

The FBI was super-sensitive to the fact that most of those inside the house were probably under twenty years old. They didn't know exactly who they were or if any had police records. There was no actual proof they were involved with the murders. It was decided that as long as we remained undetected, we'd wait until night to see if anyone left or entered. Then we would move on the house. The situation was getting sticky, maybe political, and there would be consequences if a minor got hurt or killed.

In sharp contrast, everything seemed peaceful in the woods around the house. The ramshackle building was strangely quiet, considering all the young people who were supposed to be in there. No loud laughter or rock music, no smells of cooking. Dim lights were flickering.

My growing fear was that we were already too late.

Chapter Forty-Nine

S omeone was whispering close to my ear – it was Kyle. 'Let's go, Alex. It's time to move on them.'

At four in the morning, he gave the signal to breach the house. Kyle was calling all the shots. He had authority over the locals, too.

I accompanied a dozen agents outfitted in blue wind-breakers. Nobody was feeling too secure about the raid. We moved cautiously to within seventy-five yards of the house, at the edge of the pine forest. Two snipers, who had dug in about thirty yards from the house, radioed that it was still quiet inside. Too quiet?

'These are mostly young kids,' Kyle reminded us before we went in. 'But protect yourselves first.'

We crawled on our hands and knees until we were as close as the snipers. Then we rushed the house, using three entrances to get inside.

Kyle and I went through the front, the others through the side and back. A couple of flash-bang grenades went off. There was screaming on the ground floor. High pitched. Kids. No gunshots – yet.

It was a weird, chaotic scene. Stoned kids – lots of them, most in their underwear or nude. At least twenty teenagers had been sleeping on the ground floor. No electricity, just candles. The place smelled of urine, weed, mildew, cheap wine, and wax. Clown Posse and Killah Priest posters were hung on the walls.

The tiny front hall and the living room merged into an open area. The kids had been asleep on blankets, or just the wooden floor. Now they were awake, and angry, shouting, 'Pigs! Cops! Get the fuck out!'

Agents were rousting more of them on the second floor. There were fistfights, but still no gunshots. No one seriously hurt. A sense of anti-climax.

A skinny boy screamed at the top of his voice and rushed at me. He seemed to have no fear of my drawn gun. His eyes were blood-red. Color contacts. He was growling and drooling frothy saliva. I took him down in a head lock, cuffed him, told him to chill before he got himself hurt. I doubt that he weighed much more than a hundred and forty pounds, but he was wiry and stronger than he looked.

An agent near me wasn't so lucky – a heavy-set

redheaded girl bit him in the cheek as he was attempting to restrain her. Then the girl bit into his chest. The agent howled, and struggled to get her off. She held on like a dog with a bone.

I yanked the girl away and cuffed her arms behind her back. She wore a black T-shirt with 'Merry Fuckin' Xmas Bitch' printed on it. She had tattoos of snakes and skulls everywhere. She was screaming in my face, 'You are unworthy! You suck!'

'The one we want is in the cellar! The killer,' Kyle called to me. 'Irwin Snyder!' I followed him through a dysfunctional kitchen, then out back to a slanted wooden door that led to a cellar.

We had our guns drawn. From what we knew about the viciousness and suddenness of the Irwin Snyder attacks, nobody wanted to go into the cellar. I yanked open the door and we edged inside.

Kyle, two other agents and I went down three rickety wooden steps.

It was quiet and dark. An agent worked a flashlight around.

Then we saw the killer. He saw us too.

Chapter Fifty

A well-built teenaged boy in a soiled black leather studded vest and black jeans was crouched, waiting for us in the far corner of the cellar. He had a crowbar. He leaped up and began swinging it over his head. He was growling. It had to be Irwin Snyder, the boy who had killed his parents. He was so damn young, just seventeen. What had gotten into his head?

Gold fangs protruded from his mouth. Contacts made his eyes appear blood-red. His nose and eyebrows were pierced with at least a dozen gold and silver tiny hoops. He was tightly muscled and over six feet tall. He'd been a star football player before he suddenly dropped out of school.

Snyder continued to growl at us. He stood in an oozing ground-water puddle and didn't seem aware of it. His eyes were glazed and seemed to be set way back in his skull.

'Back off!' he shouted. 'Y'all have no idea how much shit you're in. Y'all have no goddamn idea! Get the fuck out of here! Get out of our house!' He was serious; he believed every word he said.

He was still swinging the heavy, rusted crowbar. We stopped moving. I wanted to hear whatever he had to say.

'What kind of shit are we in?' I asked Snyder.

'*I know who you are!*' he shouted, spraying spit all the way across the room. He was in a murderous rage. He looked stoned beyond comprehension.

'Who am I?' I asked him. How could he know?

'You're fucking Cross, that's who,' he said, and bared long canine teeth, the smile of a madman. His answer shook me up. 'The rest of y'all are FBI dogs! Y'all deserve to die! You will! The *Cross* don't work here, assholes.'

'Why did you kill your mother and father?' Kyle asked from his place on the stairs.

'To free'm,' Snyder sneered. 'Now, they're free as little birdies in the air.'

'I don't believe you,' I said. 'That's bullshit.'

He continued to growl like a barnyard dog. 'Smarter than you look. *Cross*.'

'Why did you use metal fangs when you bit them? What does the Tiger mean, Irwin?' I asked another couple of questions.

'You already know, or you wouldn't ask,' he said, and laughed wickedly. His real teeth were yellow and nicotine-stained. His black jeans were filthy, and looked as if they'd been dipped in ashes. The leather vest had studs missing. The cellar smelled awful, like spoiled meat. What had happened down here? I almost didn't want to know.

'Why did you kill your parents?' I asked again.

'Killed them to free myself,' he screamed. 'Killed their asses 'cause I follow the Tiger.'

'Who's the Tiger? What does the Tiger mean?'

His eyes danced with mischief. 'Oh, you'll see soon enough. You'll see. Then you'll wish you hadn't.'

He reached into his jeans and I rushed him. Irwin Snyder had a stiletto knife in his right hand. He swiped the knife at me and I pivoted away.

I wasn't fast enough, and the blade sliced my arm. It burned like hell. Snyder screeched in triumph. He lunged at me again. Fast, athletic, forward.

I managed to wrestle the knife from his hand, but he bit into my right shoulder. He went for my neck! Kyle and the others were all over him now.

'Goddamn it!' I yelled in pain. I punched his face. He bit me again. This time on the back of my hand. *Damn, it hurt!*

The FBI agents had trouble pinning him down as he

hurled a stream of curses and threats at all of us. They were afraid of being bitten.

'Now you're one of us!' he screeched at me. 'You're one of us! Now you can meet the Tiger,' he howled, and laughed, grinning like a madman.

Chapter Fifty-One

M y head was aching, but I spent the next four hours questioning Irwin Snyder in a bare, white-washed claustrophobic room at a jail in Charlotte. For the first hour or so, Kyle and I interrogated him together, but it didn't work out. I asked Kyle to leave the room. Snyder was shackled, so I felt safe being alone with him. I wondered how he felt?

My arm and hand were beginning to throb, but this was more important than my flesh wounds. Irwin Snyder had known I was coming to Charlotte. How had he known? What else did he know? How was a vicious young killer in Charlotte connected to the rest of this mess?

Snyder was pale and unhealthy-looking, with a scruffy goatee and sideburns. He stared at me with eyes that were dark, very active, intelligent enough.

Then he laid his head down on the Formica table, and I

lifted him right out of his chair by his hair. He cursed at me for a full minute. Then he demanded to see his lawyer.

'Hurts, doesn't it,' I said. 'Don't make me do it again. Keep your head *off* the table. This isn't naptime. It isn't a game either.'

He gave me the finger, then put his head back down on the table. I knew he'd been getting away with this type of shit at school and in his home for years. But not here, and not with me.

I yanked him by his greasy, black hair again, even harder this time. 'You don't seem to understand the King's English. You murdered your parents in cold blood. You're a killer.'

'*Lawyer!*' he screamed. '*Lawyer! Lawyer!* I'm bein' tortured in here! I'm bein' beaten by a cop! *Lawyer! Lawyer! I want my fuckin' lawyer!*'

With my free hand I grabbed his chin. He spat on my hand. I ignored it.

'Listen to me now. *Listen!* Everybody else from the house is at the station in the city. You're the only one out here with me. No one can hear you. And you're not being beaten. But you are going to talk to me.'

I yanked his hair again – as hard as I could without actually pulling out a clump. Snyder shrieked, but I knew I hadn't hurt him much.

'You killed your mother and your father with a claw

hammer. You bit me twice. And you stink to high heaven. I don't like you, but we're going to have this talk anyway.'

'Better see somebody about those bites, pig,' he snarled. 'You been warned.'

He was still talking tough, but he cringed and pulled back when I reached out for his hair again.

'How did you know I was coming to Charlotte? How did you know my name? Talk to me.'

'Ask the Tiger, when you two meet. It'll happen sooner than you think.'

Chapter Fifty-Two

It became clear that Irwin Snyder couldn't have committed the earlier murders. He had been out of North Carolina only once or twice in his life. Most of his contact with the outside world was over the Internet. And of course he was too young to have been involved in murder going back eleven years.

The seventeen-year-old had killed his mother and father, though. He seemed to have no remorse. *The Tiger had told him to do it.* That was all I had been able to get out of him. He refused to say how he had come into contact with the person or group who had such control over him.

While I was questioning Snyder, and then the others from the house, my shoulder and hand began to itch, and then ache. The bites were puncture wounds, but there had been little bleeding. The bite to my shoulder was the deepest, even through my jacket, and had left prominent teeth marks, which I'd had photographed at the station.

I didn't bother going to the local emergency room in Charlotte. I was too busy. But the wounds soon became extremely painful. By late morning, I had trouble making a fist. I doubted I could pull the trigger of my gun. *Now you're one of us, Cross,* Irwin Snyder had told me.

I wondered what group, or cell, or cult, Snyder was part of? Where was the Tiger? Was it only one person? I attended a meeting with the FBI and the Charlotte police that lasted until eight that evening. The net result was that we were still nowhere near a solution. The FBI was scouring the Internet, searching for messages relating to the Tiger, or any kind of tiger.

I flew back to Washington later that night, and managed to sleep a little on the plane. Not nearly enough. The phone rang minutes after I stepped inside the front door of my house. *What the hell?*

'You're back, Dr Cross. That's good. Welcome, welcome. I missed you. Did you enjoy Charlotte?'

I put down the receiver and hurried outside into the night. I didn't see anyone, no movement up or down Fifth Street, but that didn't mean he wasn't lingering near the house. How else could he have known I was here?

I ran out into the street. I stared hard into the darkness. I couldn't see anyone, but maybe he could see me. Someone had definitely been watching. Someone was out there.

'I am back,' I shouted, 'come and get me. Let's settle this right here and now. Let's settle it! Here I am, you bastard!' He didn't call back to me, didn't answer.

Then I heard a footstep behind me. I whirled around to face the Mastermind.

'Alex, *what* is going on out here? When did you get home? Who are you talking to?'

It was Nana, and she looked very small and frightened. She came up and hugged me tight.

Chapter Fifty-Three

I woke up in bad shape around six the next morning. There was blotchy redness and blistering heat around the bites. The wounds throbbed. I noticed a nasty pus-like drainage from the bite on my hand. It was swollen to nearly twice its normal size. This was not good. I was sick as a dog, and it was the last thing I needed right now.

I drove myself to the St Anthony's Hospital ER, where I found out that I was spiking a fever. My temperature was a hundred and three.

The emergency-room doctor who examined me was a tall, dark-haired Pakistani named Dr Prahbu. He could have been one of the sons in the movie *East Is East*. He said that the most likely cause of the cellulitis was staphylococcus, a common bacteria found in the mouth.

'How is it that you were bitten?' he wanted to know. I suspected that he wasn't going to like my answer, but I gave it anyway. 'I was subduing a vampire,' I said.

'No, seriously, Detective Cross. How did you come to be bitten?' he asked a second time. 'I am a serious person and this is a serious question. I need to know this.'

'I am completely serious. I'm part of the team investigating vampire killers. I was bitten by a man with fangs.'

'Okay, fine, Detective. Whatever you say.'

I was given tests in the ER: a CBC and differential count, sedimentation rate, and a culture and sensitivity test on the drainage from the wound. Blood cultures would be studied. I told Dr Prahbu that I needed copies of his findings. The hospital didn't want to give them over to me, but they finally relented and faxed the results to Quantico.

I was sent home with a prescription for a drug called Keflex. I was to keep my infected arm elevated, and administer Domeboro soaks every four hours.

I was too sick to do much of anything by the time I got home. I lay in bed and listened to 'Elliot in the Morning' on the radio. Nana and the kids hovered around me constantly. Nausea swept over me really bad; I couldn't eat. I couldn't sleep, couldn't concentrate on anything except the painful throbbing in my shoulder and hand. I became delirious for several hours.

Now you're one of us.

I finally fell asleep, but woke up around one in the morning. The witching hours. I felt even worse. I was afraid the phone would ring and it would be the Mastermind.

Someone was in the room with me.

I sighed when I saw who it was.

Jannie was sitting in the chair by my bed, keeping watch over me.

'Just like you did when I was sick,' she said. 'Now sleep, Daddy. Just sleep. Rest up. And don't you dare turn into a vampire on me.'

I didn't answer Jannie. I couldn't even manage a few words. I drifted off to sleep again.

Chapter Fifty-Four

*N*o one would expect this, and that was why it was so good, so excellent. The end of Alex Cross.

It was time for it to happen. Maybe it was overdue. Cross had to die.

The Mastermind was inside the Cross house, and it was as exciting and extraordinary an experience as he had imagined it would be. He'd never felt more powerful than he did standing in the dark living room at a little past three in the morning. He had won the battle. The Mastermind had triumphed. Cross was the loser. Tomorrow, all of Washington would be mourning his death.

He could do anything – so what should he do first?

He wanted to sit and think about it. No need to rush. Where would he choose to sit? Why of course, on Cross's piano bench on the sun porch. Cross's favorite spot for relaxation and escape, the place he liked to play with his children, smarmy, sentimental bastard that he was.

The Mastermind was tempted to play something, perhaps a little Gershwin, to show Cross that even his command of the piano was superior. He wanted to announce himself in a dramatic fashion. This was so good, so delicious. He never wanted tonight to end.

But was it the absolute best he could do? It had to be a night he would never forget, something to savor always. A souvenir that would have great meaning to him, only to him.

There were two triangles that explained his complex relationship with Alex Cross, and he visualized them as he sat on the porch, biding his time, enjoying himself immensely. Christ, he was smiling like a damn fool. He was in his element, and he was happy, so happy.

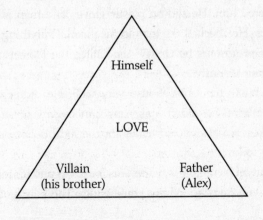

Himself

LOVE

Villain
(his brother)

Father
(Alex)

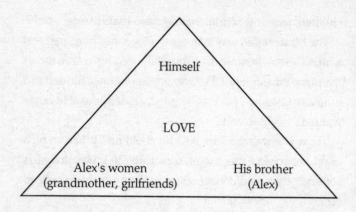

It was such a good psychological model, so concise and clear and sound. It explained everything that was going to happen tonight. Even Dr Cross would approve. It was the perfect dysfunctional family triangle.

Maybe he would explain it to Cross now. Just before he murdered him. He slid on plastic gloves and then plastic booties. He checked the load in his pistol. Everything was set. Then upstairs he went – the Caller, the Mastermind, Svengali, Moriarty.

He knew the Cross house very well. He didn't even need a light. He didn't make any unnecessary noise. No mistakes. No evidence or clues for the local police or the FBI to follow.

What an incredible way this was for Cross and his family to die. What a coup. What a chilling idea. The 'killing order' was starting to come to him as he climbed the stairs. Yes, he was sure of it.

Little Alex

Jannie

Damon

Nana

Then Cross.

He walked to the end of the upstairs hallway and stood there listening before he opened the bedroom door. Not a sound. He slowly pushed on the door.

What was this? A surprise? Christ!

He didn't like surprises. He liked precision and order. He liked to be in total control.

The young daughter, Jannie, was sitting by Cross's bed, fast asleep. Watching over her father, protecting him from harm.

He watched Cross and the girl for a long moment, maybe ninety seconds. A small nightlight had been left on in the room.

There were thick bandages on Cross's hand and shoulder. He was perspiring in his sleep. He was wounded, sick, not himself, not a worthy opponent. The killer sighed under his breath. He felt such disappointment, such sadness and despair.

No, no, no! This wouldn't do. It was all wrong, all wrong!

He closed the bedroom door, and then quickly, silently

retraced his steps out of the Cross house. No one would know he had been there. Not even the detective himself.

As usual, no one knew anything about him. No one suspected a thing.

He *was* the Mastermind, after all.

Chapter Fifty-Five

I woke several times during the night. I thought someone was in the house at one point. I felt someone there. Nothing I could do about it, though.

Then, after fourteen hours of sleep, I woke and found that I was actually feeling better. I could almost think straight again. Exhaustion still had a hold on me, though. All my joints ached. My eyesight was blurry. I could hear music playing softly in the house. Erykah Badu, one of my favorites.

There was a knock on the bedroom door and I said, 'I'm decent. Who goes there?'

Jannie pushed open the door. She was holding a red plastic tray with a breakfast of poached eggs, hot cereal, orange juice, and a mug of steaming coffee. She was smiling, obviously proud of herself. I smiled back at her. *That's my girl. What a little sweetheart she was – when she wanted to be.*

'I don't know if you can eat yet, Daddy. I brought you some breakfast. Just in case.'

'Thank you, sweetie, I'm feeling a little better,' I said. I was able to push myself up in bed, then prop a few pillows behind me with my good hand.

Jannie carried the tray over to the bed and carefully set it on my lap. She leaned in and kissed my fuzzy cheek. 'Somebody needs a shave.'

'You're being so nice,' I said to her.

'I *am* nice, Daddy,' Jannie answered back. 'You feel good enough for a little company? We'll just watch you eat – we'll be good. No trouble. Is it okay?'

'Just what I need right now,' I said.

Jannie came back with little Alex in her arms and Damon trailing behind, giving me the high sign. They climbed up on my bed and, as promised, they were very good, the best medicine around.

'You just eat your breakfast while it's hot. You're getting too skinny,' Jannie teased.

'Yeah, you are,' Damon agreed. 'You're drawn and *gaunt*.'

'Very good,' I smiled between small bites of eggs and toast, which I hoped I could keep down. I kept running my hand over little Alex's head.

'Did somebody poison you, Daddy?' Jannie wanted to know. 'What exactly happened?'

I sighed and shook my head. 'I don't know, baby. It's an

infection. You can get it from a human bite.'

Jannie and Damon grimaced. 'Nana says it's *septicemia*. They used to call it blood poisoning.' Damon contributed some scholarly research.

'Who am I to argue with Nana,' I said, and left it at that. 'I'm no match for Nana Mama right now.' *Or maybe ever.*

I looked at the puffed-up bandage and gauze covering most of my right shoulder, where I'd been bitten. The skin was a sickly yellow around the bandage. 'Something bad got into my blood. I'm okay now, though. I'm coming back.' But I remembered what Irwin Snyder had said: *You're one of us.*

Chapter Fifty-Six

I was able to make it downstairs for dinner that night. Nana rewarded my appearance at the table with chicken, gravy and biscuits and a homemade apple crisp. I made an effort to eat, and I surprised myself by doing pretty well.

After dinner, I put little Alex to bed. I went back up to my room around eight-thirty and everybody seemed to understand that I was tired, not myself yet.

I didn't sleep once I got up to my room, though. Too many bad thoughts about the murders were buzzing in my head. Right or wrong, I felt like we were getting close to something. Maybe I was just fooling myself.

I worked for a couple of hours on the computer and my concentration was fine. I was pretty certain that something had to link the cities where the murders had taken place. What was it, though? What was everybody missing? I looked at anything and everything. I studied the schedules of airplane carriers that flew into each of the cities, then bus companies, and finally railroads. It was probably just busy work, but you never know, and I had nothing better to do.

I checked out corporations that had main or branch offices in the cities and found there were a lot of matches, but it wasn't likely to get me anywhere. Federal Express, American Express, the Gap, the Limited, McDonalds, Sears, J.C. Penneys were just about everywhere, so what?

I had at least one travel book for each of the cities and I pored over them until it was almost midnight. Nothing came of it. My arm was throbbing again. I was starting to get a headache. The rest of the house was quiet.

Next, I checked on traveling sports teams, circuses and carnivals, author tours, rock-and-roll groups – and then I hit on something in the entertainment area. I had been ready to call it a night, but here was something interesting. I tried not to get excited, but my pulse quickened as I checked the West Coast information first. Then the East Coast. *Bingo. Maybe.*

I had found the kind of pattern that I was looking for – an entertainment act that worked winters and early spring on the West Coast, and then came East. Their tour cities and the murders were matching up for now. Jesus.

They had been touring for fifteen years.

I was almost certain I'd found some kind of connection to the killers.

Two magicians who called themselves Daniel and Charles.

The same ones Andrew Cotton and Dara Grey had seen on the night they were murdered in Las Vegas.

I even knew where they were scheduled to perform next. They were probably already there.

Eleven years of unsolved murders had come down to this.

New Orleans, Louisiana.

A nightclub called Howl.

A pair of magicians named Daniel and Charles.

I still couldn't travel, so I would have to remain in Washington. I hated not being able to go to New Orleans. I would miss an important time, but Kyle would be there. I knew he wanted to make this bust himself, and I couldn't blame him. This could help make his career, no doubt about it. The case was huge.

I called Kyle Craig.

Chapter Fifty-Seven

That night in New Orleans a half-dozen FBI agents circulated through the crowd that had turned out for Daniel and Charles's early performance. Howl was located in the warehouse district, off Julia Street. Usually it featured musical acts, and, even tonight, zydeco and the blues reverberated from the mortar and redbrick walls. A few tourists tried to bring 'to-geaux' cups from Bourbon Street into Howl. They were denied admission *for life*.

The used Cressidas and Colts and a few sports-utility vehicles in the parking lot were a tip-off to the presence of Tulane and Loyola college students packed inside. Smoke lay thick over the noisy and restless crowd. Several in the audience looked under-age and the club had been cited for serving minors. The owners found it easier to buy off the New Orleans police than to effectively regulate the club.

Suddenly, everything went quiet. A single voice punctuated the silence, *'Holy shit! Look at this.'*

A male tiger had walked out onto the stage, which was covered in layers of black velvet.

There was no leash on the cat. No trainer or handler was anywhere in sight. The usually raucous audience remained silent.

The big cat lazily raised his head and roared. A girl in a hot pink tank top screamed in the pit seating area. The cat roared again.

A second white tiger walked out and stood beside the first. It glared down at the crowd. The pit audience was situated directly in front of the stage. Men and women seated there scrambled away, grabbing their beer bottles.

Another unmistakable tiger roar now came from the back of the club, behind the audience. Everyone froze. How many cats were on the loose? Where were they? The crowd was silent now. What the hell was going on?

The blinding lights onstage made peripheral space a dark void. Any retreat to either side of the room was suddenly a gamble. There was a shift of the stage lights – left to right, then right to left. The lights were powerful, almost blinding. They created the visual illusion that the entire stage had moved.

The crowd's gasp was audible. Panic was in the air.

The tigers were gone!

Two magicians in shimmering black-and-gold lamé suits now stood at the center of the stage where the tigers had been just a heartbeat ago. They were both smiling; they almost seemed to be laughing at the jittery audience.

The taller of the two, Daniel, finally spoke. 'You have nothing to fear. We're Daniel and Charles, and we're the best you will ever see! That is a promise I plan to keep. Let the magic begin!'

The crowd inside Howl began to clap and cheer, and then to howl. There were two shows that night. Each was scheduled to last an hour and a half. Kyle Craig was inside the club with the FBI agents. More agents were posted outside on the street. Daniel and Charles concentrated on several trunks which they called 'Homage to Houdini'. They also performed Carl Hertz's 'Merry Widow'.

The audience response to the shows was highly favorable. Nearly everybody left the club in awe – vowing to come again, to tell friends to come. Apparently, it happened everywhere that Daniel and Charles played, coast to coast.

Now came the real work for the FBI. After the second show, Daniel and Charles were whisked away to a silver limousine idling in a sealed-off alley at the stage door. There was a lot of noise and confusion backstage. Daniel and Charles were screaming at one another.

Once the silver limousine exited the alley, a team of FBI

cars followed it through the usual crowds in downtown New Orleans, then out toward Lake Pontchartrain. Kyle Craig was in radio contact for the entire trip.

The limo pulled up in front of an antebellum mansion where a private party was in full rage. Loud rock-and-roll music, Dr John, blared across spacious lawns marked by two- and three-hundred-year-old oaks. Partygoers had spilled onto the lawns that sloped down to the dark, glimmering water of the lake.

The limo driver got out and opened one of the back doors with a theatrical flourish. As several FBI agents watched in disbelief, two white tigers jumped out.

Daniel and Charles were not in the limousine. The magicians had disappeared.

Chapter Fifty-Eight

Daniel and Charles had arrived at a small, private club inside a house in Abita Springs, Louisiana, about forty miles outside New Orleans. This particular club had never been written up in the entertainment section of the *Times-Picayune*, or in any of the glossy guide magazines available in the lobbies of just about every large and small New Orleans hotel.

A man named George Hellenga greeted his guests with great excitement and enthusiasm. Hellenga had badly pitted cheeks, the thickest black eyebrows, dark sunken eyes. He wore contacts that made his eyes appear black. Hellenga weighed more than three hundred pounds, all of it bunched tightly into black leather jacket and pants purchased at a Big & Tall shop in Houston. He bowed to the magicians as they arrived and whispered that he was honored by their visit.

'You should be,' Charles snapped. 'We're tired after a long day. You know why we're here. Let's get on with it.' Offstage, Charles often did the talking, especially when addressing someone like this pathetic underling, this cipher, George Hellenga, who immediately showed Daniel and Charles the way downstairs. They were the masters; he was the slave. There were legions of others like him, waiting in so many cities, praying for a chance to serve the Sire.

As he descended the steps, Daniel broke into a smile. He saw the captive, the slave, and he was well-pleased.

He went to the boy, who looked to be eighteen or nineteen, and spoke to him. 'I'm here now. It's so good to meet you. You're astonishing.' The boy was tall, perhaps six feet two. He had closely cropped blond hair, supple limbs, full lips that were accented with the most delicate silver rings. His lips were rosy-red, outstanding.

'He's pouting. He looks so sad. Let him loose,' Daniel commanded the slave Hellenga. 'What is the poor boy's name?'

'His name is Edward Haggerty, Sire. He's a freshman at Louisiana State. He is your servant,' said George Hellenga, who was now trembling visibly.

Edward Haggerty's slender hands were manacled to the brick wall. He wore silver thong underwear, a silver ankle bracelet. Nothing else. He was a magnificent creature, slender, toned, perfect in every way.

George Hellenga stole a nervous look at the Sire. 'He might run if we let him loose, sir.'

Daniel reached out his arms to the beautiful boy and held him tenderly, as he would a small child. He kissed his cheek, his forehead, and those astonishing red lips.

'You won't run away?' he asked in a soft, soothing voice.

'Not from you,' the boy answered, just as softly. 'You are the Sire, and I am nothing.'

Daniel smiled. It was the perfect answer.

Chapter Fifty-Nine

M y phone rang early in the morning and I snatched it
up. It was Kyle. In his slow and deliberate voice, he
told me that Daniel and Charles had disappeared the
previous night. He was furious at his agents. I'd never
heard him so angry. So far, no murders had been reported
in and around New Orleans. About six that morning, the
magicians had showed up at their house in the Garden
District. *Where had they been all night? What had happened?
Something had.*

I stayed in Washington that day, still recuperating from
the cellulitis. I studied Daniel and Charles and wrote a
preliminary profile on them to compare with the one being
done in Quantico. The first important bit of information
was that the magicians had definitely performed in Savannah and Charlotte on the nights of the murders. I was
working with a couple of techies in Quantico and they not

only matched up the timing of the magicians' tour with about half of the murders, but verified that Daniel and Charles had definitely performed in those cities, and were there when the murders had taken place. Another useful nugget was that the tigers traveled with Daniel and Charles only for bookings that lasted at least a week. The magicians were scheduled to perform in New Orleans for the next three weeks. They also owned a house there, in the Garden District.

I shared what I had found with Quantico and they put it into the file they were amassing. I also faxed everything to Jamilla Hughes in San Francisco. She was trying her best to get down to New Orleans, but her boss hadn't made a final decision yet.

I put in another call to Kyle on the matter. He hemmed and hawed, but finally promised to see if he could get Inspector Hughes sprung for a few days. After all, it had started with her case.

I was becoming frustrated at home. I felt as if I were on a stakeout in my own bedroom – with nothing to observe firsthand. The consolation was that I was with little Alex for long patches of the day, and that I got to see more of Damon and Jannie. But I was feeling a little like the forgotten man on the murder case.

I went to see Dr Prahbu at St Anthony's that afternoon. The doctor examined me, then reluctantly gave me clearance to go back to work. He told me to take it easy for the next few days.

'How *did* you get those bites?' he asked. 'You never told me, Detective.'

'Yes, I did,' I said. 'Vampires in North Carolina.'

I thanked the doctor for his help, then went home to pack for the trip to New Orleans. I was a little unsteady, but I couldn't wait to get there. Nana didn't bother to give me the business when I left Washington this time. She was angry because I'd been so ill from the infected bites.

I flew into New Orleans International Airport that afternoon, then I took an old yellow cab to the Big Easy. A message was waiting at the front desk of my hotel, the Dauphine Orleans. I opened the small envelope hesitantly, but it was good news. Inspector Hughes was on her way to New Orleans.

The message was classic. It was pure Jamilla: *I'm coming to New Orleans, and they're going down. Don't doubt it for a second.*

Chapter Sixty

Jamilla and I met up at the Dauphine Hotel that night. She was decked out in a black leather jacket, blue jeans, a white pocket-T. She looked rested and ready for anything; I didn't feel so bad myself.

We had supper together, steak and eggs and beer, in the dining room. As always I enjoyed her company. We made each other laugh. At ten-thirty we drove over to Howl. Daniel and Charles had shows scheduled at eleven and one. And then? Maybe they had planned another clever disappearing act.

We were pumped to take them down. Unfortunately, we still needed concrete evidence that they were our killers. There were more than two hundred agents and New Orleans police involved in the case. Something had to break. Presumably, Daniel and Charles would have to feed soon.

It was a Friday night and Howl was almost full when we got there. Loud music played from speakers that seemed to be everywhere in the ceiling and walls. The crowd was mostly young and restless, drinking beer, smoking, dirty dancing. Several Goths were mixed in with the more clean-cut college kids. The two groups leered at one another and the atmosphere was charged. A photographer from *Offbeat* magazine crouched in front of the stage, waiting for the show to begin.

Jamilla and I sat down at one of the small tables and ordered Jax beers. There were at least a dozen FBI agents in the club. Kyle was outside in a surveillance car. He had been inside the night before, but it was hard for Kyle to blend in with a mostly young, hip crowd. He looked too much like a cop.

The back of my throat was already beginning to burn from the smoke and the heavy perfume in the air. A gulp of beer soothed the gullet somewhat. My arm and hand still ached some from the bites.

My head was clear, though; I definitely felt a lot better than I had. I liked having Jamilla around again. She gave good counsel.

'Kyle has a six-team surveillance on the magicians around the clock,' I told her. 'They won't lose them again. Kyle guarantees it.'

'The FBI thinks they're definitely the killers?' she asked.

'No doubt about it? Lock 'em up, throw away the key?'

'Some doubt I suppose, but not much. You never know exactly what Kyle is thinking,' I told her. 'But yes, I think he believes they are. The techies at Quantico do. So do I.'

She studied me over the lip of her bottle of Jax. 'Sounds like the two of you are pretty tight, huh?'

I nodded. 'We've worked a lot of cases together in the past few years. Our success rate is good. I can't say that I really know him.'

'I've never had much luck working with the FBI,' she said. 'That's just me though.'

'Part of my job is to make sure police relations with the Bureau run smoothly in DC. Kyle is definitely smart. He's just hard to read at times.'

She sipped her beer slowly. 'Unlike somebody else at this table.'

'Unlike two somebodies at this table,' I corrected her, and we both laughed.

Jamilla glanced toward the stage. 'What's the hold-up? Where are they? Should we start stamping our feet for them to come out and show us some magic? Show us what they've got?'

We didn't have to – a moment later one of the magicians walked out onto the stage.

It was Charles, and he *looked* like a killer.

Chapter Sixty-One

Charles was wearing a skintight black bodysuit and thigh-high patent leather boots. He had a simple diamond earring and a gold nose stud. He stared contemptuously at the audience. He did this for several uncomfortable moments, his eyes full of hatred and disdain for every case he encountered.

At least twice, I thought that he looked directly at Jamilla and me. So did she.

'Yeah, we're watching you too, asshole,' she said, raising her beer in mock salute. 'You think those two pitiful creeps know we're here?'

'Who knows? They're good at this. They haven't been caught yet.'

'I hear you. Hopefully, they both have stomach cancer and will die slowly and painfully over the next few months. Cheers,' she raised her bottle again.

Charles leaned down and spoke to a college-age couple at a table near the stage. He was miked.

'What are you two airheads staring at? Watch out, or I'll turn you into a couple of toads. Upgrade you on the food chain.' He laughed, and it was deep and throaty. To my ear, it was also unnecessarily unpleasant, way over the top. The kids in the audience laughed and cheered him on. Civility seems to be dead. Nasty is chic; nasty is so cool and *real*.

I looked over at Jamilla. 'He sees them as food. Interesting how his twisted mind works.'

The second magician sauntered onto the stage a couple of minutes later. No magic gimmicks to announce the entrance, which surprised me. I had heard this was a real light-and-sound show, but not tonight. Why the style change? Was this for us? Did they know who we were?

'For the uninitiated, I'm Daniel. Charles and I have been doing magic shows since we were twelve years old and living in San Diego, California. We're very good at magic. We can do the "Vanishing Performer" – Houdini's personal favorite; the "Sword Cabinet"; Carl Hertz's "Merry Widow"; DeHolta's "Cocoon". I can catch a bullet fired from a Colt Magnum in my teeth. So can Charles. Aren't we *special*? Don't you wish you were us?'

The crowd howled and cheered. The rock music from the speakers had been lowered some. Only the beat droned on.

'The illusion you are about to witness is the same one "Harry" Robert Houdini used to close his show in Paris and New York. We're using it to *open* our show. Need I say more?'

The lights suddenly flashed off. The stage was in total darkness. A few women in the audience screeched loudly. Mock fear. Mostly there was laughter, some of it nervous. What were these two up to?

Jamilla nudged me with an elbow. 'Don't be scared. I'm right here. I'll protect you.'

'I'll remember that.'

Tiny pinpricks of light appeared everywhere on the stage. The main spots came on again. Nothing happened for the next minute or so.

Then Daniel, riding a spirited, prancing white stallion, came out onto the stage. He was dressed in royal blue glitter from head to toe. He wore a matching top hat, and he tipped it to the cheering audience.

'I must admit this is pretty cool,' Jamilla said. 'Quite the stunt. So visual. Now what?'

Daniel was followed onstage by eight men and women in crisp, white palace uniforms. And – two white tigers. It was a pretty amazing spectacle. Two female performers in white held up a huge Oriental fan in front of Daniel and his high-stepping horse. My eyes were glued to the stage.

'Jesus,' Jamilla muttered. 'What the hell is this?'

'They're ripping off "Harry" Robert Houdini, like the man said. And they're doing it well.'

When they slowly pulled the Oriental fan away, Daniel was gone. Now Charles was seated on the white horse.

'Once again – Jesus,' said Jam. 'How do they do that?'

Somehow, Charles had changed into black trash and glitter. The smirk on his face was totally, incredibly arrogant. It showed utter disdain for the audience, but they seemed to love it, to love him. A puff of smoke, and the audience gasped as one.

Daniel was back onstage, standing alongside Charles and the spirited horse. The illusion was masterful. Everyone in the audience jumped up and clapped wildly. The screams and piercing whistles hurt my eardrums.

'And that,' Daniel announced, 'is only the beginning! You ain't seen nothing yet!'

Jamilla looked at me and her mouth sagged. 'Alex, these guys are very good, and I've *seen* Siegfried and Roy. Why are they playing at these little clubs? Why are they wasting their time here?'

'Because they want to,' I told her. '*This is where they look for prey.*'

Chapter Sixty-Two

Jamilla and I watched both magic shows that night. We were amazed by the calmness and the confidence exuded by Daniel and Charles. Following the second show, the magicians went home. The agents on surveillance there said it appeared the two were settled for the night. I didn't get it, and neither did Jamilla.

Eventually, around two in the morning, she and I returned to the Dauphine. Two FBI teams would stay near Daniel and Charles's place until morning. We were becoming frustrated and confused. We had a lot of manpower working their butts off.

I wanted to ask Jamilla up for a beer, but I didn't. Too complicated for right now. Or maybe I was just getting chickenshit as I got older. Maybe I was even a little wiser. *Nah*.

I was up again at six, making notes in my hotel room. I

was learning some things I didn't want to know, and not just about magic tricks. I now knew that in the vampire underworld, the area surrounding the main home of a Regent or Elder was known as the domain. The FBI and the New Orleans police had staked out the neighborhood in the Garden District, where Daniel Erickson and Charles Defoe were staying.

Their house was located on LaSalle near Sixth. It was greystone and probably had as many as twenty rooms. The house sat on a hill, with a high, reinforced stone outer wall similar to the outer curtain of a castle. It also had a large deep cellar, which wouldn't have been possible in the swampy, sea-level terrain without the elevation of the hill. Almost no one in the task force would admit that they believed in vampires; but everyone knew that a series of brutal murders had been committed and that Daniel and Charles were the likely killers.

Jamilla and I spent the next two days surveying the house, the *domain*. We worked double shifts, and nothing could relieve the tedium. A scene that sometimes comes to mind when I'm on stakeouts is the one in *The French Connection*: Gene Hackman standing out in the cold while the French drug dealers eat an elaborate dinner in a New York restaurant. It's like that, just like that, sometimes for sixteen or eighteen hours at a stretch.

At least LaSalle Street and the Garden District were

pretty to watch. The sugar and cotton barons of the mid-nineteenth century had originally called this home. Most of the hundred- and two-hundred-year-old mansions were beautifully preserved. The majority were kept white, but a few were painted in Mediterranean pastels. Placards informing the frequent 'walking tours' about the esteemed residents were affixed to intricate wrought-iron fences.

But it was still surveillance, even sitting side-by-side with Jamilla Hughes.

Chapter Sixty-Three

During the stakeout on LaSalle Street, she and I found that we could talk about almost anything. That's what we did throughout the long hours. The topics ranged from funny cop stories, to investments, movies, Gothic architecture, politics, then on to more personal subjects like her father, who had run out on her when she was six. I told Jamilla that my mother and father had both died young from a lethal combination of alcoholism and lung cancer – probably depression and hopelessness, too.

'I worked for two years as a psychologist. Hung out a shingle,' I told her. 'At the time, not too many people in my neighborhood in DC could afford treatment. I couldn't afford to give it away. Most white people didn't want to see a black shrink. So I took a job as a cop. Just temporary. I didn't expect to like it, but once I started I got hooked. Bad.'

'What hooked you about being a detective?' she wanted to know. She was a good listener, interested. 'Do you remember an incident, any one thing in particular?'

'As a matter of fact, I do. Two men had been shot down in Southeast, which is where I live in Washington, where I grew up. The deaths were written off as "drug-related", which meant not much time would be spent investigating them. At the time, that was standard operating procedure in DC. Still is, actually.'

Jamilla nodded. 'I'm afraid it is in parts of San Francisco, too. We like to think of our city as enlightened, and it can be. But people out there are good at looking the other way. Makes me sick sometimes.'

'Anyway, I knew these two men, and I was almost certain they weren't involved in selling drugs. They both had jobs at a small local music store. Maybe they smoked a little weed, but nothing worse than that.'

'I know the types you're talking about.'

'So I investigated the murder case on my own. A detective friend named John Sampson helped. I learned to follow my gut. Found out that one of the men had been dating a woman who a local dealer thought he owned. I kept digging, following my instincts, digging a little deeper. Turns out, the dealer had murdered the two men. Once I solved that case, it was all over for me. I knew I was good at it, maybe because of all the psych training I'd had, and I liked making things right. Or maybe I just liked *being* right.'

'Sounds like you have some balance in your life, though. The kids, your grandmother, friends,' she said.

We let it go at that – didn't pursue the obvious – that Jamilla and I were both single and unattached. It had nothing to do with our jobs. If only it was that simple.

Chapter Sixty-Four

O ne comforting reality of police work is that you rarely come up against a murder situation that you've never seen or heard about before. But these killings *were* different: seemingly random, vicious, ongoing for more than eleven years, varying *modus operandi*. What made the case particularly difficult was the possibility that there were *several killers*.

I met with Kyle the following morning to talk about the case. He was in a foul mood and I couldn't wait to get out of there. We shared our pet theories and whiney complaints, then I joined Jamilla Hughes on the stakeout in the Garden District.

I brought a box of Krispy Cremes, which got major chuckles from her, and also from the FBI agents watching the house. Everybody clamored for the tasty, air-shot doughnuts, though. The entire box was gone in a matter of minutes.

'Turns out they're real homebodies,' she said as she munched on a glazed.

'It's still daylight. They're probably in their coffins,' I said.

She grinned and shook her head. Her dark eyes sparkled. 'Not exactly. The shorter one, Charles, was working in the garden out back all morning. He's certainly not afraid of the sun.'

'So maybe Daniel is the real vampire. The *Sire*. He's supposed to be the force behind the magicians' act.'

'Charles has been on the phone a lot. He's setting up some kind of party at the house. You'll love this – it's a Fetish Ball. Wear your favorite kinky things: leather, rubber, Goth, Victorian, whatever you're into. What are you into?' she asked.

I laughed, thought about it. 'Mostly denim, corduroy, jeans, a little black leather. I have a leather car coat. It's a little beat up, but it's nasty looking.'

She started to laugh. 'I think you'd look dashing as a Gothic prince.'

'How about you? Any fetishes we should know about?'

'Well . . . I'll admit to owning a couple of leather jackets, pants, one pair of long boots that I'm still paying for. I am from San Francisco, you know. A girl has to keep up with the times.'

'Same for us boys.'

It was another long day of surveillance. We continued to

watch the house until dark. Around nine o'clock, a pair of FBI agents dropped by to relieve us. 'Let's get a bite,' I said to Jamilla.

'Bad choice of words, Alex.' We both laughed a little too hard.

We didn't want to venture too far from the magicians' house, so we settled on the Camellia Grill on Carrollton Street at the River Bend. The Camellia looked like a small plantation home on the outside. Inside, it was a neat diner, with a long counter and stools screwed to the floor. A waiter in a crisp white jacket and black tie served us. We ordered coffee and omelets, which were light and fluffy and about the size of rolled-up newspapers. Jamilla had a side order of red beans and rice. When in the Big Easy.

The food was good, the coffee even better. The company was nice, too. She and I got along well, maybe even better than that. The lulls in our conversation weren't too uncomfortable, and they were infrequent. A friend of mine once defined love as finding someone you can talk to late into the night. Pretty good.

'Nothing on the beeper,' she said while we loitered over our coffee after the meal. I had heard there were lines outside the Camellia during lunch and dinner, but we had caught a slow time.

'I wonder what the two of them do inside that big, eerie

house, Alex? What do psycho murderers do in their spare time?'

I had studied enough of them. There was no set pattern. 'Some are married, even happily if you ask the spouses. Gary Soneji had a little girl. Geoffrey Shafer had three children. That's probably the scariest thing I can imagine – when a husband, or the person next door, or a dad, turns out to be a stone-cold killer. It happens. I've seen it.'

She sipped her coffee refill. 'The neighbors seem to like Daniel and Charles. They consider them eccentric but pleasant and, I love this, civic-minded. Daniel owns the house. He inherited it from his father, who was also eccentric – a portrait painter. Rumor has it that the magicians are gay, but they're often seen in the company of young attractive women.'

'Vampires aren't restricted by gender. I learned that from Peter Westin,' I said. 'These two are equal-opportunity killers, males and females. Something still isn't matching up for me, though. There's a logic hole I keep trying to fill. A few of them actually.'

'Their magical mystery tour sure matches up with a lot of the murders, Alex.'

'I know it. I can't dispute the evidence we've collected so far.'

'But you have one of your famous feelings.'

'I don't know about famous, but something feels wrong

to me. This thing isn't tracking right. The other shoe hasn't dropped. That's what worries me. Why did they get sloppy all of a sudden? They went undetected for years and now several dozen FBI agents are watching their house.'

We drank our coffee and lingered in the restaurant, which was only half full, but would be humming again when the bars closed. Nobody pressured us to leave, and we weren't in a hurry to get back to the boredom of the stakeout.

Jamilla was interesting to me for a lot of reasons, but the main one was probably that I saw so much of my own experiences in hers. We were both committed to police work. We had full lives – friends and family – and yet, in a way, we were loners. Why was that?

'You okay?' she asked. Her eyes communicated concern. I can usually intuit good people, and she was one of them. No doubt about it.

'I just went away for a minute,' I said. 'I'm back now.'

'Where do you go when you take these little mind excursions?'

'Florence,' I said. 'It's probably the most beautiful city on earth. My favorite anyway.'

'And you were just in Florence, Italy?'

'Actually, I was thinking about some of the similarities in our lives.'

She nodded. 'I've thought about it. What the heck is to

become of us, Alex? Are we both doomed to repeat the same mistakes?'

'Well, hopefully we're going to catch two real bad killers here in New Orleans. How's that?'

Jamilla reached over and patted my cheek, then she said ruefully, 'That's what I think too. We *are* doomed.'

Chapter Sixty-Five

The Mastermind watched Alex Cross get out of the car. He had him in his sights.

Cross and the lovely Inspector Jamilla Hughes had returned from a dinner break and were back on surveillance duty. Were they getting closer? Would Alex and Jamilla become lovers in New Orleans? That was an obvious flaw in Cross's character; he needed to be loved.

But now Cross was out of the car again.

Something is bothering the great Cross. Maybe he needs to walk a little after the meal. Or maybe he needs to think about the case some more, and wants to be alone. He is a loner, just like I am.

This was amazing; this was so good.

He followed Cross down a dark side street filled with modest homes in two styles – the double shotgun and the creole cottage; both were staples in this part of New Orleans.

The fragrance of honeysuckle, azaleas, jasmine and gardenias were heavy in the air. He sucked in a breath. Pleasant. A hundred years before, the scents had masked the odors of the nearby slaughterhouses. The Mastermind knew his history, knew lots about most things, and the facts flowed easily through his mind as he continued to follow Cross at a safe distance. He retained information and knew how to use it.

He could hear the rattle and hum of the St Charles Avenue streetcar as it raced along its tracks a few blocks away. It helped to cover any slight sound of his own footsteps.

He was enjoying this walk with Cross immensely. Maybe this would be *the night*. Just the thought sent adrenaline pumping through him.

He continued to move closer to Cross. Yes, this was it. Right here, right now.

He half expected Cross to spin around and look at him. That would be good, so rich, ironic, fitting. *Proof of Cross's instincts, and that he was a worthy adversary*.

The Mastermind ducked into some lurks and he circled. He was only a few yards away from Cross now. He could close the distance in an instant.

Cross came to a stop at the old Lafayette Cemetery, the

so-called 'City of the Dead'. Inside the gates were lavish above-ground vaults, multi-burial graves.

The Mastermind stopped as well. He savored this, second by second.

A New Orleans Police Department sign was posted on the gates: PATROLLED.

The Mastermind doubted that was true. And it didn't really matter, did it? He could eat the NOPD for lunch.

Cross looked around, but didn't see him in the shadows. Should he jump him now? Would they fight hand-to-hand? It didn't matter – he knew he would win. He watched Alex Cross breathe. His last breaths on this earth? What a thought.

Cross turned away from the cemetery and started down another side street. He was heading back to the surveillance car, to Inspector Hughes.

The Mastermind started forward, but then he turned away. This wasn't the night that Cross would die. He had taken mercy, spared him.

The reason – it was too dark on this street. He wouldn't be able to see Cross's eyes when he died.

Chapter Sixty-Six

Something surprising happened the next morning; an event I don't think any of us were expecting. I certainly wasn't, and it threw me for a complete loop. We had gathered at the FBI's New Orleans office for the morning briefing. There were about thirty of us in a large and sterile room that looked out on the muddy brown Mississippi River.

At nine o'clock, Kyle began to address the surveillance team that had been on the watch during the previous twenty-four hours. He finished with them and went on to the day's assignments. He handed them out and was very specific. It was a typical Craig performance: clear, to the point, efficient, never a mistake, or the hint of one.

When he was finished, or thought that he was, a hand shot into the air. 'Excuse me, Mr Craig, you didn't mention me. What am I supposed to do today?'

It was Jamilla Hughes and she didn't sound happy. Kyle was already collecting his notes, shuffling a few papers into his thick black briefcase. He barely glanced up as he said, 'That's up to Dr Cross, Inspector Hughes. Please see him.'

The remark and its delivery were unnecessarily curt, even for Kyle. I was taken aback by his rudeness, or at least the lack of any tact.

'This is complete bullshit!' She rose from her seat. 'It's unacceptable, Mr Craig. Especially that irritating, blasé tone of yours.'

The FBI agents in the room looked at her. Usually, no one dared confront Kyle on anything. After all, he was rumored to be in line for the director's job some day. Moreover, many of them felt he deserved it. He was certainly smarter than anybody else in the Bureau. He also worked harder than anyone I knew.

'Look, this is no reflection on Detective Cross,' Jamilla went on, 'but my work in California helped open this case up. I don't want anybody's pat on the back, no condescending applause, thank you, but I came all the way down here and I can contribute. So use me, and respect me. By the way, I couldn't help noticing there's only one other woman on this entire task force. Don't bother to make excuses,' she said, and waved off anything Kyle might have been ready to say in his defense.

Kyle kept his cool. 'Like the supposed vampires, Inspector Hughes, gender doesn't matter to me. I do applaud your efforts during the early stages of this case. But as I said, you can see Dr Cross about your assignment. Or you can go back home right now, if you like. Thank you, everyone,' he said as he saluted the team. 'Happy hunting. Hopefully, today will be our day.'

I was surprised, mostly by Kyle's response, but also by Jamilla's quick anger. I was uneasy when she came up to me after the meeting.

'He got me so mad. Grrrr,' she said. She shook her head and made a face. 'I have a quick temper sometimes, and he was wrong. There's something fucked-up about that man. I have a bad feeling about him. Why would he have it in for me? Because I'm working with you? So what *do* we do today, Dr Cross? I'm not leaving because he's a goddamn idiot.'

'He was wrong. I'm sorry about what happened, Jamilla. Let's talk about what we do next.'

'Don't be condescending,' she said.

'I'm not. Why don't you get off the soapbox, though.'

She still wasn't over her bad scene with Kyle. 'He doesn't like women,' she said. 'Trust me on that. He also practices the three Cs that some men are so fond of: compete, criticize, control.'

'So tell me what you *really* think about Kyle. And men in general.'

Jamilla finally managed a smile. 'I think, and I'm being pretty objective and measured about this, that your so-called friend is a total control freak and a complete asshole. As for men in general, it varies with the individual.'

Chapter Sixty-Seven

The *real* vampires had arrived and they believed they were invincible. William and Michael knew that the exotic city of New Orleans belonged to them from the instant they crossed the bridge. They were a couple of young princes with their long blond ponytails, black shirts and trousers, shining leather boots. Their mission ended here if all went well – and it would.

William drove the Red Cross van through the French Quarter – they were on the lookout for prey. The van rode slowly back and forth on Burgundy, Dauphine, Bourbon, Royal, Chartres, all of the more famous streets. The sounds of Readysexgo blared from the tape deck. 'Radio Tokyo', then 'Supernatural Blonde'.

The brothers finally got out and strolled along Riverwalk. They turned into the Riverwalk Marketplace, and it made William feel physically ill: Banana Republic, Eddie

Bauer, the Limited, Sharper Image, the Gap – mediocrity, tripe, utter stupidity everywhere he looked. 'What do you want to do?' William turned to Michael. 'Look at all this commercial crap in the middle of this beautiful city.'

'Let's take somebody out here in their putrid shopping mall. Maybe we should feed in a changing room at Banana Republic. I love that idea.'

'No!' William said. He grabbed hold of Michael's arm. 'We've been working too hard for this. I think we need a distraction.'

They couldn't take any more prey. Not now. Not so close to Daniel and Charles's domain. So William drove out of New Orleans on the Bonnet Carre Spillway. He continued on Interstate 10 into the real Louisiana. A distraction was definitely needed.

William found what he wanted about an hour outside New Orleans. The rock climb wasn't much, but at least the face was steep. You had to concentrate; if you didn't, you fell, and you were dead.

The brothers chose to free solo, the most extreme example of the sport. Also the most dangerous by far. In free solo, the climbers used no ropes, or any kind of backup protection.

'We are a couple of hardmen!' Michael laughed and shouted once they were halfway up the two-hundred-foot climb. Hardmen were the toughest climbers of all. They were the best, and it fit the brothers' self-image.

'Yes we are!' William shouted back to his brother. 'There are *old* climbers, and there are *bold* climbers.'

'But there are no *old, bold climbers*!' Michael roared with laughter.

The climb turned out to be more challenging than it had looked. It required lots of different kinds of skill. They had to do vertical crack climbing, then suddenly they were face climbing, pressing tight against the rock, using very small hand holds.

'We're in the climbing groove now!' Michael screamed at the top of his lungs. He had forgotten about hunting for prey, forgotten his hunger. There was nothing but the climb. Nothing but staying alive, survival of the fittest.

Suddenly, they had to commit – they were at a point in the climb where, once they made the next couple of moves, they couldn't go back the way they had come. There was nowhere to go but straight up. Or to quit right now.

'What do you think, little brother? You make a plan for us. You decide. What does your instinct tell you?'

Michael laughed so hard he had to grip the rock face with both hands. He looked down – and what he saw was certain death if he fell. 'Don't even think about quitting. We won't fall, brother. Not ever. We're never going to die!'

They climbed to the top and from there they could see New Orleans. It was their city now.

'We're immortal! We'll never die!' the brothers shouted into the wind.

Chapter Sixty-Eight

I stared out at the great, sweeping live oaks. Then I noticed the plump magnolias and sloppy, fanning banana trees of the Garden District. There was nothing else for me to do. The surveillance continued. Jamilla was starting to repeat herself. We both were, and that became a running gag between us. Sections of the day's *Times-Picayune* were all over the backseat of the car. We had read it cover to cover.

'There's no physical evidence tying Daniel or Charles to a single murder. Not in any of the cities, Alex. Everything we have on them is circumstantial, or theoretical, hypothetical bullshit. Does that make any sense to you? It doesn't to me.' She was talking, probably just to talk, but she was making sense. 'It just doesn't add up. They can't be that good. No one is.'

We were parked four blocks north of the house on

LaSalle. The *domain*. We could get there in seconds if anything developed, but so far, nothing had. That was the problem. Daniel and Charles rarely left their two-hundred-year-old mansion, and when they did, it was only to go shopping, or to a fancy restaurant downtown. Not surprisingly, they had good taste.

I tried to answer Jamilla's question. 'It makes some sense to me that we can't link them to the early murders. You know as well as I do – once a murder case gets old it's almost impossible to find witnesses, or compelling evidence. I don't understand why we haven't found anything on the recent murders, though.'

'That's what I'm thinking too. We have witnesses to the killings in Savannah and in Charleston, but no one recognizes photos of Daniel or Charles. Why not? What are we missing?'

'Maybe they don't commit the actual murders themselves,' I said. 'Maybe they used to, but not anymore.'

'Don't they want to feast on the kills? Drink the blood? What other purpose do the murders serve? Are they symbolic? Is this part of some arcane mythology? Are they creating a new mythology? Jesus, Alex, what the hell are these two monsters doing in New Orleans?'

I didn't have answers to her questions, or my own. No one did, unfortunately. So we sat in the car, tried to keep cool in the heat, and waited for Daniel and Charles to make their next move.

If they were so careful and so good then why did we know about them, why were we here?

Chapter Sixty-Nine

William found this laughable. God, it was good! Priceless. He was watching the police as they in turn watched the house of horrors owned by Daniel and Charles. It was too much. The young prince walked down LaSalle, puffing on a cigarette, haughty, confident, unafraid of anyone, superior in every way he could imagine. Michael was home sleeping, so he had decided to take a stroll.

This was rich. Maybe he would see one of the local celebrities who lived in the Garden District. Like the fabulous Trent Reznor of Nine Inch Nails, or some asshole from MTV's Real World house in the Big Easy.

There were two nondescript Lincolns parked on the street. He wondered if the magicians had noticed the cars. He smiled, shook his head. He wondered what the hell Daniel and Charles were thinking. They would be careful, of course. They had been committing murders for a long time, years and years. So now what? Something had to give.

He continued to the end of the street, then walked south toward Sixth. Most of the houses there had screened-in porches crawling with vines. Along the way, he saw a fine physical specimen – a male, twenty-one or so, shirt off, pecs gleaming with sweat. That picked up his spirits. The man was hosing down a silver BMW convertible, the James Bond car.

His chiseled body, the spurting water hose and the shiny car turned William on like a light switch. But he controlled himself and walked on.

And then, just down the street, he saw a young girl. She was maybe fourteen, sitting on her front porch, gently stroking a Persian cat. She was pretty, even sultry.

The girl had long brown hair that flowed down to her small breasts. A diaphanous snakeskin-print top over a belly-length tank top. Tight, dark blue jeans, hip-hugging and flared just right. Stud and hoop earrings, both gold and silver. Toe rings. Bracelets of multiple colors on one slender arm. A typical teenager – except that she was so stunning. A complete turn-on. And arrogant, just like he was.

William stopped and called out to her. 'Your cat is beautiful.' He smiled wickedly.

She looked up, and he saw that she had the same piercing green eyes as the Persian. The girl ran her eyes all over him. He could actually feel them against his skin. He knew that she wanted him. Men and women always did.

'Why do you hold back?' he asked, and continued to smile. 'If you want something, then you should take it. Always. That's your lesson for the day, free of charge.'

'Oh, and you're a teacher?' she called from the porch. 'You don't look like any teacher I've ever had.'

'A teacher, but also a student.'

He had desire for this girl. Not only was she a physical specimen, but she had good instincts. She was sexual and knowing for her age. She used her gifts, unlike most young people, who wasted their talent and potential. She wouldn't speak again, wouldn't even smile, but she didn't look away either.

William loved her confidence, the way her bright green eyes tried to mock him, but couldn't quite do it. The way she thrust her small breasts out at him, her only weapons. He wanted to go up on the porch and take the beautiful girl right there. Bite her, drink her. Spill her blood all over the whitewashed wooden planks.

No. Not now, not yet, not here. God, he hated this, hated not being himself. He wanted to exercise his power, to use his gifts.

Finally, William began to walk away. It took all his will,

all his power, to leave this beautiful prize sitting so invitingly on the porch.

It was then that the girl finally spoke again. 'Why do you hold back?' she called, and laughed pitilessly.

William smiled and turned around.

He walked back toward the girl.

'You're very lucky,' he said. 'You've been chosen.'

Chapter Seventy

Something had to break for us. At seven in the morning, I sat alone at a table outside the Café du Monde across from Jackson Square. I ate sugar-dusted beignets and sipped chickory-laced coffee. I stared off in the direction of the spire of St Louis Cathedral and listened to the bleating horns of riverboats coming down the Mississippi.

It should have been a nice time of the morning, except that I was frustrated and angry and filled with energy that I didn't know what to do with.

I had seen a lot of bad cases, but this was possibly the most difficult to comprehend. The gruesome murders had been going on for more than eleven years, but the pattern was still unclear, and so was the motivation of the killers.

As soon as I reached the FBI offices, I got the disturbing news that a fifteen-year-old girl was missing and that she lived less than six blocks from the magicians. It was possible that she was a runaway, but it didn't seem likely to me. Still, she had been gone less than twenty-four hours.

There was a briefing scheduled and I went upstairs to find out more, and also why I hadn't been alerted earlier. When I entered the session that morning, I sensed the frustration everywhere that I looked. It was hard to imagine a worse result: we suspected that we had tracked down the murderers, but there was nothing we could do about it. And now there was a possibility they had murdered another victim right under our noses.

I sat down beside Jamilla. Both of us had containers of hot coffee plus the morning edition of the *Times-Picayune*. There was nothing about the missing girl; apparently the New Orleans police had sat on the disappearance until early that morning.

Kyle was angry. He just wasn't himself. He was storming about the front of the room, his right hand nervously combing back his dark hair. I didn't blame him – everything about the investigation depended on FBI cooperation with the local police. The NOPD had broken that trust, broken it badly.

'For once, I sympathize with Mr Craig,' Jamilla said. 'The locals were way out of line.'

'We could have been working on the girl's disappearance for hours,' I agreed. 'What a mess, and it's getting worse.'

'Maybe this is our opportunity. I wonder if we could get inside the house during the party tonight. What do you think? I'd love to give it a try,' she whispered. 'Everybody who goes to the so-called Fetish Ball will be in costume, right? Somebody needs to get inside that house. We need to do something.'

Kyle stared directly at Jamilla and me. He raised his voice. 'Can we have one meeting?'

'He means can he have *his* meeting,' she whispered. I wondered why she had taken such a dislike to Kyle. He was acting strange though; the pressure of the case was getting to him. Something had him on edge.

'Tell him what you think,' I said. 'He'll listen. Especially now that the girl is missing.'

'I doubt it. But what can he do – fire me?'

She swiveled around to face Kyle. 'I think we could probably get inside the house tonight during the party. And if we don't, what do we lose? The missing girl might be in there.'

Kyle hesitated, but then he said, 'Do it. Let's see what's in the house.'

Chapter Seventy-One

It could only happen like this in New Orleans. I spent part of the afternoon securing a couple of printed invitations and then Jamilla and I prepared our costumes for that night. The ball began at midnight, but we'd heard most of the crowd wouldn't start to arrive until closer to two.

It had already been a long night for us by the time the festivities started. We waited until just past two to approach the house. Some of the partygoers were college age, a few were even younger, but at least half of the crowd looked to be thirty or older. A few arrived in limousines and other expensive cars. The dress for the night was definitely eye-catching: antique mourning coats and top hats, velvet Victorian gowns, corsets, walking sticks, tiaras.

The Goth crowd sheathed their androgynous bodies mostly in black leather and velvet. There were body piercings everywhere; frilly white and black lace on several of the women; belly rings, dog collars, black lipstick, and gobs of mascara on both the men and women.

Blood-red eyes stared out from every direction. It was difficult to avoid them. A rock song called 'Pistol Grip Pump' played from hidden speakers outside the house. Fangs were everywhere. And stage blood. A few of the women wore black or purple velvet bands around their necks, presumably to conceal bite marks.

It got more interesting and eerie as we went inside the house. People were addressing one another with titled names, 'Sir Nicholas', 'Mistress Anne', 'The Baroness', 'Prince William', 'Master Ormson'. A statuesque woman walked by and brazenly sized-up Jamilla. She was bronzed with body paint and wore a bronze-colored thong. The iron scent of blood mingled with smoky leather and pungent oil from wall torches.

Jamilla looked ready; she was definitely tough. She had on a tight, sleek black dress with leather boots and black stockings. If she'd wanted to look sexy, she'd succeeded. She had purchased black lipstick and leather wristbands at a place called the Little Shop of Fantasy on Dumaine Street. She'd also helped me with my outfit: a mourning coat that scraped the floor, cravat, black trousers, black boots that came to my knees.

No one seemed to pay much attention to the two of us.

We checked out the main floor, then flowed with the crowd down into the basement. There were flaming torches everywhere on the stone walls. The floors were dirt and stone. It was cold and damp and musty.

'Jesus, Alex,' Jamilla whispered close to my ear. She took my arm, held it tight. 'I don't think I would have believed it if I wasn't standing right here.'

I felt exactly the same. Several of those congregating downstairs wore canine teeth that were terrifying, especially in such large numbers. Electrified candelabras and the fiery torches were the only sources of light. I saw human skulls nailed into the walls, and I was sure they were real.

I started checking to make sure we could get out of here if we had to. I wasn't sure about a quick escape. The crowd was thickening and the feeling was claustrophobic. I wondered if someone was supposed to die here tonight. If so, who would it be?

Then I heard a deep voice announce, 'The Sire is here. Bow your heads.'

Chapter Seventy-Two

The cavernous underground room was quiet and tense. I had the uncomfortable feeling that I was about to see something I wasn't supposed to. Then Daniel Erickson and Charles Defoe made their grand entrance.

The magicians epitomized outrageous bohemian royalty. The audience of faithful obediently bowed their heads. Both men were physically impressive. Charles was bare-chested and wore skintight leather pants with boots. He was an erotic-looking man with a powerful build. Daniel had on a tight black frock coat, with black trousers and a black silk cravat. He was well muscled, but slender at the waist.

Tugging against a heavy metal leash in front of them was a white Bengal tiger. Jamilla and I exchanged looks. 'This is getting interesting in a hurry,' she whispered.

Daniel stopped to talk with several of the young males. I

remembered that the earliest murder victims were all men. The tiger was less than ten feet away from me. What did it mean for the vampires? Was it just a symbol – and for what?

Charles came and stood next to Daniel against the far wall. He whispered something close to Daniel's ear. They laughed and looked around the room.

Daniel finally spoke in a loud, clear voice. I could tell he expected to be listened to. His confidence was charismatic. 'I am the Sire. What a vibrant and alive gathering this is,' he said. 'I can feel the energy coursing through this room. It excites me.

'The force harnessed here knows no limits. Believe in it. Believe in yourselves. Tonight is a special night. So come with me to the next room. The next level. Come, if you believe – or even better, if you don't.'

Chapter Seventy-Three

I had never seen anything like this. Jamilla and I were quiet and wide-eyed as we entered an even larger chamber in the basement.

The room was lit by wall sconces, most of them electric. The brutal fangs gleamed everywhere. The white tiger had begun to growl, and I recalled the bites into human flesh.

If you hunt for the vampires.

What was happening in this eerie cellar? What was the purpose of tonight's gathering? Who were these ghouls – hundreds of them?

Daniel and Charles stood beside two tall, handsome, dark-haired men in satiny black robes with capes. They looked to be in their early twenties, maybe even younger. They looked like young gods. Everyone crowded forward to see what would happen next.

'I am here to anoint two new vampire princes,' Daniel

announced with grave authority. The persona was the same one he used onstage. 'Bow before them!'

A woman at the front shrieked. 'Our princes! Dark princes! I worship you!'

'Silence!' Charles shouted. 'Take that stupid cow out of here. Banish her.'

The lights suddenly blinked once, then went out completely. The few burning torches were doused. I reached for Jamilla, and we slid back toward the nearest wall.

I couldn't see anything. I felt a cold spot at the center of my chest.

'What the hell is happening, Alex?'

'I don't know. Let's keep together.'

It got crazy very fast in the darkness. People screamed. A whip cracked nearby. It was madness. Chaos. Sheer terror.

Jamilla and I had our guns out. But there wasn't anything we could do in the dark.

A minute or so passed. Everything was inky blackness. It seemed like a very long time. Too long. I was afraid of being stabbed. Or bitten.

A generator kicked in somewhere in the house. The lights in the cellar flickered, then went on again. Then off. Then on.

I saw after-images, rings of color. And then—

The magicians had disappeared.

Someone shouted, 'Our princes are dead.'

Chapter Seventy-Four

I pushed my way through the shocked crowd and didn't meet resistance. Then I saw the bodies. The two young men in black robes lay sprawled on the cellar floor. They had been stabbed and their throats cut. Blood was pooled around the bodies. Where were Daniel and Charles?

'Police!' I called out. 'Don't touch them. Back away.'

The men and women closest to the bodies slinked away. I wondered if they had been about to drink the spilled blood. Wasn't that the ritual? The pattern for the ghoulish murders so far?

'There's only two of them! Two cops!' someone shouted.

'We *will* shoot you,' Jamilla called out in a loud, clear voice.

'Back away. Do it. Where are Daniel and Charles?' I shouted.

The crowd began to close in on us, so I fired off a

warning shot. It echoed loudly. There was chaos in the cellar. Men and women began struggling to get through the doors. No one would get away though. FBI agents were waiting outside.

Jamilla and I pushed our way into a connecting room in the basement. We started down a narrow hallway lit only by candles. Daniel and Charles could have come this way when the lights went out. It seemed likely; they knew the house.

There were small rooms crowded next to each other on either side of the dusty tunnel. The layout reminded me of ancient catacombs. Everything was closed in – musty, damp, depressing as hell, scary.

'You okay?' I glanced back at Jamilla.

'I'm fine. So far anyway. This place is starting to grow on me.' She made a wisecrack, but her eyes were darting about.

I could hear Kyle's voice calling to us. The FBI agents were inside now. 'Anything up there? Alex? You see anything?'

'Not yet. Daniel and Charles took off when the lights went off. No sign of them.'

We moved cautiously, checking each of the rooms. Most of the space seemed to be used for storage. A few were completely empty. Dank and eerie, like tombs. Atmospheric, I suppose. Spooky for sure.

I kicked open another door. Jamilla and I peered in. She gasped, her mouth open in a silent scream. 'Oh Jesus, Alex! What the hell happened?'

I reached out and held onto her arm. I couldn't believe what I was looking at. I couldn't make myself believe it. My knees went weak.

Daniel and Charles were laid out on the floor of the room. They had been murdered. I was too stunned to speak. Kyle came into the room behind us, said not a word.

We moved closer to the bodies, but I knew they were dead. The throats of both men had been cut. And there were deep bites, fang marks.

So who was the Sire?

Part Four

Hunt

Chapter Seventy-Five

L ate the following afternoon, Jamilla had to return to
San Francisco. She pretty much admitted that she was
burnt-out and baffled. I gave her a ride to the airport, and
we continued to talk about the murder case all the way
there. We realized we were both obsessing.

What had happened the night before changed everything. We had tracked down the supposed killers – and
they had been killed. This was a complex and thoroughly
frustrating murder mess in which anything seemed possible. The killers weren't necessarily clever, but they were full
of surprises.

'Where do you go from here, Alex?' she asked as we
turned into the airport.

I laughed. 'Oh, now it's where do *I* go?'

'You know what I mean. C'mon.'

'Kyle has asked me to stay down here for another day or

two to help out. Everyone who was in the house is being held by the New Orleans police. That's a lot of freaks to be interviewed. Somebody has to know something.'

'If you can get anything out of them. You think the New Orleans cops are cooperating now? They sure weren't before.'

I smiled. 'You know how stubborn local cops can be. We'll get what we need. It just might take a little longer. I'm sure that's part of the reason Kyle wants me to stay on.'

She frowned at the mention of Kyle's name. I knew she was disappointed to be leaving though. 'I have to get back home, but I'm not going to drop this one. My friend Tim at *The Examiner* is doing another big piece on the California murders. Maybe it all started out there. Think about it.'

'Eleven years ago, maybe more,' I said. 'But who were the first killers? Daniel Erickson and Charles Defoe? Someone else in the cult? *Is* there a cult?'

She threw her hands up in the air. 'I have no idea at this point. I'm practically brain dead. I'm going to get on my plane and sleep all the way home.'

She lingered for a few more minutes. We talked some more about the case. Then I asked her about Tim at *The Examiner*. 'Just a friend,' she said.

Jamilla and I shook hands at the curbside luggage drop in front of the area marked for American Airlines. Then she leaned in and kissed me on the cheek.

I slid my hand behind her neck and held her for a few seconds. It was nice. The two of us had shared a lot of pain and misery in a short time. We had also been in a life-threatening situation.

'Alex, as always, an honor,' she said as she pulled away. 'Thanks for the Krispy Cremes and everything else.'

'Keep in touch,' I said. 'Will you, Jamilla?'

'Absolutely. I plan to. You can count on it. I mean that, Alex.'

Then Inspector Jamilla Hughes turned away and walked inside the bustling terminal at New Orleans International. I was definitely going to miss her. I already thought of her as a friend.

I watched her go, then headed back to the FBI offices in New Orleans to bury my head in some work. I went over everything we had with Kyle. Then we went over every-thing again, just to be sure it was as fucked-up as we thought it was. The two of us agreed that there weren't even any good theories about what had happened to Daniel and Charles. We just didn't know. No one was talking so far – or maybe no one had seen anything.

'Whoever killed them wanted to show us that they were superior. To them. To us. Physically, mentally, in terms of their ruthlessness,' I said. But I wasn't really sure about that. I was just thinking out loud.

'I don't think it was an accident that the whole thing

feels a little like a magic trick,' Kyle said. 'Doesn't that strike you, Alex? Some connection to magic?'

'Yeah, but it wasn't a magic trick. Daniel and Charles are dead, and so are a lot of other people. Going back a lot of years.'

'We're nowhere. Is that what you're saying?'

'Yeah. And I don't like it here,' I said.

Chapter Seventy-Six

I worked late that night in the FBI office. So what else was new? Around nine I was feeling lonely and edgy, all messed up. I called home, but nobody was there. That worried me a little, until I remembered that it was my Aunt Tia's birthday and Nana was throwing a party at Tia's new house in Chapel Gate, north of Baltimore.

I hadn't bought Tia a present. *Damn it. Damn me.* Ever since I had come to Washington as a kid, Tia had never forgotten my birthday. Not once. This year, she had given me the watch that I was wearing now. I called her house in Maryland, and I got to talk to most of my relatives. They teased that I was missing out on some great sock-it-to-me cake. They wanted to know where I was on Tia's birthday, and when I was coming home.

I didn't have a satisfactory answer to give them. 'Soon as

I can. I miss you all. You have no idea how much I miss being there.'

I decided I needed to stop in at the magicians' house before I went back to the Dauphine. Why did I *need* to do that? I wondered. Because I was wired. Because I am obsessive. A couple of New Orleans policemen were stationed out front. They looked bored and under-utilized, and definitely not obsessive.

I showed them ID and they let me inside. No problem, Detective Cross.

I really wasn't sure why but I had a vague feeling that we had missed something in the house. Forensics had spent hours going over the place. So had I. We hadn't found anything concrete. Still, I didn't like being in the house again. The domain. Maybe I needed a gris-gris for protection.

I walked through the over-done, very ornate foyer and living room. My footsteps made the big house sound empty. I kept wondering, what were we missing? What was I missing?

The master bedroom was situated off the hall at the top of the stairs. Nothing had changed since the first time I was in there. Why in hell had I bothered to come back here? The large, open room was filled with dark, modern art, some of it hung, but several paintings were propped up against the walls. The magicians slept in a bed, not in the coffins we'd found below in the tunnels.

As I was searching through their clothes closet again, I came across something I hadn't seen before. I was sure it hadn't been there when I'd canvassed the bedroom the first time. Lying among the shoes were effigies of Daniel and Charles – miniature dolls of the magicians.

There were slash marks across the throats, chests and faces. Just like the way they were murdered.

Where the hell had the gruesome effigies come from? What did they mean? What was going on down here in New Orleans? Who had gotten into this house after we sealed it? I was tempted to call Kyle, but I held off. I wasn't sure why.

I didn't want to go back down into the tunnels alone, and at night, but I was here, and I figured I ought to take another quick look around. There were two cops posted just outside the door, right?

What were we missing? Unspeakably violent murders that went back at least eleven years.

Our two best suspects had been murdered.

Someone had put effigies in their bedroom.

I went down to the cellar, then into the tunnels that spidered out in several directions from the main area. New Orleans is about eight feet below sea level and the cellar and tunnels were probably always damp. The walls sweat.

I heard a scraping noise, and stopped. Someone or

something was walking around. I reached into my shoulder holster, took out my Glock.

I listened closely. Nothing. Then more scraping.

Mice or rats, I thought to myself. *Probably all it was. Probably. Almost definitely.*

I had to go and look further, though. That was my problem, wasn't it? I *had* to go look, had to investigate, couldn't just walk away. What was I trying to prove to myself? That I had no fears? That I wasn't like my father, who had quit on just about everything in life, including his kids and himself?

I inched forward slowly and quietly, listening to the house.

I could hear water dripping somewhere in the dank tunnels.

I used my old Zippo to light a few of the torches hung on the tunnel walls. There were really bad images in my head. The bite wounds on the bodies I'd seen. The way Daniel and Charles had been attacked. The poisonous bites I'd suffered in Charlotte. *You're one of us now.*

The anger, the rage connected to the murders was present in so many cities.

What were the killers angry about?

Where were they right now?

I never heard them coming, never saw a movement.

I was hit, twice. The attackers had come swiftly out of the darkness. One went for my head and neck. The other hit around my knees. They were a team. Efficient.

I went down hard and it took the wind right out of me. But I fell on one of the attackers, who was still wrapped around my legs. I heard a loud crack, maybe a bone breaking. Then a scream. He let me go.

I got up, but the second assailant was attached to my back. He bit me! *Oh Jesus, no!*

I cursed and slammed him into the wall. I did it again. Who the hell were these fantastic madmen? Who was the leech riding my back?

He finally let go, the sonofabitch! I spun around at him, clipping the side of his head with my gun. I hit him again with a solid left hook. He went down like a sack.

I was breathing hard, still full of fight, though. Neither of the assailants was moving much now. I kept the gun on them while I lit another candle on the wall. That was better; light always helps.

I saw a male and female, probably no more than sixteen or seventeen. Their eyes were like dark holes. The male must have been six foot six or more.

He had on a dingy white T-shirt with 'Marlboro Racing First to Finish' printed on it, and baggy, scungy black jeans.

The girl was around five two with wide hips, wide

everything. Her black hair was stringy and greasy, with reddish highlights.

I touched my neck and was surprised that the skin wasn't broken. There was no blood on my hand.

'You're under arrest,' I yelled at the two of them. 'You goddamn bloodsuckers!'

Chapter Seventy-Seven

V*ampires? Is that what these twisted creeps were? Assas-sins? Murderers?*

Their names were Anne Elo and John 'Jack' Masterson and they had attended Catholic high school in Baton Rouge until about four months ago, when they had dropped out and run away from home. Each was seven-teen years old. They were just kids.

I spent three hours attempting to question the suspects that night, then another four hours the following morning. Elo and Masterson wouldn't talk to me or anyone else – not a word. They wouldn't say what they were doing inside the mansion in the Garden District. Why they had attacked me. Whether or not they had placed the sinister effigies in the closet of the dead men.

The teens simply glared across the plain wooden table in one or another of the interrogation rooms at police headquarters. The parents were notified and brought in, but Elo and Masterson wouldn't speak to them either. At one point, Anne Elo finally addressed her father with two words – 'Blow me.' I wondered how the cult of the vampire had satisfied her needs, her incredible anger.

In the meantime, there were still lots of others to talk to from the Fetish Ball. The commonality among most of them was that they held 'straight jobs' in New Orleans: they were bartenders and waitresses, hotel desk clerks, computer analysts, actors, and even teachers. Most were afraid to have their alternative lifestyles come out at work, so they eventually talked to us. Unfortunately, no one told us anything revealing about Daniel and Charles, *or their murderers*.

It was an extraordinarily busy night at the precinct house. More than two dozen homicide detectives and FBI agents conducted reinterviews. We exchanged notes and bios of the suspects with highlighted inconsistencies. We went hard at the most obvious liars in the group. We also kept a list of the witnesses who seemed the most likely to break under pressure. We switched interviewers on them, sent them to the cells, then summoned them back before they could sleep; we doubled up on them.

'All we need is a few rubber hoses,' one of the New Orleans detectives said while we were waiting for Anne Elo to be fetched from her cell for the sixth time that night.

His name was Mitchell Sams, and he was around fifty, a black man, hugely overweight, tough, effective, cynical as hell.

When Anne Elo was brought back into the interrogation room, she looked like a sleepwalker. Or a zombie. Her eye sockets were incredibly deep and dark. Her lips were chapped and caked with dried blood.

Sams went at her. 'Good morning, glory. It's nice to see your pasty-white face again. You look like total shit, babe. I'm being kind. Several of your friends, including your pathetic boyfriend, have broken down already tonight.'

The girl turned her vacant eyes toward a brick wall. 'You must be mistaking me for somebody who gives a shit,' she said.

I decided to try an idea that had been weaving through my mind for the past hour or so. I had used it on a few of the others. 'We know about the new Sire,' I told Anne Elo. 'He's gone back to California. He isn't here for you. He can't help you, or hurt you.'

Her face remained blank and unresponsive, but she folded her arms. She sagged a few inches in her chair. Her lips were bleeding again, possibly because she'd bitten into them. 'Who gives a shit. Not me.'

Just then, a bleary-eyed NOPD detective opened the door to the interrogation room where Mitchell Sams and I were working on Elo, and beckoned us out. The detective had dark sweat stains under both arms of his pale blue sports shirt. Heavy stubble covered his chin and cheeks. He looked about as exhausted as I felt.

'There's been another murder,' he told Sams. 'Another hanging murder.'

Anne Elo appeared at the open door, and slowly, rhythmically clapped her hands. 'That's great,' she said.

Chapter Seventy-Eight

I rode to the crime scene alone, feeling increasingly distant and unreal. The wheels in my head were turning slowly and methodically. Where did we go from here? I had no goddamn idea. Jesus, I was beat.

The house was an outbuilding for one of the Garden District's historic homes, a small carriage house with a second-story balcony. It looked like it could have been a cute, cozy B&B. Magnolia and banana trees surrounded it on the outside. So did an intricate wrought-iron fence, the kind I had seen everywhere in the French Quarter.

About half of the New Orleans Police Department was already at the scene. So were a couple of EMS trucks, their roof lights spinning and blazing. The press was beginning to arrive as we did – the late shift.

Detective Sams had gotten to the murder scene a couple of minutes before I did. He met me in the hallway outside the upstairs bedroom where the killing had taken place. The interior of the place had fine detailing on almost every surface – ceilings, banisters, moldings, doors. The owner had cared about the house, and also about Mardi Gras. Feathers and beads, colorful masks, costumes were tacked up on most of the walls.

'This is bad, even worse than we thought,' Sams said. 'She's a *detective* named Maureen Cooke. She's in Vice, but she was helping out on Daniel and Charles. Most of the department was pitching in.'

Sams led me into the detective's bedroom. It was small but attractive, with a sky-blue ceiling that someone had once told me was supposed to keep winged insects from nesting there.

Maureen Cooke was a redhead, tall and thin, probably in her early thirties. She had been hung by her bare feet from a chandelier. Her nails were painted red. The detective was naked except for a delicate, silver bracelet on her wrist.

Blood streaks were all over her body, but there was no sign of blood pooling on the floor or anywhere else.

I walked up close to her. 'Sad,' I whispered under my breath. A human life – gone – just like that. Another detective dead.

I looked at Mitchell Sams. He was waiting for me to speak first.

'This might not have been done by the same killers,' I said, and shook my head. 'The bite wounds look different to me. They're superficial. Something's changed.'

I stepped back from the body of Maureen Cooke and took in her bedroom. There were photographs that I recognized as part of E.J. Bellocq's study of the Storyville prostitutes. Strange, but fitting for the vice detective. A couple of Asian fans had been framed over the bed, which looked like it had been slept in. Or possibly the bed hadn't been made the previous day.

My cell phone rang. I hit a button with my thumb. I felt out of it. Numb. I needed sleep.

'Did you find her yet, Dr Cross? What do you think? Give me your best guess on how to stop these terrible murders. You must have it figured out by now.'

The Mastermind was on the line. How did he know?

Suddenly I was yelling into the phone. 'I'm going to take you down! I've figured that much out, asshole!'

I hung up on him, then I shut the phone off. I looked around the bedroom. Kyle Craig was watching me from the doorway.

'Are you all right, Alex?' he whispered.

Chapter Seventy-Nine

When I got back to the Dauphine Hotel it was almost ten-thirty in the morning. I was too tired and too worked up to sleep. My heart was still racing. There was a message for me: Inspector Hughes had called from San Francisco.

I stretched out on the bed and called Jamilla back. I shut my eyes. I wanted to hear a friendly voice, especially hers.

'I might have something good for you,' she said when I reached her at home. 'In my spare time, ha-ha, I've been taking a close look at Santa Cruz. Why Santa Cruz, you might ask? There have been several unsolved disappearances there. Too many. I plotted them out myself. Alex, something is happening up there. It fits in with the rest of this case.'

'Santa Cruz was on our original list,' I said. I was trying to focus on what she had just told me. I couldn't remember exactly where Santa Cruz was located.

'You sound tired. Are you all right?' she asked.

'I just got back to the hotel a few minutes ago. Long night.'

'Alex, *go to sleep*! This can wait. Goodnight.'

'No, I can't sleep anyway. Tell me about Santa Cruz. I want to hear it.'

'All right. I talked to a lieutenant with the Santa Cruz PD. Interesting conversation. Annoying, too. They're aware of the disappearances. They've also noted house pets and livestock disappearing in the past year. Lot of ranches in the area. Nobody believes in vampires, of course. *But* – Santa Cruz has a certain reputation. The kiddies call it the vampire capital of the US. Occasionally, the kids are right.'

'I need to see what you have so far,' I told her. 'I'm going to try and get a little sleep. But I want to read whatever Santa Cruz sends you. Can you send it to me?'

'My contact at *The Examiner* promised to send me the relevant files. Meanwhile, today's my day off. I might just take a ride.'

I opened my eyes wide. 'If you go, take somebody along. Your contact at *The Examiner*. I mean it.' I told her about the murder of the vice detective, Maureen Cooke, here in New Orleans. 'Don't go there alone. We still don't know what we're dealing with.'

'I'll take somebody along,' she promised, but I didn't know if I could believe her.

'Jamilla, be careful. I don't have a good feeling about this.'

'You're just tired. Get some sleep. I'm a big girl.'

We talked for a few more minutes, but I wasn't sure if I had gotten through to her. Like most good homicide detectives, she was stubborn.

I shut my eyes again and started to drift away, then I was gone.

Chapter Eighty

J amilla was remembering a line from a favorite Shirley Jackson novel, *The Haunting of Hill House*, which had been made into a really disappointing movie. 'Whatever walked there, walked alone,' Jackson had written. That pretty much summed up how she felt about the murder case. And maybe even about her life lately.

She drove her trusty, dusty Saab toward Santa Cruz. She gripped the steering wheel a little too firmly most of the way, and her hands felt numb. The kink in her neck was getting worse. This was a disturbing case, and she just couldn't let it go. The killers were out there somewhere. They were going to keep murdering until somebody stopped them. So maybe she should stop them.

She had tried to get Tim to go with her, but he was covering a bicyclists' protest for *The Examiner*. Besides, she wasn't sure that she wanted to spend the whole day with him. Tim was sweet, but, well, he wasn't Alex Cross. So here she was getting off Route 1, entering Santa Cruz all by her lonesome. *All by her damn lonesome again.*

At least she had alerted Tim to the fact that she was going to Santa Cruz, and of course she *was* a big girl, and armed to the teeth. *Ugh, teeth*, she thought. She cringed at the image of fangs, and the horrible deaths of all those who had been bitten.

She had always liked Santa Cruz, though. Maybe because it had been practically the epicenter of the Loma Pietra earthquake back in '89 – 6.7 on the Richter scale, fifty-seven dead – but then the area had come back. The gutsy little town and the people there had refused to fold. Lots of earthquake-proof construction, nothing higher than two stories. Santa Cruz was pure California, the best.

As she drove, she watched a big, blond surfer climb out of a VW with a surfboard strapped to the roof. He was finishing off a drippy slice of pizza, heading into the Book Shop of Santa Cruz. Pure California.

There was quite a mix of people here – post-hippies, high-tech start-up folks, transients, surfers, college kids. She liked it an awful lot. So where were the goddamn vampires hiding? Were they here? Did they know *she* was here in Santa Cruz looking for their gnarly asses? Were they among the surfers and post-hippies she was passing on the street?

Her first stop was the town's police department. The lieutenant, Harry Conover, was totally surprised to see her in the flesh. She guessed he couldn't imagine any detective going out of his or her way on the job.

'I told you I'd pass along everything I found on the Goths and wannabe vamps. Didn't you believe me?' he asked. He shook his head of longish blond curls, rolled his soft brown eyes. Conover was tall, well-built, probably in his mid-thirties. Around her age. Jamilla could tell that he was a big flirt, and that he had a high opinion of himself.

'Sure I believed you. But I had today off, and this case is burning a hole right through me. So here I am, Harry. Better than e-mail, right? What do you have for me?'

She sensed that he wanted to tell her to get a life, to enjoy her day off. She'd heard it all before, and maybe he was right. But not now, not with this case still on the boards.

'I read in a couple of the reports that some of the local ghouls might be living together commune-style. You have any idea where?' she asked.

Conover shook his head, and even pretended to be concerned. He was also checking her out, she could tell. Obviously, he was a breast man. 'We never got any confirmation of that,' he said. 'Kids crash together, of course, but I don't know about any *commune*. There are a couple of hot clubs – Catalyst, Palookaville. And lots of kids share cribs on lower Pacific Street.'

She didn't give up. Never. 'But if a lot of kids *were* living together – any ideas where that might be?'

Conover sighed, and actually looked a little annoyed with her for asking. Jamilla could tell he wasn't the kind of cop who put too much of himself into his work. She would have transferred him in a second if he worked for her, and Conover would have sworn it was a gender thing. It wasn't. He was a lazy, half-assed cop, and she hated that. Lives depended on how well he did his job. Didn't he understand that?

'Maybe out in the foothills. Or north around Boulder Creek,' Conover finally volunteered in a soft drawl. 'I really don't know what to tell you.'

Of course you don't, Harry. Duh.

'Where would *you* look first?' she persisted. *If you were worth jack shit as a cop.*

'Inspector, I just wouldn't be chasing this one too hard. Yes, there have been some curious disappearances around here. But that's true of just about every town up and down the coast of California. Kids are more restless now than they used to be when we were growing up. I don't believe anybody's getting seriously hurt in Santa Cruz, and I sure don't buy that this is the freaking *vampire* capital of the West Coast. It isn't. Believe me on that. There are no vampires in Santa Cruz.'

She nodded, pretended to agree. 'I think I'll try the foothills first,' she said.

Conover saluted her. 'If you're finished chasing ghouls before seven or so, give me a call. Maybe we could have a drink. It is your day off, right?'

Jamilla nodded. 'I'll do that. If I'm finished before seven, Harry. Thanks for all your help.' *Jackass.*

Chapter Eighty-One

She was pissed now. Who in their right mind wouldn't be? Here she was working her butt off in somebody else's town. She parked the Saab on a funky side street, near the Metro Center, right across from the Asti bar. She had lost track of the San Lorenzo River while she was driving, but it was around here somewhere. She could *smell* it anyway.

She had just gotten out of the vehicle when two men appeared. They walked up quickly and flanked her tightly on either side.

Jamilla winced. They almost seemed to appear out of nowhere. *Blond ponytails,* she thought. *College kids? Surfers?* She sure hoped so.

They were well-built, but they didn't look like weightlifters. More like they came by it naturally. Images of Eros, Hermes, and Apollo came to mind. Muscles that were extremely well-defined. Virility. Chiseled marble.

'Can I help you fellows out?' she asked. 'Looking for the beach?'

The taller of the two spoke with tremendous confidence, or maybe it was cockiness. 'Doubt it,' he said. 'We're not surfers, actually. Besides, we're from around here. How about you?'

Both of them had the deepest blue eyes. They were incredibly intense. One looked no older than sixteen. Their movements were deliberate and controlled. She didn't like this. There was no one around to intervene on the side street.

'Maybe you could tell *me* where the beach is?' she said.

They were crowding her physically, standing too close. She wouldn't be able to get her gun out. She couldn't move without bumping into one or the other. They wore black T-shirts, jeans, rock climbers' shoes.

'You want to back off a little?' she finally said. 'Just back off, okay?'

The older one smiled. The dent between his lip and nose was a sexy round hollow. 'I'm William. This is my brother Michael. By any chance were you looking for us, Inspector Hughes?'

Oh no, oh Jesus. Jamilla tried to reach for the sidearm in the holster strapped to her back. They grabbed her. Took away her gun as easily as if she were a child. She was astonished at how fast they moved – and how strong they were. The two of them pushed her down on the sidewalk and handcuffed her. *Where did they get cuffs? In New Orleans? The murdered detective?*

The older one spoke again. 'Don't scream, or I'll snap your neck, Inspector.' He said it so matter-of-factly. *Snap your neck.*

The second one spoke then. He was right in her face. She saw the long canine fangs. 'If you hunt for the vampire, the vampire will hunt for you,' he said.

Chapter Eighty-Two

S he was gagged, then thrown roughly onto the rear seat of a pickup truck. The truck started up and took off with a jolt.

She was being driven somewhere. Jamilla tried to concentrate on everything about the trip. She counted off the seconds, kept track of the minutes. There was stop-and-go city driving, then faster, smoother riding, possibly on Route 1.

Then a very rough road, possibly unpaved. She figured the trip took approximately thirty-seven minutes.

She was carried inside a building, some kind of ranch house or roughshod farm structure. People were laughing. At her? They wore fangs. Jesus. She was put down on a cot in a small room and her gag removed.

'You've come looking for the Sire,' the one who called himself William whispered, his face up close to hers.

'You've made a terrible mistake, Inspector. This one will get you killed.'

He smiled horribly, and she felt as if she were being both ridiculed, and, at the same time, seduced. William touched her cheek with his long, slender fingers. He lightly caressed her throat, stared into her eyes.

She was repulsed, wanted to run away, but couldn't do anything. There were a dozen or so vampires here – watching her like she was meat on a spit.

'I don't know anything about a Sire,' she said. 'What's a Sire? Help me out here.'

The brothers looked at each other, shared a knowing smirk. A few of the others laughed out loud.

'The Sire is the one who leads,' said William. He was so calm, so very sure of himself.

'Who does the Sire lead?' she asked.

'Why, anyone who will follow,' William answered. He laughed again, seemed to be enjoying himself immensely at her expense. 'Vampires, Inspector. Others like Michael and myself. Many others, in many, many cities. You can't imagine the extent of it. The Sire stands firm with simple directions on what to think, how to act, things like that. The Sire is not accountable to any authorities. The Sire is a superior being. Are you starting to understand? Would you like to meet the Sire?'

'Is the Sire here now?' she asked. 'Where are we?'

William continued to stare down at her. He was definitely seductive. Disgusting. Then he leaned in closer. 'You're the detective. *Is* the Sire here? Where are you? You tell me.'

Jamilla felt as if she might retch. She needed her space. 'Why are we here?' she asked. She wanted to keep them talking, keep them occupied for as long as she could.

William shrugged. 'Oh, we've always been here. This used to be a commune – California-dreaming hippies, mind-altering drugs, Joni Mitchell music. Our parents were hippies. We were isolated from other ways to live and think, so we depended on each other. My brother and I are unbelievably close. But we're nothing really. We're here to serve the Sire.'

'Was the Sire always at the commune?' she asked.

William shook his head, and gave her a serious look. 'There were always vampires here. They stayed apart, left the others alone. You had to join them, not the other way around.'

'How many are there?'

William looked at Michael, shrugged his broad shoulders, and they both laughed. 'Legions! We're everywhere.'

Suddenly William roared and went for her throat. Jamilla couldn't help it – she screamed.

He stopped inches away from her, still growling like an animal. Then he purred gently. His long tongue licked her cheek, her lips, her eyelids. She couldn't believe what was happening.

'We're going to hang you and drink every last drop. And the most amazing thing – you're going to enjoy it when you die. It's ecstasy, Jamilla.'

Chapter Eighty-Three

I had returned to Washington, and was taking a much needed day off. Why not? I hadn't seen enough of the kids lately, and it was Saturday after all.

Damon, Jannie and I went to the Corcoran Gallery of Art that afternoon. The little creeps fiercely resisted the museum at first, but once they were inside the Palace of Gold and Light they were completely entranced. Then they didn't want to leave. Typical of them.

When we eventually got home at around four, Nana told me I was to call Tim Bradley at the San Francisco *Examiner*. *Give me a break. This case wouldn't stop. Now I was supposed to call Jamilla's buddy?*

'It's important that you call. That's the message,' Nana said. She was baking two cherry pies. Reminding me how good it was to be home.

It was one o'clock in California. I called Tim Bradley at

his office. He picked up right away. 'Bradley.'

'It's Detective Alex Cross.'

'Hi. I hoped you'd call. I'm a friend of Jamilla Hughes.'

I knew that much already. I interrupted. 'Is she okay?'

'Why do you ask that, Detective? She went to Santa Cruz yesterday. Did you know about that?'

'She mentioned she might go. Did somebody go with her?' I asked. 'I suggested she take company.'

His answer was curt and defensive. 'No. Like Jamilla always says, she's a big girl. And she carries a big gun.'

I frowned and shook my head. 'So what's going on? Has something happened? Is something the matter?'

'No, not necessarily. She's usually careful, precise. I just haven't heard from her, and she promised to call. *Last* night. It's been another four hours since I first called you. I'm a little concerned. It's probably nothing. But I thought you would know best . . . about this particular case.'

'Does she do things like this often?' I asked.

'Investigate a case on her day off? Yes. That's Jam. But she would definitely call me if she promised to.'

I was worried now. I thought of my last two partners. Both Patsy Hampton and Betsey Cavalierre had died, and neither of the victims had had justice. The Mastermind claimed to have killed Betsey. And also detective Maureen Cooke in New Orleans. So what about Inspector Jamilla Hughes?

'I'm going to call the local police in Santa Cruz. She gave me a name and a number. I think it was Conover. I have it written down in my notes. I'm going to call him right now.'

'All right, thank you, Detective. Will you let me know?' Tim the reporter asked. 'I'd appreciate it.'

I said that I would, then tried to reach Lieutenant Harry Conover at police headquarters in Santa Cruz. He wasn't working, but I made a fuss, and dropped Kyle Craig's name. The sergeant reluctantly gave me Conover's home number.

Someone picked up at the number, and I heard loud music that I vaguely recognized as U2. 'We're having a party at the pool. C'mon over. Or call back on Monday,' said a male voice. 'Bye, bye for now.'

The line went dead.

I redialed and said, 'Lieutenant Conover, please. It's an emergency. This is Detective Alex Cross. It's about Inspector Jamilla Hughes of the San Francisco PD.'

'Awhh shit,' I heard, then, 'this is Conover. Who is this again?'

I explained who I was and my involvement in the case in as few words as possible. I had the feeling that Harry Conover was drunk, or close to it. It *was* his day off, but Jesus – it wasn't even two in the afternoon his time.

'She went up in the hills, looking for new-wave vampires,' he said and laughed derisively. 'There are no

vampires in Santa Cruz, Detective. Trust me on that. I'm
sure she's just fine. She probably headed back to San
Francisco.'

'There have been at least *two dozen* vampire-style murders so far.' I tried to sober Conover up, at least to get
through to him. 'They hang their victims, and then drain
the blood.'

'I told you what I know, Detective,' he said. 'I guess I
could call out some patrol cars,' he added.

'You do that. And while you do, I'm going to call the FBI.
They believe in vampire murders. When was the last time
you saw Inspector Hughes?'

He hesitated. 'Who knows. Let me see, must be close to
twenty-four hours.'

I hung up on Conover. I didn't like him at all.

I sat and thought about everything that had happened
since I'd first met Jamilla Hughes. The case made my head
spin. Everything about it was over the edge, completely
new territory. Having the Mastermind around made it
even worse.

I phoned Kyle Craig, and then American Airlines. I
called Tim Bradley back and told him I was on my way to
California.

Santa Cruz.

The vampire capital.

Jamilla was in trouble out there. I could feel it in my blood.

Chapter Eighty-Four

On the long flight out to California, I realized that I hadn't been tormented by the Mastermind in two days. That was unusual, and I wondered if he was traveling too. *Que pasa, Mastermind? Maybe he was on the plane to San Francisco with me?* I remembered a tired old joke about paranoia. A man tells his psychiatrist that everybody hates him. The psychiatrist says he's being ridiculous – everybody hasn't met him yet.

It got worse. At one point, I actually took a walk down the aisle and checked out the other passengers. No one looked even vaguely familiar. No Mastermind on board. No one seemed to be wearing fangs, either. I was losing it.

I arrived at San Francisco International Airport and was met by agents from the FBI. They told me that Kyle was on his way from New Orleans. Lately, Kyle had been pressuring me more than ever about making the switch to the FBI.

The change certainly made financial sense. Agents earned a lot more than detectives. The hours were usually better, too. Maybe I would talk to Nana and the kids after this was over. Hopefully soon, but why should I think that?

I left the airport with three agents in a dark blue off-road vehicle. I sat in back with the senior agent from San Francisco. His name was Robert Hatfield and he told me some of what they had so far. 'We found where some of the so-called vampires are staying. It's a ranch in the foothills south of Santa Cruz, not too far from the ocean. At this juncture, we don't know if Inspector Hughes is being held there. She hasn't been spotted.'

'What's out there in the hills?' I asked Hatfield. He could have been anywhere between thirty-five and fifty. He looked fit. His hair in a short brush cut. Appearances obviously meant a lot to him.

'Not a hell of a lot. It's rural. A couple of fairly large ranches. Rocks, desert birds of prey, a few mountain cats.'

'Not tigers?' I asked.

'Funny you should mention tigers. The ranch out there used to be a preserve for wild animals. Bears, wolves, tigers, even an elephant or two. The owners trained animals, mostly for use in feature films and commercials. They were basically hippies left over from the Sixties. The ranch was actually licensed by the Department of the Interior. It did business with Tippi Hedren, Siegfried and Roy.'

'The animals aren't still on the property?'

'Not for the past four or five years. The original owners disappeared. No one's been interested in buying the land. It's about fifty-five acres. Not good for much. You'll see.'

'What about the animals that were there? You know what happened to them?'

'Some were bought by other preserves that supply specialty animals to movies. Brigitte Bardot supposedly took some. So did the San Diego Zoo.'

I sat back in my seat and thought everything through while we drove. I didn't want to get my hopes up again. I wondered if the past owners of the ranch might have left a tiger behind. I spun a wild scenario out in my head. Actually, it was kind of interesting. Vampires in Africa and Asia supposedly changed shape into big cats rather than bats or wolves. The tiger imagery was certainly scarier than bats, and so were the ravaged bodies I had seen. Also, Santa Cruz had a reputation to uphold: the vampire capital.

We passed a farmhouse along the highway and then a small winery. Not much else to see, though. Agent Hatfield told me that in summer the hills turned brown and gold, much like the African veldt. This time of year there was lots of rain, and the terrain was a rich green, reminiscent of parts of Ireland.

I had been trying not to think about Jamilla and the

danger she might be in. *Why did she have to come up here alone? What drove her? The same things that drove me? If she was dead, I would never forgive myself.*

The car finally pulled off the main road. I didn't see a house or other building in any direction that I looked. Just barren, bright green hills. A hawk floated easily in liquid-blue skies. The scene was quiet and serene and quite beautiful.

We turned down an unpaved road and went for about a mile over bumpy, rocky terrain. We passed over the grille of a cowcatcher. A broken, split-rail fence ran alongside the road for about a hundred yards, stopped, then started again.

Suddenly, we came upon six vehicles parked on either side of the trail. All were unmarked, mostly Jeeps.

Standing right there was Kyle Craig. Kyle had his hands on his hips, and he was smiling as if he had the most amazing secret to tell me.

I suspected that he did.

Chapter Eighty-Five

'I think this is exactly what we've been working for,' Kyle said as I walked up to him. We shook hands, an old ritual that reflected on Kyle's formality. He looked calmer and more in control than he had during the past week. 'Let me show you something,' he said. 'Come.'

I followed him down along the split-rail fence until we came to a broken-down gate. He showed me a faded image. The body and head of a tiger had been branded into the gate. It was subtle, but this was it, it had to be. We had arrived at the tiger's lair.

'The group inside seems to be led by the Sire, the new and improved one, I assume. We haven't been able to establish an identity for the leader. Alex, the past Sire was the magician, Daniel Erickson. Two members of the group just returned from a trip. They were in New Orleans. Pieces are finally starting to fit.'

I looked at Kyle, shook my head. 'How did you find all of this out? When did you get here, Kyle?' *How much have you been keeping from me? And why?*

'Santa Cruz police contacted us and I came right out. We grabbed one of the "undead" when the little prick left the ranch this afternoon. He's a local high school dropout, wasn't as committed as some of the others. He told us what he knew.'

'Is the Sire in there now?'

'Supposedly. This kid has never actually seen the Sire. He's not part of the inner circle. The two males who traveled to New Orleans are in there, though. He heard they were the ones who killed Daniel and Charles. He said the two of them are total psychos.'

'Well, I believe that.' I looked down through the limbs of pine-cypress trees at the ranch. 'What about Jamilla Hughes?'

His eyes shifted. 'We found her car in town, Alex. But no sign of her. The kid we questioned didn't know about her either. He claimed there was a commotion at the ranch late last night. He was bunked in with some of the younger ghouls. They thought that someone had broken the perimeter, thought it might be the police. But then it got quiet again, according to the boy. There's no evidence that she's there.'

'Can I talk to him, Kyle?'

Kyle looked away; he didn't seem to want to answer me. 'The Santa Cruz police took him away. I guess you could go into town to see him. I talked to him, Alex. The androgynous little twerp was scared of me. Imagine that.'

Kyle was acting strange, but I reminded myself that he understood the deranged criminal mind better than any other FBI agent or police officer I had worked with. The agents who worked under him were convinced that he would run the Bureau one day. I wondered if Kyle could ever take himself out of the field, though.

'Inspector Hughes may be there. I guess we could go in right now, but I think we should wait. I want to go at them tonight, Alex. Or possibly at sun-up. I don't think she's down there.'

Kyle paused. His eyes shifted toward the distant ranch house. 'I want to find out if they hunt as a group. There are questions we need answered. What motivates these freaks? What makes them tick? I want to make sure we get the Sire this time.'

Chapter Eighty-Six

It was a long, cool, very tense night in the foothills outside Santa Cruz. I couldn't wait for it to be over, or maybe I couldn't wait for it to start. We learned something interesting right away. The woman lawyer who had been murdered in Mill Valley had been involved in a lawsuit trying to get control of this property. It was probably why she and her husband had been hung.

I watched the ranch through binoculars from the surrounding trees and rock formations. I watched until my eyes ached. No one had left as of eleven. I didn't see anyone standing lookout either. The people inside were either crazy or supremely confident. Or maybe they were innocent. Maybe this was another wrong turn.

I was trying not to worry too much about Jamilla, but it wasn't working. I couldn't bear to think that she might already be dead. Was that what Kyle thought? Was that what he was keeping from me?

At midnight, two males walked outside leading a tiger. I watched them through the night-sight glasses. I was almost certain I had seen them in New Orleans. They'd been at the Fetish Ball, hadn't they? They loped off into the flat, open fields behind the house.

One of the men got down on all fours, then rolled around in the tall grass with the cat. Jesus Christ, they were playing! How incredibly weird. I remembered that the tiger had been called off its prey in Golden Gate Park.

About twenty minutes later, the men brought the cat to a pen behind the main compound. They hugged the six-hundred-pound tiger as if it was a large dog. The lights in the main building and the bunkhouse burned brightly until past two. Loud rock-and-roll played. Then the lights were dimmed.

No one had left the house to hunt.

We still didn't know if Jamilla was inside, or even if she was alive. I stayed awake and watched. I couldn't sleep, not even for an hour or so. The FBI continued to collect information on the people inside the domain. What in God's name were they doing down there?

There was no word on the identity of the Sire. We did learn about the two blond males with the ponytails. William and Michael Alexander were the sons of a post-hippie couple who had worked at the ranch as

animal handlers. The mother had been a zoologist. The
boys had grown up comfortable around wild animals.
They attended schools in Santa Cruz until they were ten
and twelve, at which time the boys began to be home-
schooled. They wore Moroccan robes and were always
barefoot on their occasional trips to town. They were
considered bright, but odd and extremely secretive. The
boys had gotten into trouble in their early teens and been
sent off to a state correctional facility for aggravated
assault. They had been dealing drugs and had been
caught breaking and entering.

Kyle joined me in the rocks overlooking the ranch at
around three.

'You look kind of gray around the gills,' I said to him.

'Thanks. Long night. Long month. You're worried about
Inspector Hughes, aren't you?' he asked me. He seemed
like a detached observer now. Calm and cool. It was pure
Kyle. Calculated intelligence. 'I don't know anything more,
Alex. I've told you what I know.'

'I can still see the body of Betsey Cavalierre. I don't want
to see something like that again. Yes, I'm worried about
her. Aren't you? What are you feeling, Kyle?'

'If she's alive down there, they have no reason to murder
her now. They're keeping her there for a reason.'

If she's alive.

Kyle patted my shoulder. 'Get some sleep if you can,' he

said. 'Rest up.' Then he wandered off. But when I looked his way, he was watching me.

I leaned against an oak tree and covered myself with my sports coat. I must have fallen asleep at some point between three and three-thirty. I saw Betsey Cavalierre in my dream, then my partner and friend Patsy Hampton. Finally, I saw Jamilla. *Oh Christ, not Jam. I couldn't stand that.*

I was aware of someone nearby, standing right over me. I opened my eyes.

It was Kyle. 'Time to go in,' he said. 'Time to get some answers.'

Chapter Eighty-Seven

The ranch was four to five hundred yards away. The terrain in between was too open for us to sneak up on the complex. Was this where Jamilla had been murdered?

Kyle whispered, 'She might still be alive.' It was as if he was reading my thoughts. What else did he know? What was he hiding from me?

'I've been thinking about the brothers. They never had to be careful before, so they weren't. The magicians were the careful ones. They committed murders for almost a dozen years. Never got caught. There's no record that they were even suspected of any of the murders.'

'You think the new Sire set up Daniel and Charles?'

'That's part of it, I'll bet. The brothers committed murders in towns where the magicians toured. The Sire wanted us to catch up with Daniel and Charles. It was a trap.'

'Why kill them in New Orleans?'

'Maybe because the brothers are psychopaths. Maybe they had orders to do what they did. We'll have to ask the Sire.'

'They don't think anyone can stop them. Well, they're wrong about that,' Kyle said. 'They're going to be stopped.'

Which was when we got a surprise. The front door of the ranch house opened. Several men in dark clothes hurried outside. The two brothers weren't among them. The men hurried to a grassy area where pickup trucks and vans were parked in a ragged line. They started the vehicles, then drove them toward the front of the house.

Kyle was on his Handie-Talkie. He alerted the snipers waiting in the trees and rocks behind us. 'Stand ready.'

'Kyle, don't forget Jamilla.'

He didn't answer me.

The front door opened again. Shadowy figures began to move out of the house. They were clothed in hooded black gowns and they came in pairs.

One person in each pair held a handgun to the head of the other.

'Oh shit,' I whispered. 'They know we're here.'

There was no way to tell who anybody was, or if any of the robed figures were actually hostages. I tried to pick out Jamilla's shape, her walk. Was she among them? Was she alive? My heart felt heavy in my chest. I couldn't spot her from way up here.

'Everybody move. *Now!*' Kyle spoke into his radio. 'Go. *Go!*'

The black-robed figures continued to move toward the waiting trucks and vans.

One of the hostages suddenly dropped to the ground – only one.

'That's her,' I called out.

'Take out the one over her!' Kyle ordered.

A shot rang out from one of the snipers. A hooded figure slumped over in a heap. Blood was spattered all over his hood.

We charged forward, running down the steep hill toward the ranch. Some of the hooded figures fired shots at us. No one was hit. The FBI agents didn't return fire.

Then gunfire rang out from the hills. Some of the robed figures dropped to the ground, dead or wounded. A few put their hands above their heads in surrender.

I kept my eyes fixed on one robed figure. She was up again, stumbling, almost falling. The hood was pulled back and I could clearly tell it was Jamilla. She stared up into the hills. She put her hands up high.

I started to sprint. I was looking for the brothers. And the Sire.

I moved toward Jamilla. She was massaging her wrist.

She was also shivering and I gave her my jacket. 'You okay?'

'Not sure. They hung me from a beam, Alex. What an unbelievable scene. You can't imagine. I thought I was dead.' There were tears in her eyes.

'Where's the Sire?' I asked.

'Maybe still inside. I think there's another way out of there.'

'Stay right here. I'll take a look.'

She shook her head. 'No, not on your life. This is payback. I'm coming with you.'

Chapter Eighty-Eight

Jamilla and I searched the main ranch house, then we checked a large, unattached bunkhouse. We didn't find anyone there, not a straggler, not William or Michael Alexander. And not the mysterious Sire. Jamilla was still shivering some, but she refused to turn back.

'You're sure the brothers aren't out front with the others?' she asked. 'Two blonds? Ponytails?'

'If they are, Kyle has them by now. I don't think so. Let's check the smaller shack. You know what's in there?'

She shook her head. 'I didn't get the grand tour when I arrived. Just straight to the dungeon. Then they left me hanging, so to speak.'

I threw open the door of the shack and saw heaters and a water pump. The room smelled strongly of urine. A mouse scooted into a hole in the wall. I winced and shook my head at what I saw next. Three bodies lay sprawled and spread-eagled against the far wall. They were teenagers. Two were males, both naked except for a few face and chest rings.

I bent over them and took a closer look. 'Seem like street kids to me. The blood's been drained from the bodies.' There were bite marks – not just on the necks, but on the faces and limbs. The skin of both males was as pale as alabaster.

The third body was female – a teenager of about fifteen. She matched the description of the girl who had gone missing in New Orleans. I felt deeply saddened to have found her here.

I looked away from the clouded eyes that stared up at me. There was nothing we could do for them now. I noticed a reddish-brown hatch cover among the dusty machines that provided water, heat, and probably air-conditioning to the ranch.

I moved across the room, bent down low to get a better look. The cover was loose, so I was able to pull it off.

Darkness. Silence. What else was down there? *Who else?*

I looked at Jamilla, then I shined a flashlight into the hole. It was wide enough for someone to get down inside. I saw metal stairs. A tunnel.

Then I saw footprints in the dirt below. Several pairs.

'Go, tell Kyle,' I turned to her. 'Get some help.'

Jamilla was already heading out the door. She started to run. I stared down into the abyss and wondered if anybody was looking back at me.

Chapter Eighty-Nine

I waited as long as I could, then lowered myself slowly into the black hole. I fitted easily, and started to climb down the sturdy metal ladder.

There were several steps, steep and precarious. I swept the flashlight around. I could make out a dirt floor, corrugated tin walls. The ceiling bulbs had been broken. A narrow tunnel stretched out before me.

I didn't hear any sounds up ahead, so I began to make my way down the tunnel. I moved slowly and carefully. I had the flashlight in one hand, my Glock in the other. I kept looking back for Kyle and Jamilla. Where were they?

I saw a discarded carcass a short way down the tunnel. I took a breath, shined my light on it.

A single eye stared back.

What I was looking at had been a small deer. Only the head and shoulders remained. I remembered reading that tigers eat their prey starting at the rump. They consume bone and all. There were more smudged footprints in the dirt. It looked like two pairs, but I couldn't tell for sure in the dim light. There were smaller animal tracks that might be the cat's. *Oh, Jesus.*

I kept moving, trying to adjust my eyes to the semi-darkness. There were shards of glass all over the dirt. Someone had purposely smashed the overhead light bulbs.

I heard a roar, and almost dropped the flashlight. It wasn't the smoothest move of my life, but I'd never been in a closed-off area with a tiger before. The big cat's roar echoed off the tin walls of the tunnel. It was unexpected and terrifying. I didn't know what to do next.

The cat roared a second time and I found that I couldn't move. I felt nailed to the spot. I wanted to turn around and go back, but that wasn't an option right now. I couldn't outrun a tiger in this tunnel, or anywhere else for that matter.

Somewhere in the inky blackness up ahead, the cat was watching me. I debated shutting off the flashlight, but kept it on for now. At least I would see the cat coming. I concentrated, stared out into the darkness, kept very still, as if that would help me. I had the Glock pointed straight ahead. I wondered if I could bring down a big cat with a handgun, even a powerful one. No way of knowing; no practice range for this kind of shooting. I had my doubts, though.

I couldn't see the cat, but I could almost visualize the thirty-odd teeth in its mouth. I remembered the wounds a cat had made on the two bodies in Golden Gate Park.

Someone called out. Someone was there, behind me.

'Alex, where are you? Alex?'

I heard Jamilla coming up the tunnel and I let out a breath.

'Don't move,' I whispered. 'Don't do anything. The tiger's in here.'

I didn't dare move. I wasn't even sure if I could. It was a standoff. I couldn't imagine the tiger being as frightened as I was. Was the Sire there too? The two brothers? Anybody else?

'Alex?'

It was Kyle. He was whispering. But if *I* heard him—

'Stay right there, Kyle. I mean it. Listen to me. Stay where you are unless you want me dead.'

Everything happened in a terrifying instant.

Suddenly, the cat rushed at me. Full speed? Half speed? Very goddamn fast. Shadows, a blur of fur.

It seemed to leap straight up into the cone of light shining from my flashlight. The cat was tensed muscle, raw speed, gleaming teeth, and the widest, brightest eyes – tremendous focus. It was aimed at me as surely as a deadly bullet.

Its upper body twisted athletically, showing off incredible strength. It seemed to be three to four feet off the ground, coming straight at me, unstoppable.

I had no options, and no room for error. I didn't even have to think about my next move. It just happened. I squeezed the trigger of my Glock. I fired off three quick shots. All head and upper body shots, I hoped, but I was just guessing.

The cat kept coming at me. It didn't even slow down. The gunshots couldn't stop it. I had no defense and no place to run, no place to hide.

The big cat hit me hard, brought me down like a weak prey. I waited for the powerful jaws to clamp down on me, to crush my bones. I might have screamed. I don't know what the hell I did. I'd never been more afraid. Not even close.

The cat kept going past me! It made no sense. I didn't understand. A few feet up the tunnel, I heard a loud thud. It was down. I had shot and killed a tiger.

Chapter Ninety

'Holy shit! Holy shit!' Jamilla said. The words exploded out of her mouth. Then she smiled. 'Jesus. I don't believe it.' She stared down at the huge, fierce animal that had tried to kill me, and was now laying at her feet.

I pushed myself up, forced my legs to move. I took tenuous steps back to where she and Kyle were standing. The cat lay twisted across the width of the tunnel. It didn't move, and it wasn't going to.

'Are they down here in the tunnel? The Lost Boys?' Kyle asked in a whisper. 'The Sire?'

'I haven't seen anybody. Just footprints, and the cat. Let's go,' I finally said.

The tunnel was much longer than I would have thought. I wasn't even sure which direction we were headed. Toward the road? The foothills? The Pacific Ocean?

'I sent men toward the perimeters of the property, about five or six hundred yards out. It spreads us thin,' Kyle said. 'I don't like it.'

I didn't answer him. I was still shaky, not quite over my moment of truth with the tiger. My heart was pumping like an engine pushed to its limit. I wondered if I might be going into shock.

'Alex?' Jamilla spoke. 'You with us? You okay?'

'Just give me a minute. I'll be fine. Let's keep going.'

Soon we could see the faintest glimmer of light up ahead. That was hopeful. But where were we coming out of the tunnel?

'Can't tell how far it is,' I said. 'Or what's between us and the light.'

My hip brushed against something. Then my shoulder. I jumped back and my whole body shuddered. But it was only a valve sticking out from the tunnel wall. Nothing. Scared the hell out of me, though.

Then I could see part of the landscape outside – a couple of cypress pines leaning away from the wind, a streak of early morning sky.

It wasn't far, maybe thirty or forty yards. Usually, the most dangerous part of a raid was breaking in; now it was getting out of this dark tunnel.

I shined the flashlight to my face, put a finger to my lips. I pointed to my chest with the same finger. *I would go first.*

I knew I was better with a gun than Kyle, and I was physically stronger than Jamilla – at least I thought so. Besides, this was the way it had been the past few years: Gary Soneji, Casanova, Geoffrey Shafer, now the Alexander brothers and their Sire. *I keep going in first. How long am I going to keep it up? Why am I doing this?*

'Don't forget, they're human,' Jamilla said. 'They bleed too.'

I wanted to believe she was right. I moved forward quietly, quickly. I hesitated at the mouth of the tunnel. Took a breath. *One, Mississippi, two . . . then out into the big, bad world.*

I don't know why, but I yelled at the top of my voice as I burst out into the pale light. No words, just a loud scream! Actually, maybe I did know why – I was afraid of these two killers, of their merciless cult, of the Sire. Maybe they bled, but they weren't human. Not like the rest of us.

I was in a pocket chasm surrounded by low-lying hills. I saw no one out there. No sign that anyone had been here recently. They had to have come this way, though. The tiger must have been in the tunnel with somebody.

Jamilla and Kyle came out of the tunnel behind me. The looks on their faces showed their disappointment, their fatigue and confusion.

I heard it before I saw anything.

A black pickup truck came roaring around the side of

one of the hills. It was headed straight for me and I had a choice: dive back into the tunnel, or hold my ground in the face of the blond killers. They were inside the truck. I could see both of them.

I held my ground.

Chapter Ninety-One

The twisted faces of the killers glared through the curved windshield of the truck. I raised my gun, held it steady as I could. Jamilla and Kyle did the same. The black Ford truck kept coming fast, almost as if they were daring us to shoot.

So we fired. The windshield splintered. Bullets pinged off the roof and hood. The roar of the guns was deafening in my ears. The acrid smell of cordite filled my nostrils.

Suddenly, the truck stopped, then shot into reverse. I kept shooting, trying to hit the driver as the target distanced itself, the vehicle backing away, veering left then right then left. I took off, running up the hill, my legs leery, as if my shoes held lead weights.

I couldn't let them get away. We'd come too far, gotten too close. These two would kill again, and again. They were madmen, monsters, and so was whoever had sent them on their mission.

Jamilla and Kyle were climbing up the steep, grassy terrain a few steps behind me. The three of us seemed to be moving in slow motion. The pickup truck was weaving wildly, its rear end fishtailing. I was hoping, praying that it would flip as it climbed in reverse up the steep side of the hill. I heard the grinding of gears and suddenly the truck flew *forward*. It was coming at us again, picking up speed.

I went down on one knee, aimed carefully, and put three shots into the windshield. The glass was blown away.

'Alex, get out of the way!' Jamilla shouted. 'Alex, move it! Now! *Alex!*'

The pickup kept coming. I didn't move away. I put a shot right where I figured the driver had to be. Then another. Then the final shot in my clip.

The big black truck was almost on top of me. I thought that I could feel heat from the engine. My face and neck were in a sweat. I had the irrational thought that a vampire can only be killed by a stake, fire, or by destroying its domain.

I didn't believe in vampires.

I believed in evil, though. I had seen it enough times to believe. The two brothers were twisted murderers. That's all they were.

I jumped sideways just before the pickup would have

run me down. I rushed down the hillside behind the truck. I was hoping it would flip – and then it did! I felt like shouting.

The truck bounced heavily on its side, then on its roof – then continued to roll over several times. Finally it stopped, resting on its passenger side, teetering slightly. Black smoke coiled up from the engine. No one got out at first.

Then the younger brother climbed out of one door. His face was streaked with blood and soot. He didn't speak, just glared at us, and then he roared like an animal. It seemed as if he had gone insane.

'Don't make us shoot you!' I shouted at him as I quickly reloaded.

He didn't seem to hear. He was in a blind rage. Michael Alexander wore long, sharp canine fangs, and they were bloody. His own blood? His eyes were red. 'You shot William! You killed my brother!' he shrieked at us. 'You murdered him. He was better than all of you!'

Then he charged – and I couldn't bring myself to shoot. Michael Alexander was insane; he wasn't responsible anymore. He kept growling, frothing at the mouth. His eyes were wild, rolling in their sockets. Every muscle on his body was tightly flexed. I couldn't kill this tortured man-child. I braced myself to tackle him. I hoped I could bring him down.

Then Kyle fired – once.

The shot struck him where his nose had been just an instant before. A dark, bloody hole appeared at the center of his face. There was no surprise or shock, just sudden obliteration. Then he crumpled to the ground. There was no doubt he was dead.

I had been wrong about Kyle – he could shoot. He was an expert, full of surprises. I needed to think about that, but not right now.

Suddenly, I heard another voice. It was coming from inside the pickup. Someone was trapped. William? Was the brother alive?

I approached the overturned vehicle slowly, gun in hand. The engine was still smoking. I was afraid the truck might blow.

I climbed onto the teetering wreck and managed to pull open a bent, badly damaged door. I saw William – shot to death, his face a sorry, bloody mask.

Then I found myself staring into the angriest, most arrogant eyes. I recognized them immediately. It was almost impossible to shock me anymore, but this was another jolt. 'So you're the one,' I said.

'You killed them, and you will be killed,' a voice threatened. 'You'll die. You *will* die, Cross!'

I was looking at Peter Westin, the vampire expert I'd met weeks before in Santa Barbara. He was cut-up, injured and bleeding. But he was in total control, even with my gun aimed at his face. He was cool and superior, so confident. I remembered sitting across from him at the Davidson Library up in Santa Barbara. He had told me he was a *real* vampire. I guess I believed him now.

I finally found the right words. 'You're the Sire.'

Chapter Ninety-Two

I tried a couple of sessions with the creepy and surreal Peter Westin that night in the jail at Santa Cruz. Kyle was attempting to get him transferred to the East Coast but I doubted he would be successful. California wanted him. Westin wore a long-sleeved black velvet shirt and black leather pants. He was as pale as paper. Thin blue veins were visible under the translucent skin of his temples. His lips were full and the pigment appeared redder than most people's. The Sire almost didn't seem human, and I was pretty sure that was the effect he wanted to convey.

It was emotionally disturbing and draining to be in the same room with him. Jamilla and I had talked about it briefly, and we both felt the same thing. Westin had none of the usual qualities that we associated with humans: conscience, sociability, deep emotion, sympathy and empathy. His entire persona was that of the Sire. He was a killer, a ghoul, a real life bloodsucker.

'I'm not going to try and scare you with interrogation room threats,' I said, low-key.

Westin appeared not to be listening. Bored? Indifferent? Smart as hell? Actually, as the Sire, he was an extraordinary person to encounter: haughty, superior, intense, physically striking. He had the most piercing eyes. He'd put on an act for me in Santa Barbara – the harmless scholar recommending books about vampires.

He cocked his head and stared intently into my eyes. He was looking for something; I couldn't tell what. I held his gaze and that seemed to irritate him. 'Fuck off,' he hissed.

'What is it?' I finally asked. 'What's on your mind, Peter? Is it that I'm not worthy to question you now?'

He smiled – and there was even a hint of warmth in it. He could be charming, I knew. I'd found that out in the library in Santa Barbara.

'*If* I talked to you, *if* I told you everything that I feel and believe, you wouldn't understand,' he said. 'You would be even more lost and confused than you are now.'

'Try me,' I said.

He smiled again, but said nothing.

'I know that you miss William and Michael. You don't show it, but you loved them,' I said. 'I know that much about you. I know you feel things deeply.'

Peter Westin nodded, almost imperceptibly. The gesture was regal. He did miss William and Michael. I was right about that. He was sad that they were dead.

Finally, he spoke again. 'Yes, Detective Cross, I *feel* more deeply than you can begin to imagine. You have no idea. You have no clue how someone like me thinks.'

Then he was quiet again. The Sire had nothing more to say. We mere mortals just wouldn't understand. I left him like that.

It was over.

Part Five

Violets Are Blue

Chapter Ninety-Three

I was feeling partially relieved, better anyway. The murder case seemed to be solved at least. Peter Westin was in jail. We'd done everything we could about his cult. The pressure had been eliminated. We'd stopped the bleeding.

Jamilla had left the previous night; we promised to keep in touch and I knew we would. I was headed out to the airport that morning to catch a flight to San Francisco, and then another to DC. I was going home and that felt good.

The details were still coming in, but I feared we would never know everything about the strange, murderous cult that had sprung up in California. It was usually that way in Homicide. You never knew as much as you wanted to. That's the basic truth about being a detective, and you never see it on TV or in the movies. I guess the endings wouldn't be as satisfying if they were closer to reality.

Peter Westin had met Daniel and Charles when they had

played in Los Angeles. Westin already had his own followers in Santa Cruz and Santa Barbara, but he feigned
allegiance until he felt he was strong enough to be the
Sire. Then he dispatched William and Michael Alexander to
do his dirty work. Supposedly there were followers in
nearly a hundred cities, especially now that the Internet
had brought us all so close together.

Something was still bothering me. I couldn't figure out
exactly what it was, but it troubled me all the way to San
Francisco. It was eating me from the inside out. Fear and
dread. But about what?

There was a forty-five-minute layover, and I got off the
plane. A jumble of bad thoughts played through my brain.
I felt wired, itchy.

*The original San Francisco vampire murders were still on my
mind.*

And the fucking Mastermind.

*Jamilla was here in San Francisco. But that was a whole
other subject.*

What was bothering me?

Then I thought I knew what it was. Maybe I'd known all
along. I called Jam at her office in the Hall of Justice. I was
informed that she had the day off.

I called her apartment, but there was no answer. Maybe
she was out on one of the five-mile runs she bragged
about. Or maybe she had a date with Tim Bradley from *The*

Examiner, as if that was any of my business.

But maybe not.

Where was she?

Had something happened to her, or was I just being paranoid beyond belief? I was definitely working too hard. I didn't need this. I really didn't need this.

I couldn't take the chance. I hurried to the American Airlines counter and canceled my flight out of San Francisco. I called Nana and told her I had to stay in California for a few hours. I would be in later tonight.

'Someone out here might be in trouble,' I said.

'Yes, and that someone is you,' Nana said. 'Goodbye, Alex.' She hung up on me again. She was right to want me home; but I was right in not wanting anybody else to be hurt.

I rented a car from Budget, and I was beginning to feel that I was completely losing it. Charles Manson's words came to mind: *Total paranoia is just total awareness.* I had always thought that Manson was wrong about everything, but maybe he wasn't; maybe he was dead-on right about paranoia.

I had a powerful gut feeling that Jamilla Hughes was in danger right now. I couldn't shake it off. Couldn't ignore it, even if I wanted to. The vibrations in my head were too strong, overwhelming. It was one of my famous feelings, and I had to go with it.

I thought about my former partner, Patsy Hampton – *and her murder*.

I remembered Betsey Cavalierre – *and her murder*.

And Detective Maureen Cooke in New Orleans.

A long time ago as a homicide detective, I had just about stopped believing in coincidences. Still, I had no logical reason to believe that a psychopathic killer could be out here in California, possibly stalking Inspector Jamilla Hughes.

I just felt it.

Total awareness.

The Mastermind was out here. It was the sense I had. I waited for his call. I was ready to nail him once and for all. I was so ready.

Chapter Ninety-Four

I drove from the airport to Jamilla's apartment at several
miles above the posted speed limit. On the way, I used
my cell phone. There was still no answer at her place. I was
already in a cold sweat. I had never followed a hunch quite
like this one.

I thought about what I could do right now. One possibility was to call in help from the SFPD, but I didn't like it.
Police officers are logical creatures, and coldly suspicious of
gut feelings. My track record with psychopaths might buy
me some credibility in Washington, but not out here in
California.

I could call the FBI – but I chose not to. There were a
couple of reasons why. More gut feelings that I wanted to
keep to myself for a while longer.

I decided to park a block over from Texas Street, where
Jamilla lived. But I took a ride up the steep Potrero Hill

first. I turned onto the street about half a dozen blocks south of her place, then I toured the connecting streets. There was a mixed style of row houses: the more charming wooden ones from the early 1900s, and the boxier three- and four-story ones with lots of aluminum detail. I could see the bay, the loading docks of Pier 84, and Oakland in the distance. I passed the New Potrero Market, J.J. Mac's, the North Star restaurant – Jamilla's home turf. But where was Jamilla?

The traffic was fairly heavy. I hoped my rented sedan wouldn't be spotted easily. And that I'd see Jamilla lugging groceries, or jogging home from a nearby park where she'd worked out.

But I didn't see her. Damn it, where was she? Not that she didn't have a right to a day off.

I couldn't imagine anything happening to her, but that was the way I had felt about Patsy Hampton, and then about Betsey Cavalierre.

Two dead partners in two years.

I didn't believe in coincidences.

Patsy Hampton had been murdered by a British diplo- mat named Shafer. I was almost certain of that. Betsey's murder remained unsolved, and that was the one that worried me. I kept thinking about the Mastermind. Some- how I had become a part of his story, his fantasy world. How? Why? I had received a late phone call from him one night that summer, just after I'd learned of Betsey's murder: *'I'm the one you call Mastermind. That's a name I can live with. I am that good.'*

The killer had used a knife on her, everywhere, even between Betsey's legs. He hated women. That was clear. I had encountered only one other killer who hated women so much: Casanova in North Carolina. But I was sure Casanova was dead and couldn't have killed Betsey Cavalierre. Still . . . I felt some kind of strange link to what had happened in North Carolina. What was the connection?

I found a spot and parked about two blocks from Jamilla Hughes's apartment on the hill near 18th. Her building was older, a remodeled yellow Victorian, with the familiar three-sided bay windows you often see in San Francisco. Very nice, very homey. There were neat little signs on the trees: *'Friends of the Urban Forest.'*

I called her again on the cell. Still no answer.

My heart was pumping fast. The cold sweat continued. I had to do something. I went to the front door of the house, rang the bell, but no one answered. *Damn it. Where was she?*

Safe Neighborhood signs were stuck in bright green patches of grass up and down the street. I hoped the street was very safe. I prayed to God that it was as safe as it looked.

I went back and waited in the car. Fidgeted. Grew even more nervous and impatient. I thought about who the Mastermind might be, then about Betsey's murder. I thought about Casanova, the Gentleman Caller, about Kate McTiernan, who'd been abducted in North Carolina. Why was *that* on my mind now? What was the connection? I couldn't get the lurid and devastating murder scenes out of my head.

Not Jamilla. Don't let this happen again. Don't let her get hurt.

While I sat there worrying, my phone rang. I answered immediately.

It was him. He was playing his cruel games. He seemed so close.

'Where are you, Doctor Cross? I thought you were heading home to kith and kin. Maybe it's time that you did. Your work is done out here. There's nothing more you can do. Nothing at all. We wouldn't want anything to happen to Nana Mama and the kids, would we? That would be the worst thing, wouldn't it? *The absolute worst.*'

Chapter Ninety-Five

I immediately called Nana in Washington. Either she wasn't there, or she was still mad at me and wasn't picking up the phone. *Damn it. Answer the phone, Nana.*

I frantically called again, but there was still no answer. *Pick up, pick up! Damn it – pick up the phone!*

Sweat had begun to coat my neck and forehead. This was my darkest nightmare, my worst fear come true. What could I do from out here?

I called Sampson and told him to rush over to my house, then get back to me immediately. He didn't question me for a second.

'I'm sending a squad car now. It will be there in minutes. I'll be right behind it. I'll get back to you, Alex,' he said.

I sat in the car and anxiously waited for Sampson's call. My head was spinning with all kinds of terrible thoughts and images. There was nothing I could do – not for Jamilla, if she was in trouble; not for my own family back in Washington.

I thought about the Mastermind and the way he'd operated in the past. There were always dramatic taunts and barbs – and then, when I least expected it, he would act; he would make a strike to the heart.

When I least expected it.

Action, not words.

Horrible murders.

He knew I hadn't returned to Washington; did he know for sure that I was in San Francisco?

I couldn't focus as much as I needed to. Was it possible that he was right here on Jamilla's street? Was the killer watching me now? He had shown that he was smart enough to follow me and not be seen. Did he want a showdown?

The cell phone rang again. My heart jumped in my chest. I fumbled with the buttons.

'Cross,' I said.

'Everybody's okay, Alex. I'm at the house with Nana and the kids. They're safe and sound. They're with me now.'

I shut my eyes and sighed with relief. 'Put her on,' I told Sampson. 'Don't take no for an answer from her. I need to talk to Nana about what we're going to do next.'

Chapter Ninety-Six

Sampson promised to stay with Nana and the kids until I could get home. There was no one that I trusted more, no one in the world they would be safer with. Still, I couldn't be sure, and that was a terrible weight to carry. I didn't feel I could leave California until I had at least located Jamilla, and knew she was safe.

Finally I called Tim Bradley at *The Examiner*. He didn't know where she was, or even that she'd taken a day off work. Maybe she had needed to get away from town – to get away from being a homicide detective.

I was beginning to feel that maybe I had made a mistake by stopping in San Francisco. The longer I sat on the street, outside her house, the more convinced I was of it. Maybe the job was finally getting to me. The instincts go first.

But every time I considered leaving, I remembered the

night I arrived at Betsey Cavalierre's house, seeing her dead body.

And instincts had gotten me here in my career.

Feelings, gut reactions, experiences from the past.

Maybe just plain stubbornness.

I stayed on surveillance, stayed at my post. I got out of the car a couple of times, walked up and down the block a little. Climbed back in the car. Waited some more. I felt more than a little ridiculous, but I wouldn't give in to it. I checked in with Sampson again. Everything was okay at home. Another homicide detective I knew, Jerome Thurman, had arrived at the house, too. Double duty against the Mastermind. Was that enough protection?

Then I saw Jamilla coming up the street in her Saab. I actually clapped my hands together. I smacked the dashboard with my palm. *Yes. Thank God she was safe. There she was!*

She parked about half a block from her house on Texas Street, got out, pulling a University of San Francisco gym bag behind her. I wanted to run up and hug her, but I stayed in my car. Her hair was up in a ponytail. She was wearing a dark blue tee and loose gray workout pants. She was all right; she hadn't been hurt. *Jamilla hadn't been murdered by the Mastermind.*

I stared through the car windshield, waiting to see if anyone was watching her, stalking her. Part of me wanted to leave well enough alone now, to go home to Washington. But I kept remembering what had happened to Betsey Cavalierre after we finished our case together.

Why then? Why my partner? I almost didn't want to go there.

I gave Jamilla time to get inside – then I called her on my cell.

'This is Jamilla Hughes. Your message is important to me. Please leave it at the beep.'

Damn it! I hated those machines.

'Jamilla, this is Alex Cross. Call me. It's important. Please—'

'Hi, Alex. Where are you? *How* are you?' I could hear the smile in her voice, and it sounded inappropriate because of the emotional state I was in.

'Please be careful.' I continued with what I was going to leave her as a message. I told her why I was concerned. Finally, I had to admit the worst: that I was on the street outside her apartment.

'Well, come inside for God's sake,' she said. There were no recriminations, not even any surprise in her voice. 'I think you're over-reacting. Maybe. Let's talk about it, though. Let's talk this thing through.'

'No, let me stay out here for a while. I hope you don't think I'm being too crazy. Whoever killed Betsey has been contacting me ever since her death. The Mastermind could be here in San Francisco. He killed her right after we finished our case. Detective Cooke was murdered after the magicians were killed in New Orleans.'

That gave her pause. 'Maybe I think you're a little crazy, Alex. But I understand why you would be. I see where you're going with this. I'm also touched that you came here to watch over me. And what happened to your last partner *does* scare me.'

It helped that I knew where Jam was, and that I had actually talked to her. After we spoke, I continued watching her street. I don't know how many times I had thought about Betsey Cavalierre's murder and wondered who the killer was, but I did it again as I sat in the car.

I stayed there for several hours. Jamilla and I talked a couple of times. She urged me to come up to her apartment. I said no. 'Let me do it my way, Jam.'

It was getting late, though, and I was beginning to fade. I saw the lights in her apartment go off. Good for her. At least one of us was acting sane.

I continued to wait. Something powerful, dramatic, haunting was nagging at me. Something I almost didn't want to face. The clues had been there, but I hadn't wanted to see them for what they were. I'd wanted to follow my 'famous instincts'. Look where it had gotten me. I had blown it for so long.

Then I saw him, and everything made sense. Suddenly the puzzle was clear; all the pieces fit. Not just Betsey's murder – the Casanova murder, the stalking of Kate McTiernan, the fact that he'd been able to keep a step ahead of me.

The killer was here on Jamilla's street.

The Mastermind was here in San Francisco.

I was sure, and it made me dizzy with fear. But also with incredible disappointment, sadness, confusion. I felt like I might throw up.

It was Kyle Craig. He was watching Jamilla's place, stalking her like the madman that he was. The goddamn *Mastermind* had come here to kill her.

How could I stop him?

Chapter Ninety-Seven

'Jamilla, are you awake?' I said in a low, tense voice. I felt a shudder run through me. It couldn't get any worse than this. I still had my eye on Kyle. He was definitely watching Jamilla's building. *Goddamn him to hell.*

'I am now. No, I was awake. Where are you, Alex? Don't tell me you're still outside? Please don't tell me that. Alex, what the hell is going on?'

'Listen to me. The Mastermind is outside your place. I can see him. I think he'll try to get inside soon. I want to come up there and I don't want him to see me. Is there a back way?'

Then I told her who the killer was.

She exploded with anger, most of it directed at Kyle. 'I knew there was something seriously wrong with him – but not this wrong. We have to stop that sonofabitch. I don't care how smart he's supposed to be.'

She told me where to look for a service entrance and then a fire escape that would take me to her floor. I hurried around in the shadows. I didn't think that Kyle had seen me. I hoped not. But then – he was the Mastermind.

He was smart, as clever as anyone I'd ever worked against.

He knew about surveillance, probably a lot more than I did.

He didn't make mistakes, at least not until now.

I found the back entrance of her building easily, and I hurried up the stairs. I tried not to make a sound. I had no way of knowing where Kyle was right now.

When I got to her apartment the door was open. My stomach dropped, and I felt sick. 'Jamilla?'

She immediately peeked out through the doorway. 'Come inside. I'm fine, Alex. We've got him now, not the other way around.'

I hurried inside the apartment, and we kept all the lights off. I could still see most of the living room and kitchen, the doorway to a small terrace. A bay window with bench seating. Her home. The place where he wanted to violate her. I snuck a look outside – I didn't see Kyle on the street. He was on the move.

Jamilla didn't look frightened, just perplexed, and angry. She had her service revolver out. She was ready for whatever might happen.

I don't think that I had fully taken in what had just happened. Everything felt unreal; my vision was tunneled. My nerves were shredded and raw. Kyle Craig had been my friend. We had worked a half-dozen cases together.

'*Why* is he outside, Alex?' Jamilla finally asked. 'Why is he coming after me? I don't understand that asshole. What did I do to him?'

I stared into her eyes, hesitated a second or two, then finally spoke. 'He's not really here to get you, at least I don't think so. It's about me – it's about Kyle and me. I've become part of his fantasy, the story he tells himself every day. He's proving how much better than me he is. He has to prove that he really is the Mastermind.'

Chapter Ninety-Eight

The Mastermind had already made his next move, though he knew it was only a half-step in the greater scheme of things. He had pulled back. He was six blocks away from Jamilla Hughes's apartment, standing on a San Francisco hill past the Jackson Playground. It allowed him to watch her building, the bay windows, the small terrace on one side.

He enjoyed this – the intractable imposition of his will, his ego on the world. It had been this way for more than a dozen years. No one had come close to capturing him, or even suspecting who he really was.

Cross was inside now, and that made everything either very hard or, perhaps, easier. There was another decision to be made soon. Should he risk everything at this point? Change everything? For years, he had been living a complicated double life. He'd done whatever he wanted, wherever, whenever. He had enjoyed his freedom, and how many others had even tasted that forbidden fruit? He had been the cop and the criminal. But maybe it was time for a change? Maybe his life had become too safe, too predictable. Kyle loved the hunt – and in that way he was like Casanova and the Gentleman Caller, two very talented killers he had known well, one working in North Carolina, the other in southern California. He found that he agreed with Casanova that men needed to be hunters by nature. And so he hunted – men and women – and found he enjoyed killing both sexes; but he went an important step farther.

He hunted their killers as well. He eliminated his competition. He beat them at their own game.

He had known Casanova years before the meticulous and very nasty killer was caught by himself and Dr Cross. He had played murder games with Casanova and with the Gentleman Caller. *Kiss the girls and make them cry.* Kyle had even fallen in love with one of the victims – young Kate McTiernan. He still had a soft spot for dear, sweet Kate. He had been so many things to so many people, played so many roles, and he had only just begun.

He had been the Mastermind – but he'd also helped capture the man believed to be the Mastermind. How could you beat that for puzzle-making and puzzle-solving.

He'd been an elusive killer in Baltimore; in Cincinnati; in

Roanoke, Virginia; in Philadelphia, until he tired of those cities and the minor roles he played in them. He was husband to Louise, father to Bradley and Virginia. He was on the fast track inside the FBI, with one significant problem: he believed they were finally on to him. He was sure of it – though God, they were such obvious, plodding fools.

So many exciting roles, so many poses that sometimes Kyle Craig wondered who he actually was.

Now the game with Alex Cross had to end. He'd felt the need to taunt and torture Cross, to prove he was the homicide detective's master. And then he had gone over the edge a little himself.

It happened when he killed Betsey Cavalierre, one of his own agents. Actually, the killing couldn't be helped. Cavalierre had become suspicious of him while she was chasing the Mastermind with Cross. She had to go, had to die.

And so did Cross. Cross was loyal to his friends, trusting, and it had become his greatest flaw, his singular weakness. But Cross would have caught on to him, even if he hadn't yet. And, of course, Cross's instincts had brought him here to watch over Inspector Hughes. Cross *needed* to be a good man, an ethical cop, a protector. What a waste of intellect. What a pity that Cross couldn't have been an even better adversary.

Alex had seen him on the street – so what came next? Whatever it was, it certainly had his adrenaline flowing. This was so good. Kyle knew he had a little time to figure it out. What to do? They were inside Hughes's apartment. He had the edge on them.

He wouldn't lose his edge, his advantage.

He made his next move.

Chapter Ninety-Nine

'**Y**ou know, I never liked him, Alex,' Jamilla said as we waited in the semidarkness of her apartment. 'He seemed so cold, almost mechanical to me. And I'm telling you, he doesn't like women. I felt it instantly.'

'Well, unfortunately, I did like Kyle. He's clever as hell. He even rigged calls from the Mastermind when he and I were together. Now I need to figure out who he really is. There's no psychosis involved, at least I don't think so. He's organized. He can obviously work out elaborate plans. For once, I wish he would call.'

'Be careful what you wish for,' Jamilla said.

She and I were sitting beside a shelving unit on the hardwood floor in her living room. There was also a workout bench; nothing too fancy, an older model. Five- and ten-pound free weights were scattered on the floor. So were magazines and sections of the *Chronicle*.

I hoped that Kyle couldn't see into the apartment, that he didn't have binoculars. Or possibly a nightscope attached to a rifle. I knew he could shoot from the way he'd taken down Michael Alexander. He was good at a lot of things.

Just in case, Jamilla and I tried to keep away from the windows.

'It makes me dizzy to think about what he's done so far. I wonder if we'll ever know the extent of it?' she asked.

'If we catch him, he'll want to talk. Kyle will want to show off what he's done. If he comes after us tonight, maybe we'll find everything out.'

'You think he knows you're here?'

I sighed, shrugged. 'Probably. Maybe tonight is his coming out party. I know one thing, he won't do what we expect. The Mastermind never does. That's the only real pattern he has.'

We talked about calling in reinforcements, but Jamilla thought it would probably scare Kyle off. He wanted the two of us, right? That's what he would get. *Do you want to taunt me any more, you bastard? Go for it. Bring it on, Kyle.*

So the two of us sat there in the dark, and it was almost cozy. Jamilla finally reached out and touched my hand. Then we moved together, leaned against one another. We waited.

'At least it's comfortable,' Jamilla whispered. 'As stakeouts go.'

'No place like home, right?'

It was a little before four when we heard noises above us. Jamilla turned and looked at me. We raised our guns.

For the first time, I confronted the idea of shooting Kyle, a man I had thought was my friend. I didn't like the feeling. I wasn't sure how I would react, and that scared me too.

There were soft footsteps outside on the terrace. In a way, I was relieved. This was the showdown Kyle wanted. He was coming. I figured that the story he'd been telling for so long, his fantasy life, had finally taken over. Maybe he was psychotic now. That would give us an advantage.

'Real careful,' I whispered, and touched the back of Jamilla's hand. 'Try to look at it the way he does. Kyle thinks he has us where he wants us.'

He picked the lock quickly and expertly. A minimum of effort. I realized that he had been watching her place. He knew enough to come up the back stairs, and then he'd climbed a metal ladder onto the terrace.

The lock made a soft *click*. Then nothing happened.

'We're good, everything's cool,' Jamilla whispered. 'This time, we win.'

We waited in the dark near the door. It finally opened, oh-so-slowly. Kyle came inside. He moved toward us in a low crouch. Obviously, he couldn't see where we were, but we could see him.

I hit Kyle with all my weight, full force, every ounce of strength that I had. I slammed him hard against the living-room wall. The whole apartment shook. Books and glasses fell to the floor from open shelves. I was surprised we didn't go right through the wall.

I clipped his chin with an elbow as hard as I could. Felt good. Kyle was wiry and strong, but I was pumped to take him. I hit him with a hard, short right hand. It snapped into his jaw. I hit him in the solar plexus. A real gut-wrencher.

I was going to hit him again. But then Jamilla flicked on the room lights. My brain caught fire. My body shuddered.

It wasn't Kyle Craig.

Chapter One Hundred

'Get down, get down! Get below the windows!' I yelled at Jamilla.

I was afraid she might be hit by rifle fire. Kyle could be out there, and I knew that he could shoot. She went down and lay facing me, and also the man I had tackled coming in the door. He looked as confused as I felt. *Who the hell was he? What had just happened? And where was Kyle?*

Jamilla had her service revolver pointed at his chest. Her hand was amazingly steady. His nose was bleeding badly from where I'd hit him. He was well-built, probably early thirties, short-haired, a light-skinned black man.

Everything was complete chaos in my brain.

'Who the hell are you? *Who are you?*' I yelled at the dazed, bleeding man on the floor.

'FBI,' he panted. 'I'm a Federal agent. Put down the gun. Put it down now.'

Jamilla was yelling too. 'I'm San Francisco PD, and I'm definitely not putting down my gun, mister. What are you doing in my apartment?' she shouted. I could almost see her mind working and she wasn't thinking nice thoughts. 'Talk to us!'

He shook his head. 'I don't have to answer your questions. Wallet's in the rear left pocket. Badge and ID. I'm FBI, goddamnit!'

'Stay down,' I yelled. 'There could be someone outside with a gun. Did Kyle Craig send you here?' I asked.

The look on the agent's face answered the question for me, but he refused to confirm or deny. 'I told you, I don't have to answer questions.'

'You sure as hell do.' Jamilla got in the last word.

I did the only thing I could under the circumstances – *I called the FBI.*

Four agents from the San Francisco office got to the apartment at a little past five in the morning. We were wary of the windows, though I doubted that Kyle was still nearby. Or even in San Francisco. The Mastermind was a step ahead. I should have known, and in a way I *had* known that he wouldn't do the expected.

During the next couple of hours, exasperated agents from the Bureau tried to reach Kyle Craig. They couldn't and it shook them up. They began to give some credence to my story that Kyle might be the man behind murders going back several years. Kyle had sent the agent to Jamilla's apartment and ordered him to break in. He'd told the agent that someone had murdered an SFPD Inspector and Alex Cross inside.

Then things started to get really hot.

I was the one who heated them up.

Chapter One Hundred and One

A t seven-thirty in the morning I was on the receiving end of a phone call from FBI director Ronald Burns in Washington. Burns was cautious and wary, but I knew he wouldn't call me himself unless he had evidence that there were serious problems with Kyle. I was still confused, and hurt, but I recognized the emotions as appropriate and sane. Kyle Craig was the madman, not me.

'Tell me whatever you know, Director,' I said. 'I know a lot about Kyle, but you know things that I don't. Tell me what they are. It's important that I know everything.'

Burns didn't answer right away. There was a long pause at his end of the line. I knew him well enough to know that he was a friend of Kyle's. At least he thought he had been. We'd all been wrong for so long. We'd been fooled, and betrayed by someone we had trusted.

Finally, Burns began to speak. 'We have been getting

worried about Kyle recently. This could go back to the days of the "Kiss the Girls" case. Maybe even before it. We know his files suggest he had a troubled adolescence, but when he joined the FBI, his psychological profile showed he had got through all that. You know that Kyle was an undergrad at Duke University. It's now become apparent that he knew Will Rudolph – the Gentleman Caller – from his student days at Duke. During the case, Kyle may have been responsible for the death of a reporter named Beth Lieberman with the *LA Times*. She was closing in on Will Rudolph.'

I shut my eyes and shook my head. I had helped solve the 'Kiss' case. I knew that Kyle had attended Duke, but not about his relationship with the Gentleman Caller, a killer who had terrorized LA.

'Why didn't you talk to me?' I asked Burns. I was trying to understand the FBI's position. So far, I couldn't.

'We didn't begin to really suspect Kyle until the murder of Betsey Cavalierre. We had no proof, even then. We weren't sure if he was a possible killer or the best agent in the Bureau.'

'Jesus, Ron, we could have talked. We should have talked. He's on the run now. You should have told me. I hope you're telling me everything now.'

'Alex, you know what we know. Maybe more. I hope you're telling *us* everything.'

After I finished with Burns, I called Sampson in Washington. I told him the latest and it blew John's mind. He had moved Nana and the kids out of our house on Fifth Street. Only he and I knew where they were now.

'Everything okay there?' I asked. 'Everybody settled in all right?'

'Are you fucking kidding, Alex? Nana is pissed off like I've never seen her before. If Kyle Craig came after her, I'd put my money on Nana. The kids are cool, though. They don't know what's happening, but they've guessed it isn't good.'

I cautioned him again. 'Don't leave them for a minute, not a second, John. I'm coming back to Washington on the next flight. I don't know how Kyle could trace you there, but don't under-estimate him. He's loose. He's very dangerous. For some reason, he wants to hurt me, and maybe my family. If I can figure out why that is, maybe I can stop him.'

'And if not?' Sampson asked.

I let the question hang.

Chapter One Hundred and Two

I had to say goodbye to Jamilla Hughes again, and each time it was a little harder. We'd been through so much together in such a short time. I made her promise to be extremely careful, even paranoid, for the next few days. She promised. Finally I got on another plane out of San Francisco International.

The mysterious phone calls had stopped, but that was scary and unsettling too. I didn't know where Kyle was, or what he was doing.

Was he still watching me? Had he somehow followed me back to Washington? I shouldn't be having thoughts like that, but I was, and I couldn't stop them from coming.

Did he have binoculars focused on me as I walked up the sidewalk to my Aunt Tia's house in Chapel Gate, Maryland, about fifteen miles from Baltimore? How could he know I was here? Why, because that's what he did for a living. Could he get past Sampson and me? I didn't think so. But how could I know with complete certainty?

The kids were enjoying their short vacation with Aunt Tia. She had always spoiled them, just as she had spoiled me as a kid. 'Same old, same old,' she liked to say when she served you a piece of hot pie in the middle of the afternoon, or gave you an unexpected present. Nana was more understanding than I thought she would be. I think she liked being with her 'little sister'. Tia was younger than Nana, 'only seventy-eight', but she was spry, very contemporary in her outlook, and she was a fabulous cook. That night, she and Nana made penne with gorgonzola cheese, broccoli rabe, and sock-it-to-me cake. I ate as if it were my last meal.

Then the kids and I played and talked until the outrageous hour of eleven o'clock, way past their usual bedtime. They are by no means perfect, but the good times with them certainly outweigh the bad. I tend to talk more about the good, and why not. I'm a father and I love Damon, Jannie and little Alex more than life itself. Maybe that says something, too.

I went back to Washington the following morning. A team of FBI agents had been assigned to my family. It was the kind of attention I'd hoped we would never need. Frankly, it scared the hell out of me.

That afternoon, I attended a meeting at the FBI building

and learned that more than four hundred agents were assigned to finding and capturing Kyle Craig. So far, nothing had gotten out to the press, and Director Burns wanted to keep it that way. So did I. More than that, I wanted to catch Kyle quickly, hopefully before he killed again.

But who would he kill? Who might Kyle go after next?

Chapter One Hundred and Three

'Christine, it's Alex,' I said. I had butterflies in my stomach. 'I hate to bother you like this. It's important or I wouldn't call.' That was sure the truth. God, I hadn't wanted to make this call.

'Is little Alex okay?' she asked. 'Is it Nana?'

'No, no. Everybody's fine.' I told a half-truth.

There was a brief, uncomfortable silence. Christine and I had been engaged to be married. She was the one who had broken it off, because she couldn't handle my life as a homicide detective. Too many bad scenes just like this one.

'Alex, this isn't good news, is it? Geoffrey Shafer? Is he back in the country?' she asked. She sounded afraid and I felt for her. Geoffrey Shafer had kidnapped her.

'No, this isn't about Shafer.'

I told her about Kyle Craig. She knew him, liked Kyle, and I could tell she felt violated. She had been hurt badly by the monsters I had met in my work. She couldn't completely forgive me for that, and I didn't blame her much. I couldn't forgive myself sometimes. Talking to Christine made me remember how much I'd loved her. Probably still did.

'Is there somewhere safe you can stay for a while? It's important that you go there,' I finally said. 'I hate to do this to you. Kyle is extremely dangerous, Christine.'

'Oh, Alex. I came out here to be safe. I felt I was safe, but now you're back in my life.'

She said she would stay with somebody she trusted, a friend. I asked Christine not to say who or where it was over the phone. When she hung up, she was crying. I felt so bad for her; so terrible about what had happened. The call brought back everything that was wrong between us.

I kept calling people I cared about. I talked to everyone I could think of who had had some contact with Kyle.

I called Jamilla next. My excuse was that I wanted to remind her to be careful – even now. But I think I just wanted to talk to her. She'd been in on so much of this. Unfortunately, she was out when I called. I left a message that I was worried about her, and to please be careful.

I warned a few detective friends – Rakeem Powell and Jerome Thurman – who were still on the DC force. I doubted Kyle would go after them, but I didn't know for sure.

I phoned my chief contact at the *Washington Post*, a writer named Zachary Scott Taylor. Zach was also one of my best friends in Washington. He wanted to interview me, but I told him not to come. Kyle was jealous of the stories Zach had written about me. He had told me as much. For whatever reason, he didn't like Zach.

'This is serious,' I told Zach. 'Don't under-estimate how crazy this man is. You're on his shit list, and that's a bad place to be.'

I spoke to FBI agents Scorse and Reilly who had worked with me on the kidnapping of Maggie Rose Dunne and Michael Goldberg. They knew about the manhunt for Kyle, but hadn't been concerned for their own safety. Now they were.

I called my niece, Naomi, who'd been kidnapped by Casanova. Naomi was practicing law in Jacksonville, Florida. She was living with a good guy named Seth Samuel Taylor. They were planning to marry later this year. 'He likes to ruin other people's happiness,' I told Naomi. 'Be careful. I know you will be.'

I called Kate McTiernan in North Carolina. I remembered the meal she'd had with Kyle and me. Did it mean anything more than what it seemed on the surface? Who knew with Kyle. Kate promised to be extra careful, and reminded me she was a third-degree black belt now. Kyle had always liked Kate, and *I* reminded her of that. Actually, the more I talked to Kate, the more worried I was about her. 'Don't take any chances, Kate. Kyle is the craziest person I've ever met.'

I contacted Sandy Greenberg, a good friend at Interpol who had worked with Kyle several times. She was shocked to learn that Kyle was a murderer. She promised to be extra careful until he was caught; she also offered to help in any way that she could.

Kyle Craig was a cold, heartless murderer.

My partner at times, my friend, or so I'd thought.

I still couldn't believe it. Not completely. I tried to make up a possible hit list for Kyle.

1. Myself
2. Nana and the kids
3. Sampson
4. Jamilla

I realized I was making the list from my point of view, and although Kyle seemed focused on me, his obsessions might extend even farther. I tried another list.

1. Kyle's family – every member
2. Myself – and my family
3. Director Burns of the FBI
4. Jamilla
5. Kate McTiernan

I sat in my empty house on Fifth Street and wondered what the hell he would do next. It was driving me crazy; I felt like I was running in circles.

Kyle was capable of anything.

Chapter One Hundred and Four

He finally called again.

'I killed them, and I don't feel a thing. Nothing at all. You will, though, Alex. In a way, you're to blame. Nobody but you. I didn't even want to kill them, but I had to do it. That's the way the horror story has to go. It's out of control now. I'll admit that.'

The horrifying confession came at quarter past five in the morning. I had been asleep about three hours when the phone rang. Panic raced through my body. My heart was pounding so hard I could hear it.

'Who did you kill?' I asked Kyle. 'Who? Tell me who it was. *Tell me*.'

'What difference does it make? They're dead, slaughtered. It's someone you care about. There's nothing you can do now – except catch me. I suppose I could help you. Isn't that what you want to hear? Would that make this more interesting for you? Would it make it *fair*?' He started to laugh uncontrollably. Christ, I had never seen him lose control.

I let him go on. Inflate his ego. That's what he wanted and needed, wasn't it?

Who had Kyle killed? Oh God, who was dead? It was more than one person – slaughtered.

'We always worked as a team. In a way, it would be my crowning moment, to catch myself. I've thought about it, actually. Fantasized. What better challenge could there be? I can't think of one. Me against myself.' He started to laugh again.

I had to force myself not to ask again who he had murdered. It would just make Kyle angry. He might hang up. Still, my mind was grinding. I was incredibly afraid. Christine? Kate? Jamilla?

Someone at the FBI? Who? Oh God, who was it? Jesus, have some mercy, have pity. Show me that you're human, you bastard.

'I'm not a highly trained psychologist like yourself, but here's one amateur's theory anyway,' Kyle said. 'I think this whole rage thing might be about sibling rivalry. Could it be? You know, Alex, I have a younger brother. He came along at the height of my Oedipus complex, when I was a mere lad of two. He displaced me with my mother and father. Check into it, Alex. Consult with Quantico. Could be important.'

He was so calm, and he was ridiculing me – as a detective and as a psychologist.

My hands were starting to shake. I'd had enough. 'Who did you kill this time?' I yelled into the phone. *'Who is it?'*

Kyle broke my heart. He told me in great detail about the murders he'd just committed. I was certain that he was telling the truth.

Then he hung up, even as I cursed him to hell.

Minutes later I was in my car, bleary-eyed, numb, rushing across Washington to the terrible murder scene.

Chapter One Hundred and Five

No, no, no!

It was like a knife thrust into my heart, then twisted until I screamed. Kyle had hurt me badly, and he wanted me to know something: *there was worse to come. This was just the beginning.*

I stood silent and transfixed in the bedroom of Zach and Liz Taylor. My eyes were blurred by tears. Two of my dearest friends were dead. I had been to their house dozens of times before – for parties, dinner, late-night talks. Zach and Liz had visited on Fifth Street many times. Zach was Godfather to little Alex.

My only consolation was that they had died quickly. Kyle was probably nervous about getting caught. He knew he had to get in and out of their apartment in the Adams-Morgan section of Washington quickly.

Whatever his reason, he had killed the Taylors with

single gunshots to the head. He hadn't bothered to muti-
late the bodies. I thought the message was clear: *This
wasn't about them.*

It was about the two of us.

Zach and Liz Taylor hadn't mattered one way or the
other to him. Maybe that was the worst thing of all. How
easily he could kill. How much he wanted to hurt me.

This was just the start of it.

It would get worse.

There was no evidence of rage, no passion at this crime
scene. I almost got the sense that once he was inside their
bedroom he'd had second thoughts. *Oh Kyle, Kyle. Have
mercy on us.*

I made mental notes – no need to write any of this
down. I knew every horrifying detail by heart. I would
never forget any of it until the day I died.

The gunshots had blown away the sides of their faces. I
had to force myself to look. I remembered how in love
they had always seemed to me. Zach had once told me
that 'Liz is the only person I know who I enjoy being with
on a long car ride.' That was the test for him. They never
ran out of things to say to one another. I felt incredibly
hollowed out as I stared at them. They were gone now.
What a terrible waste, what a horror show.

I walked past their bodies to a large casement window
that looked out on the street. I was feeling so unreal. I saw

the marquee sign for Café Lautrec, closed now. I thought about Kyle on the run, what he must be thinking, where he might go next.

I wanted to catch him, to stop him. *No, I wanted to kill him. I wanted to hurt him in the worst way possible.*

Someone from the Crime Scene Unit edged up to me, a sergeant named Ed Lyle. 'Sorry about your loss. What do you want from us, Detective? We're ready to get to work here.'

'Sketch, video, photograph,' I told Lyle. But I really didn't need any of it. I didn't need any more graven images, or even any evidence.

I knew who the killer was.

Chapter One Hundred and Six

I got home around one that afternoon. I needed to sleep, but I couldn't stay down for more than a couple of hours. I got up and paced through the empty house on Fifth Street.

I kept walking from room to room. I felt the need to stop a terrible disaster from happening, but I didn't know where to start. The possible hit lists for Kyle were continually running through my head: my family, Sampson, Christine, Jamilla Hughes, Kate McTiernan, my niece Naomi, Kyle's own family.

I couldn't get the image of Zach and Liz out of my head. They had been executed in the prime of their lives – because of me. Finally, I was able to throw up, and it was the best thing that had happened to me that day. I pushed out my guts. Then I slammed the bathroom mirror with the heel of my hand and nearly broke it.

Kyle was always a fucking step ahead, right? It had been that way for so many years now. He was such an unbelievable bastard.

He had complete confidence in his abilities, including his power to elude us any time he wanted to. What would be next? Who would he kill? Who? *Who?*

How could he make himself disappear after the killings? How did he blend in and become invisible when so many people were looking for him?

He had money; he had taken care of that when he'd played the role of the Mastermind. So what was next for him?

I worked at my computer late into the night and early morning. The computer was beside my bedroom window. Was he outside watching? I didn't think even Kyle would take that kind of chance now. But hell, how could I rule anything out?

He was capable of large-scale mass murder. If that was his plan, where would he strike? *Washington? New York City? LA? Chicago? His old hometown of Charlotte, North Carolina? Maybe somewhere in Europe? London?*

Was his family safe – his wife and his two children? I had vacationed with them in Nags Head one summer. I'd stayed at their home in Virginia a few times over the years. His wife Louise was a dear friend. I had promised her I would try to bring Kyle in alive if I possibly could. But now

I wondered – did I want to keep that promise? What would I do if I ever caught up with him?

He might go after his own parents, especially since he put part of the heavy blame for his behavior on his father. William Hyland Craig had been a general in the army, then chairman of the board of two Fortune 500 companies in and around Charlotte. Nowadays, he gave lectures at ten to twenty thousand a pop; he was on half a dozen boards. He had beaten Kyle as a boy, disciplined him ruthlessly, taught him to hate.

Sibling rivalry? Kyle had brought it up himself. He had been highly competitive with his younger brother until Blake's death in a hunting accident in 1991. Had Kyle actually killed Blake? What about the older brother, who still lived in North Carolina?

Did he think of me as a younger brother? Did Kyle see Blake in me? He was competing with me, and he'd tried to control me from the start. The women in my life might have represented a threat to him, an extreme variant of sibling rivalry. Was that why he had killed Betsey Cavalierre? What about Maureen Cooke in New Orleans? And Jamilla?

I made a note to think carefully and plot out one particular angle, a dysfunctional family triangle, with both Kyle and me a part of it.

One step ahead.

So far anyway.

If he came after his family, or his parents, we would have him. They were being closely protected in Charlotte. The FBI was all over them.

Kyle knew that. He wouldn't do anything stupid – just cruel and nasty.

One step ahead.

That seemed to be the key to Kyle's fantasy life, at least as I understood it so far. He wouldn't make the obvious move. He would go at least one move, maybe two, beyond that. But how did he stay a step ahead, especially now? A very bad thought had been running through my head lately. Maybe there was someone in the FBI helping him – maybe Kyle had a partner.

I had finally drifted off to sleep when the phone in my bedroom woke me. It was three in the morning. *Goddamn him. Doesn't he ever sleep?*

I picked it up, clicked it off, then unplugged the phone from the wall.

No more phone tag, Kyle. Fuck you.

I was setting the rules now. This was my game, not his.

Chapter One Hundred and Seven

I n the morning, I drank too much black coffee and thought about our last case together: the Tiger, Daniel and Charles, Peter Westin, the Alexander brothers. What did it mean in Kyle's fantasy? The macabre story he was plotting out involved both of us. He had asked me into the investigation, then used it to control me. Was that where it ended for him, and me?

I kept trying to piece together the puzzle from a psychologist's point of view. The rest might flow from that. *Might*. With Kyle, there was no knowing for sure. If he saw a clear pattern, he might reverse it; if he understood his own pathology, and maybe he did, he would use that in his favor too.

Around noon, I called Kyle's older brother, Martin, a radiologist living outside Charlotte – where we had once believed that Daniel and Charles had begun their murder spree. Did Kyle have a previous connection with them? Was that a possibility?

Martin Craig tried to help, but he finally admitted that he and his brother hadn't spoken during the past ten years. 'We saw one another at my brother Blake's funeral,' Martin said. 'That was the last time. I don't like my brother, Detective Cross. He doesn't like me. I don't know if he likes anybody.'

'Was your father especially rough on Kyle?' I asked Martin.

'Kyle always said so, but to tell the truth, I never saw much of it. Neither did my mother. Kyle liked to make up stories. He was always the big hero, or the pathetic victim. My mother used to say that Kyle had an ego second only to God's.'

'What did you think about that? Your mother's assessment of your brother?'

'Detective Cross, my brother didn't believe in God, and he wasn't second to anyone.'

The continuing theme throughout the three brothers' relationship had been competition, and Kyle had always believed that Martin and Blake won in the eyes of his parents. Kyle had been a starter on the high school basketball team, but Martin had been the clever all-county point guard, who also played bass guitar in a local band, and had an enviable social life. There had once been a feature story in the local paper about the basketball-playing brothers, but the article dealt mostly with Blake and Martin. They had all attended Duke Undergraduate, but Martin and Blake went on to medical school. Kyle became a lawyer, a career choice his father deplored. Kyle had talked to me about sibling rivalry, and maybe I was beginning to understand a little of the origins of his fantasy world.

'Martin,' I finally asked, 'is it possible that Kyle murdered your younger brother, Blake?'

'Blake died in a hunting accident – supposedly,' Martin Craig said. 'Detective Cross, my brother Blake was an incredibly responsible and careful man, *almost as careful as Kyle*. He didn't accidentally shoot himself. I've always believed with all my heart that Kyle had something to do with it. But who would believe me? That's why he and I haven't spoken in ten years. My brother is Cain. I believe he's a murderer, and I want to see him caught. I want to see my brother go to the electric chair. That's what Kyle deserves.'

Chapter One Hundred and Eight

Nothing ever starts where we think it does. I kept remembering that Kyle had done nearly all of the TV and print interviews after the capture of Peter Westin in the foothills outside Santa Cruz. He'd wanted the praise. He'd wanted to be the star, the only one. In a way, that's what he was now: the brightest star of all.

I had one decent idea about what to do next, something pro-active that might bother Kyle. I contacted the FBI and discussed it with Director Burns. He liked it too.

At four o'clock that afternoon, a press conference was called in the lobby of the FBI building. Director Burns was there to speak briefly and then to introduce me. Burns stated in no uncertain terms that I would be involved in the manhunt until Kyle Craig was brought to justice, and that Kyle would definitely be caught.

I was wearing a black leather car coat and I buttoned it

up as I stepped up to the mikes. I was playing this for all it was worth. I wanted to look self-important. I wanted to look like the star. Not Kyle. This was my manhunt. Not his. He was the prey.

There was the usual mechanical buzz and hum of cameras, the incessant flashes, and all those inquiring minds of the press, those cynical eyes staring up at me, waiting for answers that I couldn't give them. It set my nerves on edge.

My voice was as grave and important-sounding as I could make it. 'My name is Alex Cross. I'm a homicide detective in DC. I've worked closely with Special Agent In Charge Kyle Craig over the past five years. I know him extremely well.' I went into some detail on our past together. I tried to sound like a pompous know-it-all. The doctor detective.

'Kyle has been helpful in solving a few murders. He was a competent number two, excellent support for me. He was an over-achiever type, but a tireless worker.

'We will capture him soon, but Kyle, if you can hear me, wherever you are, I urge you to listen closely. Give yourself up. I can help you. I've always been able to help. Give yourself up to me. It's the only chance you have.'

I paused and stared into the TV cameras, then I stepped back slowly from the microphones. The camera flashes were everywhere. They were treating me like the star now.

Just as I had hoped they would.

Director Burns said a few more words about his concern for public safety and the extent of the FBI manhunt. He thanked me profusely for being there.

As I stood beside Director Burns, I continued to stare out into the TV cameras. I knew that Kyle would be looking right at me. I was sure that he'd see this segment, and that it would infuriate him.

I was sending Kyle a clear message, a challenge.

Come and get me, if you can. You're not the Mastermind anymore – I am.

Chapter One Hundred and Nine

N ow, I waited.

    I went to visit Nana and the kids early the next morning. A team of three FBI vehicles traveled with me. We were hoping that Kyle might take the bait and follow. Not surprisingly, he didn't show. No one really expected that he would, but we were willing to try anything at this point.

Aunt Tia had a small clapboard house that was painted yellow with white aluminum shutters. It was located on a quiet street in Chapell Gate, which she called 'the country'. As I drove up to the small house, I saw no evidence of the FBI, which was a good sign, I thought. They were doing their job well.

The special agent in charge was a man named Peter Schweitzer. He had an excellent reputation. Schweitzer met me at the front door and introduced me to the six other agents inside Tia's house.

When I was fully satisfied about security, I went to see Nana and the kids. 'Hello, Daddy.' 'Hello Dad.' 'Hello, Alex.' Everybody seemed especially glad to see me, even Nana. They were having a big breakfast in the kitchen and Tia was busy making pancakes and hot sausages. She put out her arms for a hug and then everybody grabbed hold of me and wouldn't let go. I must admit, I liked the attention; I needed the hugs.

'They can't get enough of you, Alex,' Tia laughed, and clapped both hands, just the way she'd been doing for years.

'That's 'cause we don't see enough of him,' Damon taunted.

'The job's almost done,' I said, hoping that was true, not completely believing it. 'At least you're all getting three squares a day.' I laughed and gave Tia an extra hug.

I ate some breakfast and stayed at Tia's for more than an hour. We never stopped talking the whole time, but only once did anyone bring up the current difficult and scary situation. 'When can we go back home?' Damon asked.

They all stared at me, waiting for a good answer. Even little Alex held me in his gaze. 'I won't lie to you,' I said finally. 'We have to find Kyle Craig first. Then we can go home.'

'And it can be just like before?' Jannie asked.

I recognized a trick question. 'Even better than that,' I told her. 'I'm going to make some big changes soon. I promise you.'

Chapter One Hundred and Ten

I left for Charlotte, North Carolina, on a ten o'clock flight out of DC. I was heading south to visit Craig family members. Maybe Kyle was there as well. It wouldn't surprise me.

His father, William Craig, chose not to be home when I arrived at the estate where Kyle and his brothers had been raised. It was a gentleman's farm with a rambling stone and wood house set on over forty acres in horse country. Someone on the staff told me it cost over fifteen dollars a yard just to paint all the white fences running around the pastures.

I spoke with Miriam Craig on a rear porch, which overlooked wild-flower gardens and a rock-filled brook. She seemed very much in control of her emotions, which surprised me, but maybe shouldn't have. Mrs Craig told me a great deal about her family.

'Kyle's father and I had no idea, no clue about his darker side, if indeed the terrible allegations are true,' she said. 'Kyle was always distant, reserved, introspective I suppose you could say, but there was nothing to suggest that he might be this troubled. He did well in school, and in athletics. Kyle even plays the piano with a beautiful touch.'

'I never knew he played,' I said, and yet Kyle had often commented on my playing. 'Did you and his father tell him how well he was doing – in school, for example? In athletics? I suspect that boys need to hear that more than we know.'

Mrs Craig took offense. 'He didn't want to hear it. He'd say, "I know" and then walk away from us. Almost as if we had disappointed him by stating the obvious.'

'His brothers did better than Kyle in school?'

'In terms of grades, yes, but the boys were all high-honor students. Most teachers saw Kyle as being deeper. I believe that he had the highest IQ, one-forty-nine if I remember correctly. He chose not to apply himself to every subject. He had a strong will, even as a young boy.'

'But there were no obvious signs that he was severely troubled?'

'No, Detective Cross. Believe me, I've thought about it a lot.'

'Kyle's father would agree?'

'We talked about it just last night. He agrees. He's just too upset to be here. Kyle's father is a proud man, and a good one. William Craig is a very good man.'

Next, I went to see Kyle's brother in Charlotte. I talked to Dr Craig in a white-on-white conference room at the clinic where he was a partner.

'I found Kyle to be caustic and very cruel. I know that Blake did as well,' he confessed over tea.

'Cruel in what way?' I asked.

'Not to small animals or anything obvious like that – to other people. Actually, Kyle liked animals just fine. He was vicious at school, though. Both verbally and physically. A real prick. Nobody liked him much. He had no close friends that I remember. That's odd, isn't it? Kyle never had a single close friend. Let me tell you something, Detective, during Kyle's sophomore and most of his junior years, our father made him sleep in the garage because he was so unpleasant to have around.'

'That seems a little severe,' I commented. Nothing I'd heard so far was so revealing. Kyle had never mentioned the punishment, though. Neither had Mrs Craig. All she'd said was that Kyle's father was a good man, whatever that meant.

'I don't think it was severe, Detective. I think it was fair, and much less than he deserved. Kyle should have been thrown out of our house when he was around thirteen. My brother was a goddamn monster, and apparently, he still is.'

Chapter One Hundred and Eleven

*W*ho would Kyle go after next? It was the question that obsessed me. I couldn't let it go. When I got home that night, I began to think about going out to Seattle. I had a bad feeling. Lots of them, actually. Would Kyle go after Christine Johnson next? He knew how to strike to cause the most hurt. Kyle knew me so well – but apparently, I didn't know Kyle at all.

Would he go after Christine? Or maybe Jamilla? Was I thinking the way Kyle would?

One step ahead.

God damn him to hell.

Maybe he would just come after me; maybe all I had to do was stay in the house on Fifth Street and wait for him to show up.

The question was burning inside my head. What was everybody missing? What did Kyle want – more than anything else? What motivated him? Who was on Kyle's vicious hit list – besides me?

Kyle wanted to exert his will, but he also craved the most exquisite and forbidden pleasures. What had moved him in the past was sex, rape, money – millions of dollars – revenge against those he hated.

I finally went to bed at one-thirty, but *surprise, surprise,* I couldn't sleep. I kept seeing Kyle's face every time I shut my eyes. His look was smug and confident. He was the most arrogant human being I had ever met. Possibly the most evil. I thought back about all our times together, all our long, philosophical talks, anything I could remember. I turned on the bed table light and scribbled more notes. Kyle was methodical and logical, but then he could surprise me with a tactic or strategy completely off the charts. I thought about the raid in Santa Cruz. The vampire murders seemed far away already. He had wanted me there so that I could see him be the hero. That was the whole point, wasn't it? He needed me to see how good he was. He wanted to take down Peter Westin by himself.

Suddenly, a question popped into my head. A really good one.

Where had he been unable to exert his will?

What were Kyle's darkest fantasies? What were his daydreams? His secret desires? Where had he been thwarted in the past?

The worst is yet to come. He was only starting with Zach and Liz Taylor. Was he about to go on a bloody rampage?

And then I recalled a particular fantasy that Kyle had shared with me one night after we had finished one of our worst cases. I remembered something he'd said, and couldn't get it out of my head.

I snatched up the phone and began to dial long distance. I hoped that I wasn't too late. I thought I knew who he was going to kill next.

Oh no, Kyle. Oh God, no!

Chapter One Hundred and Twelve

Maybe I was just going crazy. I drove for nearly six hours on I-95 headed to Nags Head, North Carolina. I kept changing radio stations to keep myself alert. I was thinking to myself that Kyle didn't want this to end – he was having too much fun; he was in his glory.

I had been in this part of North Carolina before, with Kate McTiernan. So had Kyle. We were trying to stop the sadistic killer named Casanova. He had kept as many as eight women captive in the woods near Chapel Hill, North Carolina. Kyle had been on our team, or so I had believed. But Kyle had also been Casanova's partner in murder.

I made it to Nags Head just before nightfall. As I drove toward the ocean, I remembered odd things: the sticky buns from the Nags Head Market; my long walks with

Kate McTiernan along Coquina Beach; the lovely, almost supernaturally picturesque beaches in Jockey's Ridge State Park. I remembered how much I admired Kate. We were still good friends, talked at least twice a month. She sent my kids imaginative presents on their birthdays and at Christmas. She was working at the Regional Medical Center in Kitty Hawk and living with a local bookseller whom she was going to marry. Their home was in Nags Head, only a couple of miles away.

Kyle had a deep, obvious crush on Kate McTiernan. He'd hinted at it: 'I could love that girl, if I didn't have Louise and the kids. Maybe I should dump them for Kate. She could make me a happy man. Kate could save me.'

He had come to visit Kate in Nags Head. I think he'd come to watch her. It bothered him that he couldn't have her, that he had been *denied* Kate McTiernan. He also knew how much Kate meant to me.

Kyle was here, wasn't he? Or he was coming.

I had warned Kate, but on the drive down I called again and explicitly told her to get the hell out of Nags Head. I didn't care how much karate she knew, or how many black belts she had accumulated. I was going to stay at her place. I thought that Kyle might be coming, too. I didn't think he wanted to *watch* anymore. If he was coming here, he wanted to kill Kate.

I took a deep breath as I finally drove into town. It all

looked so familiar, serene and beautiful, like nothing bad should ever happen here.

The worst is yet to come, I kept thinking. *That's why he killed Zach and Liz Taylor first. He set up his pattern with them. The Taylors were just the beginning. A warning of things to come.*

I drove down a narrow, paved road that weaved its way alongside wind-blown sand dunes. I was looking for any sign of Kyle. Number 1021 was a two-story clapboard beach house directly across from the ocean. Very quaint and stylish, very Kate McTiernan. If Kyle got to her, I would never forgive myself.

A Scottish flag was flying above the rooftop, and that was pure McTiernan, too. As I had asked, her six-year-old Volvo was still parked in the driveway; the houselights were on, shining like beacons to guide me – and maybe Kyle as well.

It made it look like somebody was home, and now somebody was.

Everything felt surreal to me. My nervous system was spiking. My hairs were standing on end. I had a sixth sense that Kyle was nearby. I just knew it, felt it in every inch of my body. Was he, though? Or was I just crazy? I wasn't sure which outcome would be worse.

I drove my car inside the garage and pulled down the heavy wooden door. There was a cold spot at the center of my chest. I was having difficulty catching a breath. Or thinking in a straight line.

Then I went inside Kate McTiernan's house. My sense of balance was off. I was listing to the right.

The telephone started to ring.

I pulled out my Glock and looked around the kitchen for Kyle. I didn't see anything. Not yet.

Where was he?

The worst is yet to come.

Was I ready for it this time?

Chapter One Hundred and Thirteen

I picked up the jangling phone, then hit my knee hard against the kitchen table.

'I've been looking all over for you, Alex.' Kyle was so very calm and cocksure. He had no conscience, no guilt whatsoever. His arrogance was stunning to me, even now. I wished he was here, so I could pound his face.

'Well, I guess you found me. Congratulations. I can't hide from you. You're so impressive. You *are* the Master-mind, Kyle.'

'You know, I am. You had me concerned, worried there, partner. I wanted to say goodbye in a proper and civil fashion. I'm leaving after this little adventure of ours is ended. It's almost over. *Whew*. Isn't that a relief?'

'Want to tell me where you are?' I asked him.

He paused for a half-second, and I could feel a fast river of adrenaline rushing through me. My legs were unsteady.

Suddenly I was afraid of what Kyle might have already done.

'I suppose it couldn't hurt to tell you. Let me think about it. Hmmm. There's blood everywhere, Alex. I will tell you that much. It's stunning, a masterpiece of carnage. I've outdone myself this time. Outdone Gary Soneji, Shafer, Casanova. This is my best work. I think it is, and I should know. I'm very objective about these things, but of course you know that.'

My heart was pounding and I felt dizzy. I could feel the blood rushing from my brain. I steadied myself against the kitchen counter. 'Where, Kyle? Tell me where you are. Where the hell are you?'

'Perhaps I'm at your Aunt Tia's outside Bal'more,' he said. Then he laughed like a madman. 'Chapell Gate. Such a pretty little town.'

A moan escaped from my mouth and my knees buckled. I flashed an image of my family – Nana, Jannie, Damon, Alex. I needed to be there with them. How could he have gotten past the FBI teams? And Sampson? He couldn't have. It wasn't possible.

'You're lying, Kyle.'

'Oh, am I now? Why would I lie? Think about it. What would be the point?'

The worst is yet to come. I needed to call Tia's. I should never have left them.

I heard a terrifying high-pitched scream above me in the kitchen. What in hell?

I looked up. Couldn't believe my eyes. Kyle leaped out of the trapdoor to the attic. He was still screaming. He had an ice pick clasped in his right hand, cell phone in the other.

I tried to get an arm up to shield myself. I wasn't fast enough. He'd taken me by surprise. I hadn't thought to look up there.

He plunged the blade into my chest at an odd angle. A shock of pain traveled through me. I went down hard on the kitchen floor. Had he struck my heart? Was I going to die? Was this the way it ended?

With his free hand, Kyle punched me in the face. I felt bone crunch. The left side of my face, my cheek seemed to cave in.

Kyle raised his fist to strike again. He was madman-strong, and he wanted to punish me. I was such an important character in his fantasy. He was so sick, so insane. I couldn't believe the things he'd done.

A voice inside screamed, *Take him out, find a way!*

A second punch glanced off the side of my forehead. I moved just enough to make him miss. I was in a living nightmare. This was almost surreal. The stainless steel handle of the ice pick was sticking out of my chest.

I grabbed the hood and collar of Kyle's windbreaker with one hand, his black hair with the other. I yanked him sideways, got him off me for a moment.

Somehow I managed to get up and pull Kyle with me. We were both grunting, gasping loudly for breath. I felt myself getting weaker. Blood was spreading on my shirt from the wound.

Still, I carried him forward, headfirst, right into Kate's well-organized glass kitchen cabinet. It shattered on impact. Splinters of glass and wood flew everywhere.

I pulled his head back out of the cabinet, cutting his face on nasty shards of the glass. I wanted to hurt him too. For Betsey Cavalierre, for Zachary and Liz Taylor, for all the others he had murdered along the way. So many dead at the hands of this heartless monster. The Mastermind. Kyle Craig.

He screamed, 'My eyes! My eyes!' I'd hurt him – finally.

I crunched a looping roundhouse right into his fore-head. I moved in closer. I hit him again and again, then I held him up so I could hit him some more. I wouldn't let him go down. I kept body-punching Kyle Craig, body-punishing him. I don't know where I got the strength. I wanted to keep hitting Kyle, for everything he'd done, the murders, the cruel betrayals, for stalking me all these months, the terrible hurt he'd inflicted on my family, on other families like mine.

He was out on his feet, so I finally let him drop to the kitchen floor. I stood over the unconscious body, exhausted, winded, afraid, and in pain. Now what? I felt as if I weren't myself anymore. Who was I? What was I becoming? What had all the brutal murders I'd seen done to me?

I stepped away from the crumpled body. The spike of the ice pick was still imbedded in my chest. It had to come out. I knew I couldn't, shouldn't, do it myself. I needed to get to a hospital. Maybe Dr Kate McTiernan would take care of me.

I made a phone call. A very important call.

This was just the *beginning*, wasn't it? Sure it was.

The Mastermind and I were alone at last. We had so much to talk about. I'd been waiting so long for this, and maybe so had he.

Chapter One Hundred and Fourteen

It was a hollow feeling to stand over Kyle and realize that I had no idea who he really was. He was an obsessively cruel psychopath; he had been stalking me for years; he had killed so many times, including friends of mine. 'You fucking bastard,' I whispered through my teeth.

The first case we had worked on together was a double kidnapping in Washington. Later, he cleared the way for me to help in the investigation of a kidnapper/killer who called himself Casanova, and who worked in the Research Triangle around the University of North Carolina and Duke. That was when we had first met Kate McTiernan. Kyle kept me close to him after that. He was the one responsible for my getting named as the VICAP liaison between the FBI and the Washington Police Department. I didn't know why at the time. Now I did.

He was conscious now. A mocking, falsely sympathetic

look crossed his face. His eyes leveled on me as he spoke. 'I know, I *know* how it hurts. You thought we were close, you thought we were friends.'

I didn't say anything, just looked into cold blue eyes edged with gray. What did I see there? Nothing except for his hatred and disdain. He was incapable of feeling guilt, or compassion.

Then Kyle smirked, and I wanted to hit him again. He began to laugh. What was the joke? What did he know? What else had he done?

He started to clap his hands together. 'Very good, Alex. You're still studying me, aren't you? You should bear in mind, I did beat you every time.'

'Except this time,' I reminded him. 'This time you lost.'

'Oh, are you so sure?' he asked. 'Are you positive that you have the upper hand, partner? How can you be certain? You can't be.'

'I'm sure. *Partner*. I do have a few questions, though. Clear some things up for me. You know what I want to hear about.'

He continued to smirk. Of course he knew. 'North Carolina. You didn't know I had attended Duke with the Gentleman Caller. I knew both killers. God, did I know them. I killed with them, hunted with them. But you let me off the hook, Detective Cross. Then there were the perfect bank robberies. The Mastermind at work. And, of course, I did kill the lovely Betsey Cavalierre. Great fun. That one's on you, Alex.'

I stared into those pitiless eyes. My voice came out in a rasp. 'Why did you have to hurt her?'

Kyle shrugged indifferently. 'That's how I win the game, by inflicting the most pain imaginable, then watching the torment and suffering. You should see the look in your eyes right now. It's priceless, a thing of beauty.

'Not that I want any pity, Doctor Cross, but did you ever see me with my shirt off? I'll answer that question. You haven't. That's because of the scars and welts there. My father, the great and respected general, the corporate chief executive officer, he beat me for years. He thought I was a very bad boy. And you know what, he was right. Father did know best. His son was a monster. Now what does that say about him?'

Kyle smiled again. Or was it a grimace? He shut his eyes.

'Getting back to Agent Cavalierre, she was investigating my whereabouts during all the robberies and kidnappings committed by the Mastermind. Smart little chippie. Pretty, too. And she really liked you, Alex. Thought you were so fine, her sweet brown sugar. I couldn't have that. She was a danger to me and a rival for your attention.

'Are you following this, Cross? Am I going too fast for you? Everything is very logical, no? I put a knife deep inside her. I was going to do the same to your friend Jamilla. Maybe I still will.'

I raised my Glock and pointed it into his face. My hand was shaking. 'No, Kyle, you won't!'

Chapter One Hundred and Fifteen

Everything had been leading up to this moment – the last few years, all of Kyle's tricks. My hand was still trembling as I moved the gun forward until it touched Kyle's forehead. To be honest, I didn't know what I would do next.

'I was hoping it might come to this. One of us in control of the situation. This is where it gets interesting to me,' he said. 'What do you do now?'

Kyle pressed his skull into the gun barrel. 'Go ahead, Alex. If you kill me like this, then I win. I like that, actually. Suddenly, *you're* the murderer.'

I let him talk – the Mastermind, the total control freak.

'Let me tell you a harsh truth,' he said. 'Can you take a little truth? How much truth can you stand?'

'Go ahead, enlighten me. I think I can take it, Kyle. I want to hear everything.'

'Oh, and you shall. What I do . . . it's what all men want to do. I live out their secret fantasies, their nasty little daydreams. I completely control my environment. I don't live by rules created by my so-called peers. I live a full fantasy life. Everything I do is motivated by self-interest. It's what everybody wants, trust me on that. So stop being so self-righteous. It irritates the shit out of me.'

I shook my head. 'I have some news for you. It isn't what I want, Kyle. It's a self-centered adolescent's fantasy.'

'Oh, spare me the provincial pop psychology. And yes, it *is* what you want to do. The chase, the thrill. It's your life, too. Don't you see that? Jesus Christ, man. You love the hunt. You love it! *You love this!*'

We studied each other in the small kitchen for several minutes. The hatred between us was so obvious now. Then Kyle began to laugh again – he roared. He was laughing at my expense.

'You still don't get it, do you? You're a fool. You're so inferior. You have nothing, not a shred of solid evidence on me. I'll be out on the street in a few days. I'll be free to do whatever I like. Imagine the possibilities. Anything I can dream up. Isn't that a consoling thought, *Alex*? Old buddy, old pal.

'I *wanted* you to know who and what I am. It's no fun unless somebody knows. I wanted this to happen.

Desperately. More than anything. I set it up. And once I'm out, you'll know that I'm somewhere . . . waiting and watching. You see, I won this time, too. *I wanted you to catch me, you asshole.* What do you think of that?'

I stared into Kyle's eyes and it was like that game kids play – who's going to look away first? Who's going to blink?

Finally, I winked at him. 'Gotcha,' I said.

'What I think,' I continued, 'is that you just made your first big mistake. You didn't think of everything. You missed an important detail, Mastermind. Know what it is? C'mon, you're a smart guy. Figure it out.'

I stepped away from Kyle. Now I was the one who smiled, maybe even smirked. I stared into his eyes and let him think about it. I could see he had no idea. 'Watch closely.'

I took my cell phone from my pocket. I held it up for Kyle to see. I showed him that it was turned *on*.

'I called my home phone before we started to talk. The phone has been on speaker. Everything you just told me is on my voice mail. I have your confession, Kyle. Everything, every word. You lose, you sick, pitiful sonofabitch. You lose, *Mastermind*.'

Kyle suddenly sprung up from the floor at me – and then I got to knock him out again. I hit him with the best punch of my life, at least it felt that way. His body lifted up off the floor and he lost a couple of front teeth.

That was how he looked in the news photograph after his capture, the great Mastermind, missing two front teeth.

Chapter One Hundred and Sixteen

I finally got to rest up, to stop being a cop for a while. Kyle Craig was in a maximum security cell at Lorton Prison. The district attorney was confident there was more than enough evidence to convict. Kyle's expensive New York lawyer was screaming that he had committed no crimes, that he'd been framed. Isn't that amazing? The murder trial would be one of the biggest that Washington and the rest of the country had ever seen.

The thing was, I didn't want to think about Kyle, or his trial, or some other psychopathic killer anymore. I hadn't been to work in weeks, and it felt good. I felt real good. My ice pick wound was healing pretty well. The scar would be a souvenir. I was spending as much time as I could at home. I'd put on most of a new roof. I'd been to two of Damon's concerts in a row. I was on a roll.

I was working on a jump shot with Jannie; reading

Goodnight Moon and *Fox in Socks* to little Alex; taking cooking lessons from the best chef in all of Washington, or so Nana bragged. I was also making some time for myself. I'd even had a couple of nice talks with Christine Johnson. I told her I was sending the cutest pictures of Alex. Jamilla Hughes was coming East for a seminar and would visit next week. Everything was going well with her life.

It was around eleven o'clock, and I was playing the piano on the sun porch. The house on Fifth Street was quiet, everybody sleeping except for me.

The phone didn't ring, and what a sweet, simple pleasure that was.

No one came to the door with bad news that I didn't want to hear right now, or maybe ever again.

No one was watching me from outside, in the shadows, or if they were, at least they weren't being a nuisance about it.

I concentrated on getting into some songs by D'Angelo, and I was doing a pretty good job of it. 'The Line', 'Send It On', 'Devil's Pie'.

Tomorrow? Well, tomorrow was a big day, too.

I was going to resign from the DC police force in the morning.

And something else, something good for a change, I thought that maybe I was falling in love.

But that's another story, for another time.

Headline hopes you have enjoyed VIOLETS ARE BLUE, and invites you to sample James Patterson's latest thriller, 2nd CHANCE (with Andrew Gross), out now from Headline.

The Choir Kids

Chapter 1

Aaron Winslow would never forget the next few minutes. He recognized the terrifying sounds the instant they cracked through the night. His body went cold all over. He couldn't believe that someone was shooting a high-powered rifle in this neighborhood.

K-pow, k-pow, k-pow . . . k-pow, k-pow, k-pow.

His choir was just leaving the Harrow Street church. Forty-eight young kids streamed past him onto the sidewalk. They had just finished their final rehearsal before the San Francisco Sing-Off, and they had been excellent.

Then came the gunfire. Lots of it. Not just a single shot. A strafing. *An attack.*

K-pow, k-pow, k-pow . . . k-pow, k-pow, k-pow.

'Get down . . .' he screamed at the top of his voice. 'Everybody down on the ground! Cover your heads! Cover up!' He almost couldn't believe the words as they left his mouth.

At first, no one seemed to hear him. To the kids, in their white blouses and shirts, the shots must have seemed like firecrackers. Then a volley of shots rained through the church's beautiful stained-glass window. The depiction of Christ's blessing over a child at Capernaum shattered, glass splintering everywhere, some of it falling on the heads of the children.

'Someone's shooting!' Winslow screamed. Maybe more than one person. *How could that be?* He ran wildly through the kids, screaming, waving his arms, pushing as many as he could down to the grass.

As the kids finally crouched low or dove for the ground, Winslow spotted two of his choir girls, Chantal and Tamara, frozen on the lawn as bullets streaked past them. 'Chantal, Tamara, get down!' he screamed, but they remained there, hugging one another, emitting frantic wails. They were best friends. He had known them since they were little kids, playing four-square on blacktop.

There was never any doubt in his mind. He sprinted towards the two girls, grasping their arms firmly, tumbling them to the ground. Then he lay on top of them, pressing their bodies tightly.

Bullets whined over his head, just inches away. His eardrums hurt. His body was trembling and so were the girls shielded beneath him. He was almost sure he was about to die. 'It's all right, babies,' he whispered.

Then, as suddenly as it had begun, the firing stopped. A hush of silence hung in the air. So strange and eerie, as if the whole world had stopped to listen.

As he raised himself, his eyes fell on an incredible sight. Slowly, everywhere, the children struggled to their feet. There was some crying, but he didn't see any blood; no one seemed to be hurt.

'Everyone okay?' Winslow called out. He made his way through the crowd. 'Is anyone hurt?'

'I'm okay . . . I'm okay,' came back to him. He looked around in disbelief. This was a miracle.

Then he heard the sound of a single child whimpering.

He turned and spotted Maria Parker, only twelve years old. Maria was standing on the whitewashed wooden steps of the church entrance. She seemed lost. Choking sobs poured from her open mouth.

Then his eyes came to rest on what had made the girl hysterical. He felt his heart sink. Even in war, even growing up on the streets of Oakland, he had never felt anything so horrible, so sad and senseless.

'Oh, God. Oh, no. How could you let this happen?'

Tasha Catchings, just eleven years old, lay in a heap in a flowerbed near the base of the church. Her white school blouse was soaked with blood.

Finally, Reverend Aaron Winslow began to cry himself.

Book 1

The Women's Murder Club – Again

Chapter One

O n a Tuesday night I found myself playing a game of crazy-eights with three residents of the Hope Street Teen House. I was loving it.

On the beat-up couch across from me sat Hector, a barrio kid two days out of Juvenile; Alysha, quiet and pretty, but with a family history you wouldn't want to know; and Michelle, who at fourteen had already spent a year selling herself on the streets of San Francisco.

'Hearts,' I declared, flipping down an eight and changing the suit, just as Hector was about to lay out.

'Damn, badge lady,' he whined. 'How come each time I'm 'bout to go down, you stick your knife in me?'

'Teach *you* never to trust a cop, fool,' laughed Michelle, tossing a conspiratorial smile my way.

For the past four months I'd been spending a night or two a week at the Hope Street House. For so long, after the terrible bride and groom case earlier that summer, I'd felt completely lost. I took a month off from Homicide; ran down by the Marina; gazed out at the Bay from the safety of my Potrero Hill flat.

Nothing helped. Not counseling, not the total support of my girls – Claire, Cindy, Jill. Not even going back to the job. I had watched, unable to help, as the life leaked out of the person I loved. I still felt responsible for my partner's death in the line of duty. Nothing seemed to fill the void.

So I came here . . . to Hope Street.

And the good news was it was working a little.

I peered up from my cards at Angela, a new arrival who sat in a metal chair across the room, cuddling her three-month-old child. The poor kid, maybe sixteen, hadn't said much all night. I would try to talk to Angela before I left for the night.

The door opened and Dee Collins, one of the House's head counselors, came in. She was followed by a stiff-looking black woman in a conservative gray suit. She had Department of Children and Families written all over her.

'Angela, your social worker's here.' Dee kneeled down beside her.

'I ain't blind,' the teenager said.

'We're going to have to take the baby now,' the social worker interrupted, as if completing this assignment was all that kept her from catching the next CalTran.

'No!' Angela pulled the infant even closer. 'You can keep me in this hole, you can send me back to Claymore, but you're not taking my baby.'

'Please, honey, only for a few days,' Dee Collins tried to reassure her.

The teenage girl drew her arms protectively around her baby, who, sensing some harm, began to cry.

'Don't you make a scene, Angela,' the social worker warned. 'You know how this is done.'

As she came towards the girl, I watched Angela jump out of the chair. She was clutching the baby in one arm and a glass of juice she'd been drinking in the other hand.

In one swift motion she cracked the glass against a table. It created a jagged shard.

'Angela,' I leapt up from the card table, 'put that down. No one's going to take your baby anywhere unless you let her go.'

'This *bitch* is trying to ruin my life,' she glared. 'First, she lets me sit in Claymore three days past my date, then she won't let me go home to my mom. Now she's trying to take my baby girl.'

I nodded, peering into the teenager's eyes. 'First, you gotta lay down the glass,' I said. 'You *know* that, Angela.'

The DCF worker took a step, but I held her back. I moved slowly towards Angela. I took hold of the glass, then I gently eased the child out of her arms.

'She's all I have,' the girl whispered and then started to sob.

'I know,' I nodded. 'That's why you'll change some things in your life and get her back.'

Dee Collins had her arms around Angela, a cloth wrapped around the girl's bleeding hand. The DCF worker was trying unsuccessfully to hush the crying infant.

I went up and said to her, 'That baby gets placed somewhere nearby with daily visitation rights. And by the way, I didn't see anything going on here that was worth putting on file . . . *You?*' The caseworker gave me a disgruntled look and turned away.

Suddenly, my beeper sounded, three dissonant beeps punctuating the tense air. I pulled it out and read the number. *Jacobi, my ex-partner in Homicide. What did he want?*

I excused myself and moved into the staff office. I was able to reach him in his car.

'Something bad's happened, Lindsay,' he said, glumly. 'I thought you'd want to know.'

He clued me in about a horrible drive-by shooting at the LaSalle Heights Church. An eleven-year-old girl had been killed.

'Jesus . . .' I sighed, as my heart sank.

'I thought you might want in on it,' Jacobi said.

I took in a breath. It had been over three months since

I'd been on the scene at a homicide. Not since the day the bride and groom case ended.

'So, I didn't hear,' Jacobi pressed. 'You want in, *Lieutenant*?' It was the first time he had called me with my new rank.

I realized my honeymoon had come to an end. 'Yeah,' I muttered back. 'I want in.'

Chapter Two

A cold rain started to fall as I pulled my Explorer up to the LaSalle Heights Church on Harrow Street in the predominantly black section of Bay View. An angry, anxious crowd had formed – a combination of saddened neighborhood mothers, and the usual sullen homeboys huddled in their bright 'Tommy's' – all pushing against a handful of uniformed cops.

'This ain't goddamn Mississippi,' someone shouted as I forced my way through the throng.

'How many more?' an older woman wailed. '*How many more?*'

I badged my way past a couple of nervous patrolmen to the front. What I saw next absolutely took my breath away.

The façade of the white clapboard church was slashed with a grotesque pattern of bullet holes and lead-colored chinks. A huge hole gaped in a wall where a large, stained-glass window had been shot out. Jagged edges of colored glass teetered, like hanging ice. Kids were still scattered all over the lawn, obviously in shock, some being attended to by EMS teams.

'Oh, Jesus,' I whispered under my breath.

I spotted medical techs in black windbreakers huddled over the body of a young girl by the front steps. A couple of plainclothesmen were nearby. One of them was my ex-partner, Warren Jacobi.

I found myself hesitating. I had done this a hundred times. Only months ago I had solved the biggest murder case in the city since Harvey Milk, but so much had happened since then. I felt weird, like I was new at this. Balling my fists together, I took a deep breath and went over to Jacobi.

'Welcome back to the world, Lieutenant,' Jacobi said, with a roll of the tongue on my new rank.

The sound of that word still sent a surge of electricity through me. Heading Homicide had been the goal I had pursued throughout my career: the first female homicide detective in San Francisco; now its first lieutenant. After my old LT Sam Roth opted for a cushy stint up in Bodega Bay, Chief Mercer had called me in. *I can do one of two things, he'd said to me. I can keep you on long-term adminis-trative leave and you can see if you find the heart to do this job again. Or I can give you these, Lindsay.* He pushed a gold shield with two bars on it across the table. Until that moment, I don't think I had ever seen Mercer smile.

'The lieutenant's shield doesn't make it any easier, does it, Lindsay?' Jacobi said, emphasizing that our three-year relationship as partners had now changed.

'What do we have?' I asked him.

'Looks like a single gunman, from out in those bushes.' He pointed to a dense thicket beside the church, maybe fifty yards away. 'Asshole caught the kids just as they came out. Opened fire with everything he had.'

I took a breath, staring at the weeping, shell-shocked kids scattered all over the lawn. 'Anybody see the guy? Somebody did, right?'

He shook his head. 'Everyone hit the deck.'

Near the fallen child a distraught black woman sobbed into the shoulder of a comforting friend. Jacobi saw my eyes fix on the dead girl.

'Name's Tasha Catchings,' he muttered. 'In the fifth grade, over at St Anne's. Good girl. Youngest kid in the choir.'

I moved in closer and knelt over the body. No matter how many times you do this, it's a wrenching sight. Tasha's school blouse was soaked with blood, mixed with falling rain. Just a few feet away a rainbow-colored knapsack still lay on the grass.

'She's it?' I asked incredulously. I surveyed the scene.

'She's the only one who got hit?'

Bullet holes were everywhere, splintered glass and wood. Dozens of kids had been streaming out to the street . . . *All those shots, and only one victim.*

'Our lucky day, huh?' Jacobi snorted.

Chapter Three

Paul Chi, one of my Homicide crew, was interviewing a tall, handsome black man, dressed in a black turtleneck and jeans, on the steps of the church. I'd seen him before, on the news. I even knew his name: Aaron Winslow.

Even in shock and dismay, Winslow carried himself with a graceful bearing – a smooth face, jet-black hair cut flat on top, and a football running back's build. Everyone in San Francisco knew what he was doing for this neighborhood. He was supposed to be a real-life hero, and I must say, he looked the part.

I walked over.

'This is Reverend Aaron Winslow,' Chi said, introducing us.

'Lindsay Boxer,' I said, extending my hand.

'*Lieutenant* Boxer,' said Chi. 'She'll be overseeing the case.'

'I'm familiar with your work,' I said. 'You've given a lot to this neighborhood. I'm so sorry for this. I don't have any words for it.'

His eyes shifted towards the murdered girl. He spoke in the softest voice imaginable. 'I've known her since she was a baby. These are good, responsible people. Her mother ... she brought up Tasha and her brother on her own. These were all young kids. Choir practice, Lieutenant.'

I didn't want to intrude, but I had to. 'Can I ask a few questions? Please.'

He nodded blankly. 'Of course.'

'You see anyone? Someone fleeing? A shape, a glimpse?'

'I saw where the shots came from,' Winslow said, and he pointed to the same thicket of bushes where Jacobi had gone. 'I saw the trailer fire. I was too busy trying to get everyone down. It was madness.'

'Has anyone made any threats recently against you or your church?' I asked.

'Threats ...?' Winslow screwed his face. 'Maybe years ago, when we first got funding to rebuild some of these houses.'

A short distance away, a haunting wail came from Tasha Catchings' mother as the girl's body was lifted onto a gurney. This was so sad.

The crowd was growing edgy. Taunts and accusations

began to ring out. 'Why are you all standing around? Go find her killer!'

'I'd better get over there,' Winslow said, 'before this thing goes the wrong way.' He started to move, then turned with tight-lipped resignation on his face. 'I could have saved that poor baby. I heard the shots.'

'You couldn't save them all,' I said. 'You did what you could.'

He finally nodded. Then he said something that totally shocked me. 'It was an M-16, Lieutenant. Thirty-six-round clip. The bastard reloaded twice.'

'How would you know that?' I asked, surprised.

'Desert Storm,' he answered. 'I was a field chaplain. No way I would ever forget that awful sound. No one ever does.'

Now you can buy any of these other bestselling
books by **James Patterson** from your
bookshop or *direct from his publisher*.

FREE P&P AND UK DELIVERY
(Overseas and Ireland £3.50 per book)

Roses Are Red	£6.99
Pop Goes the Weasel	£6.99
Cradle and All	£6.99
When the Wind Blows	£6.99
Cat and Mouse	£6.99

TO ORDER SIMPLY CALL THIS NUMBER

01235 400 414

or e-mail <u>orders@bookpoint.co.uk</u>

Prices and availability subject to change without notice.